CAT AND MOUSE

Katherine met the earl's gaze and saw pure, naked desire. He was doing nothing to hide it, showing her blatantly how much he wanted her. The power in his look was almost hypnotic and Katherine did not think she could glance away even if she wished. His thumb rubbed a sensuous pattern along her palm and every nerve in he body tingled.

"Katherine," he whispered hoarsely.

The sound of his voice jolted her back to her senses. She wrenched her gaze and hand away, and jumped to her feet. "Good night, my lord," she said.

"Edward," he said as he politely rose.

"Edward," she whispered as she fled through the doorway . . . knowing all too well that she could run but she could not hide how she had responded . . . not from him or from herself . . .

MELINDA McRAE holds a master's degree in European history and takes great delight in researching obscure details of the Regency period. She lives in Seattle, Washington with her husband and daughter.

A Highly Respectable Widow

by

Melinda McRae

A SIGNET BOOK

SIGNET
Published by the Penguin Group
Penguin Books USA Inc., 375 Hudson Street,
New York, New York, 10014, U.S.A.
Penguin Books Ltd, 27 Wrights Lane, London W8 5TZ, England
Penguin Books Australia Ltd, Ringwood, Victoria, Australia
Penguin Books Canada Ltd, 10 Alcorn Avenue, Toronto, Ontario, Canada M4V 3B2
Penguin Books (N.Z.) Ltd, 182-190 Wairau Road,
Auckland 10, New Zealand

Penguin Books Ltd, Registered Offices:
Harmondsworth, Middlesex, England

First published by Signet, an imprint of New American Library,
a division of Penguin Books USA Inc.

First Printing, January, 1992

10 9 8 7 6 5 4 3 2 1

Copyright© Melinda McRae 1992
All rights reserved

To Ron.
For allowing me to shirk all my
household responsibilities
in the name of "stress reduction."
And I still think you're
cuter than Kevin Costner.

Prologue

For *ennui* is a growth of English roots,
  Though nameless in our language—we retort
The fact for words, and let the French translate
  That awful yawn which sleep cannot abate.
                                             —Byron, *Don Juan*

It was time to find a new mistress. Edward Warrenton
Beauchamp, the ninth Earl of Knowlton, stared up at the
watered-silk canopy stretched over his head, the delicate floral
pattern dimly visible in the shaded candlelight. The lady sleeping
soundly beside him, despite having been under his protection
for less than a month, already bored him. Her throaty lisp, which
he had once thought so enticing, now grated on his ears like
the raucous cries of a Billingsgate fishwife. Her voluptuous
curves, which had promised much, now reminded him of the
rotund peasant women he had seen in Belgium. Even her not-
inconsiderable talents in bed inspired no more than a brief burst
of lust. Yes, it was time.

Knowlton rose from the massive bed and quietly dressed. He
pulled the newly fashionable gray trousers over his tautly
muscled legs. The crumpled linen shirt—had he really been so
careless as to drop it in such a heap?—settled easily upon his
shoulders. He did not even bother to button the front of his richly
embroidered white satin waistcoat, and he stuffed the limp cravat
into his pocket. From the inner pocket of his impeccably tailored
coat of black superfine he removed a small, flat box and placed
it on the dressing table. Picking up his shoes, he left the room
without a backward glance at the sleeping woman.

Easing his weary body against the soft velvet squabs of his
carriage, he found it strange that even such a virtuoso performance as La Belle Marie had given last night should leave
him so unmoved. He made a wry grin. Well, perhaps not com-

pletely unmoved, he thought as he recalled just how actively he had joined into the exercise. He had the aching muscles to prove it. But the pleasure had fled in an instant, leaving him vaguely dissatisfied, as if there was something more he wanted. Or needed.

He wondered if a long life of excess with women of every shape, size, hue, and class had finally caught up with him. Was this some perverse god's idea of a joke? To turn the once major pleasure of his life into a tedious routine devoid of the element of excitement, imagination, even satisfaction? For there was more to pleasure than that brief physical release, he knew. But now the act of physical union with a woman had become commonplace, almost dreary.

He glanced outside the carriage to the still-deserted streets of London. Knowlton had a fondness for these early-morning hours, having seen enough of them over the years. He liked watching the harsh outlines of the buildings emerge from the concealing shadows of the night. It was unfortunate that people could not be stripped of the shadows they hid behind as well.

A grimace of disgust crossed his face at his maudlin ramblings. He needed something to restore his spirits. Invitations to nearly every estate in the kingdom lay piled on his desk, but somehow he sensed that the discomfort that had so dogged him this spring in London would follow him as long as he remained with the *beau monde*. The thought of a solitary journey across Europe briefly excited him, but then he dismissed that idea as well. Touring alone could be devilish uncomfortable without a companion to take off the rough edges of Continental travel. He absently ran his hand through his light brown hair while he considered. It must be something closer to home.

Of course! He laughed at the sudden realization. Home. The perfect place to restore his restless spirits in comfort and privacy. He had not intended to go to Warrenton until harvest, but what would it matter if he made the journey a few months earlier than planned?

Excitement, which had so long been missing from his life, crept in again. Surely at Warrenton he would find the peace he found so difficult to obtain in London. The placid countryside would be a balm to his soul. Knowlton endured the remainder of the carriage ride to Upper Brook Street with eager anticipation, prepared to issue the order to pack for Warrenton as soon as he crossed the doorstep. He was going home.

1

. . . the soft breeze can come
To none more grateful than to me; escaped
From the vast city, where I long had pined
A discontended sojourner: now free
—Wordsworth, *The Prelude*

"What the blazes?"

Knowlton ducked instinctively while his temperamental
stallion reared in shock and surprise at the sudden attack. As
plums flew through the air, Knowlton struggled to keep his seat,
grabbing frantically for a handhold as his horse plunged, kicking
and stomping at the fruit rolling under his feet.

"Down, you fool," he commanded, swaying in the saddle
to the skittered dancing of his horse. Knowlton made a darting
grab at the dangling right rein, but at the same moment his mount
veered left and he found himself unhorsed. He landed with an
ignominious plop in a muddy remnant of yesterday's shower.

"Damn." Knowlton scrambled to his feet, angrily surveying
his mudsplattered clothing. Keeping a wary eye on the orchard
from whence the attack had come, he sidled toward his mount.

"You are a disgrace to your kind," he said in mock disgust
to his horse, who now stood peacefully in the middle of the lane,
nuzzling the crushed fruit at his feet.

Knowlton bent down and picked up one of the bruised and
battered plums that had so startled his mount, gingerly
extricating the pit. He extended the plum cautiously toward the
nose of his horse, who sniffed it apprehensively at first, then
with relish as he recognized the fragrant smell. Fear forgotten,
he grabbed it with his teeth.

"That's better," Knowlton murmured, giving the animal a
soothing pat. Carefully tying the reins to a bush, he stood back
to survey the trees bordering the lane. Plums did not fly through

the air on their own. Someone had tossed them. And he intended to find the culprit.

This section of the estate orchard was little maintained, but the old tree limbs bent groundward with their still-abundant load of fruit. Knowlton quickly scanned the field but noted nothing out of place. The assailant must be hiding, hoping his target would move on. Knowlton advanced with determination. One did not throw ripe plums at the Earl of Knowlton with impunity.

Finding a toehold with his boot, he clambered awkwardly over the low stone fence surrounding the orchard. Once on the other side, he searched the ground and trees, looking for some sign of an intruder. Most suspiciously, he discovered a neat pile of purple fruit under one tree, nestled among the tufts of grass. He knew very well that plums did not fall from trees in clumps.

Those well-timed missiles had put him in perilous danger for a few frightening moments, and Knowlton itched to get his hands on his assailant. There would be no more fruit tossed at unwary passersby from this orchard if he had anything to say about the matter.

Knowlton walked carefully to the base of the tree, circling it cautiously lest any more bombs came his way. Catching a flash of movement in the upper branches, he allowed himself a quick smile of satisfaction. He ducked under the low-hanging limbs and squinted up into the dancing leaves.

"I know you are up there," he said sternly. "It will go easier with you if you come down at once." A deep silence answered his offer.

"I will not ask again," Knowlton said, his irritation mounting. "Climb down and present yourself!"

Some tenant was going to get a tongue-lashing for letting his child run wild, Knowlton mused as he quickly searched for an advantageous foothold. Reaching upward to grab a low branch, he pulled himself up into the tree. Leaves and plums bounced against his head as he scrambled onto the branch. A decidedly loud rustle told him his quarry was above.

Twisting under one branch, Knowlton cautiously sought to rise to his full height. As he did so, a foot came into view and he clamped his hand around the ankle with an iron grip.

"Got you!" he cried. "You come down here now!"

A quick jerk pulled the foot free from Knowlton's grasp, and with a loud crackling of broken twigs, accompanied by the soft thumps of falling plums, a dark shape slipped through the branches with surprising speed.

Knowlton jumped to the ground as the young lad took off running through the overgrown orchard. It took only a few long-legged steps to put the boy within reach and Knowlton grabbed a handful of coat, pulling the lad up short and whirling him about.

An immediate appraisal of the red-haired, freckled-faced youth of perhaps ten told Knowlton he had been wrong about one thing—this was no tenant's son. His shirt, jacket, and breeches, although worn and dirty, were that of a young gentleman.

"You could have caused me serious harm," he thundered at the trembling boy, in mock fury,

"I didn't plan to! I didn't think I could hit you from that distance! I never would have thrown anything if I'd known." The words slid out rapidly.

Something in the boy's glib protestations made Knowlton suspect he was in the presence of a master at apologizing for mischievous behavior. No child with hair that flaming shade of red could be anything else but a rascally scamp.

"Are you familiar with the local magistrate?" Knowlton maintained his stern tone.

The boy shook his head.

"Well, I suspect it is high time you became acquainted. There are the small matters of trespassing, assault, attempted theft . . . If you are lucky, it might only result in trans-portation."

"Transportation?" The boy's eyes grew wide in alarm.

"You look like an adventurous sort of lad," Knowlton continued, barely able to suppress his grin. "Just the type to enjoy a long sea voyage. Why, I daresay you would find it the adventure of a lifetime."

"I don't want to be transported," the lad protested. "I have to stay here and take care of my mama."

"Oh, I am certain we could arrange for her to travel with

you too,'' Knowlton agreed amiably. "I don't hold with the practice of splitting families up on these occasions.''

"I bet if you went to the earl he would not mind too much that I took some of his plums,'' the boy said. "Everyone says he's a right'un. Maybe if you told him I would never do it again, he would not object.''

"I hate to disillusion you, my boy, but I *am* the Earl of Knowlton.''

The boy's eyes widened with surprise and he bowed hastily. "It is an honor to meet you, my lord. I could pay you for the plums,'' he offered eagerly. "Leastwise, not with money, but I could do some work for you. Anything you want. I can pull weeds or scrub pots.'' He looked at Knowlton with eager apprehension.

Knowlton rubbed his chin as if deep in thought. "I don't know. I have a whole staff of gardeners to pull my weeds. And there is more than one scullery maid to scrub my pots. What else can you do?''

"I could write your letters! Even Mama says I have a neat hand.'' Then his face fell. " 'Course, you might have to help me with the spelling.''

"A secretary who cannot spell. Just what I need.''

"I could carve you a whistle.''

Knowlton looked skeptical. "A whistle?''

The lad nodded eagerly. "From the willows down by the pond. They make the most marvelous sound when you cut them just right. Mama won't even let me blow them in the house,'' he announced proudly.

"Well enough, then, you can make me a whistle to pay for the plums. And I will concede you do not know your own strength and did not mean to hit my horse with your missile. But there is still the trespassing . . . although I suspect,'' said Knowlton, unable to keep a grin from his face, "that someone's mother is going to be extremely perturbed about the state of his clothes.''

The lad looked down in chagrin at his dirt-bespattered breeches. "I guess she is going to be angry.'' He looked up, brightening. "She might not mind as much if I bring her lots of plums.''

Knowlton threw back his head and laughed at the logic. He put his arm companionably around the boy's shoulder.

"I remember a few times in my youth when I received a thrashing for ruining my clothes," he confided. "I think plums just might do the trick for you."

"Do you really think so?"

"It is worth a try. Come, I will help you. How many plums does your mother need?"

The lad shrugged. "There are just the two of us. How many can two people eat?"

"Where do you live?" Knowlton asked in curiosity as he reached up to pull a ripe plum from its branch.

"Down across that field there," the boy said, pointing. "In the Rose Cottage."

Knowlton nodded in recognition. He recalled there had been a new renter in the spring.

"If that is the case, you may feel free to help yourself to as many plums as you like, anytime," Knowlton said. "Do you have a name, lad?"

"Robert Mayfield, my lord," he replied. "My mama calls me Robbie. That's 'cause I'm named for my father and it was too confusing to have two Roberts."

"Your father is not living with you?"

"He's dead," Robbie said quietly.

"I am sorry, Robbie," replied Knowlton, berating himself for his curiosity.

"He was killed at Salamanca," Robbie said with a proud air. "He was a captain in the cavalry. I have his sword, except Mama won't let me play with it. And when I am old enough I am going to join a cavalry regiment."

"An admirable goal," said Knowlton. So Mrs. Mayfield was a widow? It might behoove him to look in on his latest tenant. Widows could often be *very* lonely. He stripped off his coat.

"We can use this to carry the plums to your house," he said easily.

Robbie stared at him. "Won't your mama be mad if you ruin your coat?"

Knowlton laughed. "She would if she were still here, Robbie

my boy. But I can ruin my coats without fear these days. She died many a year ago.''

"I am sorry, sir,'' said Robbie.

His evident sincerity touched Knowlton. He reached down and picked out a ripe plum from the pile upon the ground. Polishing the fruit on his sleeve, he bit into it and savored the satisfying, juicy tartness. He gestured toward the stack. ''Have one.''

Robbie eagerly complied. Knowlton eased himself to the ground, stretching out his tall frame on the sweet-smelling grass, leaning back on one elbow while he savored his plum. Lord, it was good to be home.

After the dirt and noise of the city, the country seemed even more peaceful than he remembered. The sound of the breeze rustling the leaves overhead, the nearby trill of a bird, all brought back in a rush memories of his own childhood here at Warrenton. When every new day was an adventure and all was new and exciting. He had never been bored in those days. Maybe he could recapture some of that youthful enthusiasm during his stay this time.

With a disgruntled sigh, Knowlton flung the pit into the far reaches of the orchard, wiping his sticky fingers on his now-filthy buckskins. Between his coat and breeches, his valet would have a fit. That brought a grin to Knowlton's face. The man was far too concerned with his master's consequence.

Knowlton cleared his throat. ''Now, Robbie, if you can manage to hold on to the plums, we can probably get that foolish beast of mine to carry us both. I will escort you home and explain matters to your mama.'' And he could avail himself of the opportunity of meeting the widowed Mrs. Mayfield. Would she have the same flaming red hair as her son? In his experience, the old adage about the passionate nature of redheads held true. With renewed interest, Knowlton started back toward the lane, Robbie half-running to keep up with the lengthy strides.

Knowlton untied his horse and held the reins, then looked expectantly at Robbie.

''Up, boy. We haven't got all afternoon.''

"I have never been on a horse, sir."

The revelation astounded Knowlton. "You want to join a cavalry regiment amd you do not know how to ride? I think you had better set your sights on a rifle brigade. Of course, you probably have not fired a gun either."

Robbie shook his head. "Mama says both are too dangerous."

Knowlton sighed in exasperation. Hen-witted women could be the death of little boys. He took the parcel of plums and set them on the ground, gave his horse a stern admonition to remain still, and put his hands together. "Step here and I will boost you up."

Robbie did as ordered and managed to creditably scramble into the saddle. Knowlton handed him the coat full of plums, then climbed up behind him.

"This is prodigiously wonderful," Robbie exclaimed with awe, surveying the world from his new vantage point.

"Prodigiously?"

"That is my new word this week," the lad explained proudly. "Mama has me learn a new one every week. The vicar says it is an admirable plan."

"You are friends with the vicar?"

"He is giving me my lessons."

Knowlton's brow furrowed. "You have lessons in the summer?"

"Mama said I missed too much time last spring when we made the move here, so I needed to study all summer if I wasn't to fall too far behind."

"And what is the vicar teaching you?"

"Oh, Latin, Greek, a little history. But I think Mama knows more history than he does."

"And how do you find Latin and Greek?" Knowlton asked impishly.

"Truly?" Robbie asked warily.

"Truly."

"Not very well."

Knowlton laughed. "I shall tell you a secret, Robbie, my boy. I loathed Latin and Greek when I was your age. Hated them. Detested them."

"And did your mama make you study them anyway?"

He nodded. "Not only my mama, but my father and my tutor. And if my lessons were not perfect, I was thrashed. The vicar does not thrash you if you make a mistake, does he?"

"No," said Robbie, with obvious relief. "Do you still hate Latin and Greek?"

"Promise me you will not tell your mother?" Knowlton whispered conspiratorially.

"I promise."

"I still loathe them."

Robbie grinned. "Mama would be very angry if she heard you say that. She says education is very important."

"I did not say education was unimportant," Knowlton said. "I merely meant that cramming Latin and Greek into children's heads is an abominable practice. I much more approve of learning a useful language like French or Italian."

"Or Spanish!" said Robbie excitedly. "I can still remember one time when Papa was home he taught us a few words of Spanish. *Buenas tardes*—that means 'good afternoon.' And *gracias* is 'thank you.' "

"A sight more useful than Latin, I am certain," muttered Knowlton as the Rose Cottage came into view. Stopping his horse at the gate, he dismounted and carefully assisted Robbie down. So Mrs. Mayfield was a mother who did not approve of horses and rifles—yet knew history and insisted her son have a gentleman's education. His interest piqued, Knowlton followed the racing boy down the front path. It was time to make the acquaintance of this intriguing lady.

2

She was a Phantom of Delight
When first she gleamed upon my sight.

—Wordsworth

Katherine Mayfield rubbed the end of her nose with the back of her hand, leaving a smudge of flour behind. She returned to her rhythmic kneading with renewed determination. Soon she could turn the loaves into the pans, pop them into the oven, and direct her attention to . . .

A frown marred her pale face. There were so many things she needed to accomplish: the washing, the mending, letting out Robbie's clothes for what must be the hundredth time. She shook her head in dismay as she thought how rapidly he was growing. The clothes he had now would last until the weather turned this fall, but then she would be faced with providing him an entire head-to-foot wardrobe. And that meant money. Which meant she must turn from her own chores to her work for Mrs. Gorton, the local seamstress. One more afternoon of stitching delicate lace trim onto some squire's daughter's gown.

Gazing longingly at the bright sunlit yard outside, Katherine wished she could afford to toss her sewing work aside and take the afternoon for herself. It would be heaven to free her mind for a few hours from the never-ceasing struggle to survive. She could pretend she was a grand lady whose servants took care of every minute detail of running the house while she spent her time as she wished.

Katherine shook her head at her futile longings. She could only attach the blame to herself for the state she and Robbie were in. The knowledge that she had done the right thing provided cold comfort when they lived so close to the edge.

With the bread tucked safely into the oven, Katherine turned to wash the flour from her hands. Hearing Robbie's excited chattering through the window, she paused to listen. He had been gone most of the afternoon and she prayed he had not got into any more mischief this week. She froze in mid-step when she heard a strange masculine voice. Robbie had been up to something, the wretch! Hastily rinsing her hands, Katherine dried them on her apron as she hastened through the narrow passageway to the front hall.

Pulling open the door, she saw Robbie dancing down the cobbled pathway, followed by a tall stranger whose demeanor and bearing belied his disheveled appearance.

"Mama, Mama," cried Robbie. " 'Tis the earl; I met him today in the orchard and he says we can have as many plums as we want."

Katherine wanted to sink into the stone steps. How many times had she warned Robbie against trespassing on the earl's property? Instead, she gathered her skirts and bobbed a deferential curtsy to her new landlord, keeping her eyes carefully averted.

"I am pleased to make your acquaintance, my lord."

The standard greeting he had planned froze on his lips as Knowlton obtained his first close look at Mrs. Mayfield. Dear God, an angel had landed on his doorstep! His polite social smile transformed itself into a wide grin of male appreciation as he perused her from head to toe. He easily looked past the drab dress, cap-covered head, and flour-smudged nose to what lay beneath. Mrs. Mayfield was quite one of the most stunning women he had ever seen. The straggling red curls peeking out from under her cap set off a flawless complexion unmarked by the trace of a freckle. And her form . . . It looked to be ample in all the right places, soft, and curving where it should.

Returning his gaze to her face, he found himself staring into the loveliest pair of blue eyes he had ever seen. The mingled expression of anger and wariness he saw there bemused him.

Katherine lifted her gaze and caught her breath at the appreciative look in the earl's eyes. Was it going to start all over again here? She struggled against her anger. "Have you seen quite enough, my lord?"

Her tone was icy, but as Knowlton expected, the accent was cultivated.

"You don't have to call him 'my lord,' " Robbie piped up. "He's not toplofty at all. See all the plums we gathered? And I got to ride on his horse! It was ever so high in the air. And I did not fall off. Can I get a horse of my own now?"

"Do not bombard your mother with so much information at once, you scamp," Knowlton said, ruffling the boy's hair. "If you know what is good for you, you will run off and make yourself more presentable before your mother has a chance to take a good look at your appearance."

Katherine caught only a brief flash of Robbie's stained clothing as he raced by, and she grimaced in dismay. Turning back to the earl, she smiled coolly.

"I can only surmise you found him stealing plums in your orchard," she said. "I am very sorry, my lord. He has been told time and time again not to wander onto the estate grounds, but he—"

Knowlton raised a forestalling hand. "I do not mind in the least. He was in the oldest portion of the orchard. I always allow my tenants free access to the fruit there. He did nothing he should not have." Knowlton had already determined not to alarm her with the plum-throwing incident. He thought Robbie had already been properly chastened for that indiscretion.

"Thank you, my lord," Katherine replied. She noted the expectant gleam in his cool gray eyes. "Was there another matter?"

"It is a hot afternoon," he said. He wanted to linger in her presence, to determine if his first reaction had been overhasty. He could simply not believe his good fortune. "Perhaps a glass of something cool . . . ?"

He watched carefully as dismay momentarily flitted over her face; then her previous closed expression returned.

"I beg your pardon, my lord. Please come inside. I can bring you a glass of water, or there is some May wine, if you prefer."

"Water would be most welcome," he said, following her over the threshold and into the parlor.

Katherine hastily retreated to the kitchen, searching to find a glass that was not cracked or chipped. So here was the great Earl of Knowlton. He did not look at all like she had imagined. In his shirtsleeves, with the casually open collar, stained buckskins, and windblown hair, he looked more like a country squire than one of the richest men in the kingdom. And one of the most notorious womanizers. A frisson of apprehension gripped her. Katherine prayed there would be no trouble here, as there had been in the last two places she had lived. She had been all too aware of his appreciative appraisal on the front steps. Those scrutinizing gray eyes made her uncomfortable.

She hoped the intentional drabness of her costume had given him pause. It was only a pity she could not do something to her hair. One sight of that color and all men thought one thing. She did want to stay in this neighborhood for a while, at least; another move would be ruinously expensive.

During her absence, Knowlton's sharp eyes appraised the shabby parlor, noting the worn upholstery on the two chairs and the tallow candles on the highly polished but conspicuously bare table. It was very clear that Mrs. Mayfield was not a widow of means. She might have an interest, then, in improving her financial station. This promised to be a most propitious situation.

When Mrs. Mayfield reappeared with his water, Knowlton gestured for her to sit, sensing her wariness. He did his best to put her at ease.

"Is the cottage to your liking?" He noted approvingly that a few recalcitrant locks of hair crept from beneath her kitchen cap, giving her a less-than-matronly appearance. Particularly since her hair was the same flaming shade as Robbie's. There was something elementally exciting about red hair on a woman.

Katherine nodded politely, uncomfortably aware of his close examination.

"No leaking roof? Sticking windows?" He arched a quizzing brow.

"Everything is satisfactory, my lord."

"You have only to speak to Mr. Taggert if you encounter any difficulties." Knowlton smiled easily. "I want my tenants to be happy. Any justified repairs will be performed."

"Thank you, my lord." Katherine relaxed her guard slightly. If he remained true to his word, Lord Knowlton would be a vast improvement over her last landlord. She suppressed a shiver at the memory of the old, drafty, and damp cottage in which she and Robbie had spent the previous winter.

"You have a lively son," Knowlton commented. "He must lead you on a merry dance."

She smiled and he observed how that action brought a glow to her pale face. He longed to reach over and pull off that ridiculous mobcap so he could see her hair in all its glory.

Robbie bounded into the room at that moment, his face and hands showing signs of a less-than-thorough wash.

"Robbie!" Katherine exclaimed in dismay, forgetting the earl for a moment. "Look at your clothes!"

He looked down sheepishly at his filthy breeches, with a tear across one knee. "I am sorry, Mama." He set down the bundle of the earl's coat on the table. "Here are the plums we picked. Will you make a pie for us, Mama?"

She looked in horror at the misshapen garment. "What did you wrap these in?"

"My coat," said Knowlton with a grin.

"You will have ruined it," she scolded.

He shrugged. "It was not my favorite coat."

She stood up, reaching for the bundle. "I will do what I can to clean it for you," she said, and whisked her armload out into the hall before he could protest. She was grateful for another excuse to leave the earl's presence.

Katherine dumped the plums into a bowl and surveyed the ruin of the earl's coat. Brushing off a stray leaf, she grimaced in discouragement. It was not terribly dirty; a good brushing would remove most of it. But the weighty plums had done things to the coat that its tailor had never intended. The earl would never wish to be seen wearing it in polite company again. With a shake of her head at the folly of the nobility, she took her clothes brush to the inside. The price of this coat would have kept her and Robbie in clothes for years.

"I fear your coat is ruined," she said woefully when she returned to the parlor. "I did what I could."

"And much more than you needed to, Mrs. Mayfield. I thank you." His gray eyes twinkled with suppressed amusement.

Robbie was bouncing on the edge of his seat. "The earl says I can visit him at his house anytime I want."

"That is very kind of you." Katherine eyed the earl with a wary glance, her suspicions reawakened.

"Truly, I mean it," Knowlton interjected, hearing the doubt in her voice. "I do not stand on ceremony with my tenants. There are a good many things at Warrenton to interest a sharp lad like Robbie. He is welcome at any time." As are you yourself, he thought silently. Most welcome.

He saw a fleeting spasm of alarm cross her face and feared he had acted too precipitately by inviting Robbie. True, it was not the thing one would expect an earl to do, but Knowlton thought he had explained himself well enough. Robbie did amuse him, and he was sorely in need of amusement. But Mrs. Mayfield sat there glaring at him as if he had asked her to dance naked on the table. His reputation, no doubt. The country gossips would surely have apprised her of that. It might take some time to repair the damage, but he already suspected it would be a worthwhile campaign.

"Thank you for the water, Mrs. Mayfield." His mouth curved into a sensual smile. "And for the chance to meet your son."

"Thank you again for the plums," Katherine replied, quickly rising to her feet to hasten his departure. His smile disconcerted her. With relief, she escorted the earl to the door. "We will very much enjoy the preserves they will make."

"Ah, yes, I surmised you were an accomplished cook," he said with an air of mystery.

Katherine's expression became puzzled.

"I might have said it was the delicious aroma of baking bread with which you tortured me throughout this visit," he said with a roguish twinkle in his eyes. "But actually, it was the dab of flour on your nose that gave it away." He reached out and brushed the offending spot with his finger, gratified to see the blush that rose to her cheeks. She looked even lovelier with color in her face.

Katherine willed her voice to remain calm, the skin on her nose still tingling from that gentle touch. "Thank you for pointing out that flaw in my appearance, my lord. I would hate to think that an important person might happen by and find me in such disarray."

He admired her aplomb and his grin widened. "It was no less a social crime than having your landlord drop in uninvited and in his shirtsleeves. Shall we call it even, Mrs. Mayfield?''

She nodded, amused in spite of her wariness. He sketched her a low bow and exited the cottage. Katherine returned to the kitchen, sinking weakly into the corner chair.

This was far, far worse than she could ever have imagined. In the other places where there had been difficulties, at least she had been personally repelled by the men. But the earl . . . It was not difficult to see why he was such a success with women. That devastating smile had sent even her pulse racing. He was handsome, witty, and knew exactly how to set off his not-inconsiderable charms to best advantage. In short, he was every inch the rake his reputation labeled him. She had the sinking feeling that remaining impervious to his charm would be one of the most difficult tasks of her life. But ignore him she must. Men of his station had only one use for poor widows.

Robbie followed the earl into the yard, watching with worshipful eyes as he mounted his horse and rode away with a farewell wave. He slowly sauntered back into the house, heading straight for the stairs.

Katherine waited at the bottom. ''There is a *small* matter we need to discuss,'' she said sternly. ''Were you not told to stay off the estate grounds?''

Robbie nodded glumly.

''And haven't I asked you countless times to take better care of your clothes?''

He nodded again.

''Robbie, those clothes have to last you until I make your winter ones.'' Katherine shook her head in dismay. ''You are already starting to look like a ragamuffin. You will be reduced to wearing your Sunday best soon, and that will mean you shall be confined to the house. I will not allow you to ruin those.''

''Yes, Mama.'' He turned to make his escape.

''Robbie?''

''Yes?''

''Three pages in your Latin grammar. For disobeying me.''

''The earl didn't mind,'' he protested. ''He said it was all right.''

''But I did not, and it is my word that counts in this house.

Now, you march into the study this minute and finish that work, or there will be no supper for you.''

"Yes, ma'am.''

Knowlton nearly laughed aloud as his horse trotted toward home. He had not been so highly diverted in an age. Robbie was a scamp. In fact, he reminded Knowlton all too clearly of himself at that age, when his mother had sworn he would be the death of her and his father had birched him regularly for some transgression or other. He was willing to bet Mrs. Mayfield did not birch Robbie. She had probably devised some equally devilish punishment for the lad—like incarceration in his room on a bright, sunny summer's day. Knowlton had much preferred a birching to that.

He was captivated by his short acquaintance with Mrs. Mayfield. She had done nothing to dash the hopes that had blossomed when he had first heard that a widow lived on his property. He could not wait to see her with her hair down. The color reminded him of firelight and sunlight mixed and would look most enticing spread out upon a white pillow.

Her demeanor, however, gave him pause. He suspected she was exactly what she appeared—a very respectable widow, struggling to raise her son alone on too little money. He would have a quick word with Taggert and see what assistance they could offer her.

Yet there had been a brief glimpse of something else—her flash of wit at his departure showed there was more to Mrs. Mayfield than first appeared. There had been a hint of mocking amusement in her voice when she gently chastised him for arriving uninvited on her doorstep. She was not afraid to trade barbs with an earl. He liked that.

The more he thought on it, the deeper his interest grew in Robbie's mother. Knowlton had little experience with ladies of her ilk—he preferred experienced women of the *ton* to impecunious widows, for the former knew the rules of the game. He had heard too many tales of the danger of going outside that tight circle, of raising expectations that would never be met.

But Mrs. Mayfield posed a challenge. He had ample proof

of the stories of redheaded women, that they had a nature more
fiery and passionate than even his own. Why else did so many
ladies of less-than-virtuous honor dye their hair that color? He
rather thought he liked the idea of testing Mrs. Mayfield to see
if that adage always held true.

In fact, it would be a welcome challenge. Could he overcome
her widow's reticence to expose the sensual woman that lay
beneath? A lazy smile crept over his features. It was exactly
the scheme he needed to bring himself out of his boredom. A
true test of his seductive skills. He had no doubt of his success—
the only question would be the length of time it would take to
bring Mrs. Mayfield to his bed. Cheered as he had not been
in weeks, Knowlton whistled a lively tune as he guided his horse
toward home.

3

And, after all, what is a lie? 'Tis but
   The Truth in masquerade;

   —Byron, *Don Juan*

"My lord?" Knowlton's imperious butler stood immobile inside the study door.

"What it is, Hutchins?" the earl drawled in a bored voice.

"There is a young person here, my lord." The butler's tone clearly indicated his disapproval. "He insists he is here at your invitation and wishes to see you."

Knowlton looked up with interest. "And what does this importuning guest call himself?"

"He says he is Robbie Mayfield, my lord."

"As I thought," said Knowlton, lowering his booted feet from his desk. "Send him in, Hutchins. And, Hutchins . . . unless I give instructions otherwise, Mr. Mayfield is to be admitted whenever he calls."

"As you wish, my lord."

Knowlton grinned as Hutchins departed. So, the rascal was here already. He pushed away the London papers he had been reading.

Robbie walked into the study, his head swiveling this way and that as he examined every corner of the room.

"Good morning, Robbie." Knowlton's smile widened at the boy's avid perusal.

"This whole house is yours?"

"Every inch of it," replied Knowlton.

"How many people live here?" Robbie breathed.

"Only myself," said Knowlton.

Robbie's eyes widened. "You live here all by yourself?"

"Only if you discount an army of servants."

"Don't you ever get lonely?"

Knowlton laughed. "Rarely. I usually am not here long enough to grow lonely. If I am, I invite a houseful of guests to stay with me."

"How do you keep them from getting lost inside the house?"

"I have to be very careful of that," the earl admitted. "I always count heads at the dinner table. I would hate for someone to starve to death and die in some lonely corner." He casually walked to the far wall and opened a cupboard door, peering cautiously inside. "I always like to double-check," he told Robbie in a confidential tone. "Just in case there is the skeleton of some former guest that I missed."

Robbie shuddered at the thought.

"I am roasting you." Knowlton clapped the lad on the back. "Come, I am certain you did not wish to spend the morning in the house. I will show you the stables."

Robbie ran to keep up with the earl's long strides as they crossed the rear lawn. The boy stared in wide-eyed wonder at the paddock, where several horses frolicked and gamboled in the morning sunlight.

"How many horses do you have?" he asked with awe as they stepped into the seemingly endless stable block.

"Several," replied the earl blandly. He was growing uncomfortable with Robbie's awestruck wonder at every sight. Knowlton had always taken Warrenton's magnificence and the excellence of its stables for granted.

"What do you do with them all?" Robbie inquired as they walked past grays, bays, blacks, and chestnuts.

"They all have their special purposes," the earl explained patiently. "There are riding horses, horses for hunting, horses for the light carriages, horses for the heavy carriages, and horses for whatever other special need may arise."

"I would like to learn how to drive a carriage someday," Robbie said.

"You had better learn how to ride first," Knowlton reminded him. "You are getting a late start as it is, for a cavalry officer."

Robbie scuffed his boot against the packed dirt floor. "Mama says we cannot afford a horse," he said glumly.

"You do not need your own horse to learn on," the earl said, making an instant decision. What better way to gain the boy's confidence? "There must be some beast in this stable that would be quite suitable for you."

"You mean you would allow me to ride one of your horses?" Robbie's eyes grew big.

"I think I can arrange it," the earl said, smiling at the boy's unfeigned eagerness.

"And you will teach me how to ride?"

Knowlton hesitated for a moment, then nodded, offering up a silent self-congratulation at this unexpected opportunity. What better way to get on Mrs. Mayfield's good side than to take an interest in her beloved son?

"Frank, have Alecto saddled," Knowlton ordered.

"Alecto?" Robbie asked. "Wasn't she one of the Furies?"

Knowlton smiled. "Far enough in your Greek studies for that, eh? An apt name for a mare, don't you think?"

The groom soon led out the medium-size bay, saddled and bridled.

Seeing the eager expression on the lad's face, Knowlton remembered how he had been set on his first horse before the age of three, and felt a brush of compassion for Robbie. How long had Mrs. Mayfield lived on the edge of poverty? Long enough that her son had never learned the basic points of horsemanship. He gave Robbie an encouraging smile. "Ready for your first lesson?"

Robbie nodded.

"The first thing to remember is: never jerk on the reins," Knowlton explained to his avid listener. "It hurts the horse's mouth. Use gentle pulling. And always be firm in your intentions. A horse will sense your hesitation and will use it to take advantage."

"Firm but gentle," Robbie repeated as the groom led the horse over to the mounting block. Now that he stood next to the horse, her back looked a long way up. There would be no Knowlton in the saddle to hold him on this time. Swallowing hard, he stepped onto the block and grabbed the reins. Knowlton helped him slip his foot into the stirrup, then Robbie swung his right leg up and over.

Knowlton waited patiently while the groom adjusted the stirrups to accommodate Robbie's short legs. Then he nodded to have the mare led about the yard. He watched Robbie with a critical eye, seeking to take his measure as a potential horseman. He was pleased with what he saw. Despite the lad's understandable nervousness, his seat was natural and unforced.

"Take up more slack in the reins," he commanded. "Hold your hands low, in a relaxed position."

Robbie complied readily, looking eagerly at Knowlton for approval.

The earl nodded his satisfaction. The lad would learn fast, Knowlton thought. He just might make the cavalry after all, despite the fact he was a good seven to eight years late sitting on his first horse. With careful instruction . . .

"Try a trot, Frank," Knowlton instructed the groom. "Hang on tight, Robbie."

Knowlton grinned as Robbie bounced along at the quickened pace. He saw the gleam of excitement in the boy's eyes and felt an unfamiliar sense of satisfaction at Robbie's pleasure. Remembering his own early riding lessons, and the grateful fondness he retained for the old groom who had taught him, Knowlton experienced an odd wish that perhaps someday this boy would look back with the same emotion on the man who had first set him on a horse.

"You are looking good, lad," he called in encouragement, rewarded by Robbie's wide grin of pleasure at the commendation.

Katherine was pleased that Robbie applied himself so diligently to his studies these days—and if he worked hard only to make certain he would have more time to get into mischief, at least his work was not suffering. She could not ask more of him; she knew how much she already asked by insisting on schoolwork in the summer.

She knew he spent most of his time with Sam Trent, one of the farmers' sons. Katherine did not mind the difference in social station; Robbie needed to be with boys of his own age, and if only farmers' sons were available, well, they would do.

Sighing, she picked up her basket, preparing to walk to the village. It was probably debatable exactly which class she and Robbie belonged to anymore. The requirements of survival were more important than paying homage to the beliefs of one's class. Food was more important than status. She had learned that lesson well.

Katherine accomplished her errands at a leisurely pace, knowing there was no need for haste this day. It was warm and sunny and the sky the brilliant blue of high midsummer. She could not blame Robbie a bit for wanting to be out on such a glorious day. Even she was tempted to follow some childish pursuit—like wading barefoot in the stream or climbing a tree to reach the topmost fruit.

Unfortunately, neither pursuit was suited to the image of responsibility she assiduously tried to cultivate. With a regretful toss of her head, she ambled down the lane toward home. Mothers were not allowed to behave like children, no matter how much they might wish to.

Katherine heard the sound of an approaching carriage, and she stepped automatically to the side of the road to let it pass, hoping it would not leave her covered in dust. She relaxed when she heard the vehicle slow.

"Good day to you, Mrs. Mayfield."

Katherine turned in surprise at the sound of the earl's voice. "Good day, my lord."

"Fine weather, is it not?" He doffed his hat.

"Very fine," Katherine assented, willing him to drive on.

"Almost too fine a day for driving," the earl continued, holding his horses at a standstill. "But alas, without my groom I am doomed to be a-wheel. Should you care to join me?"

"Thank you, but I will walk."

Her reluctance spurred his determination. This was a perfect opportunity to allay her apprehensions. "Oh, come now, Mrs. Mayfield. You have been to the village, I see, and I suspect your basket is growing heavier by the moment."

"I am quite capable of carrying my basket," she protested, firmly intending to resist his cajolery. Lord Knowlton only boded danger for her.

"Now, do not be churlish, Mrs. Mayfield. I am only trying to be a good neighbor." Knowlton gave her his most innocent smile. "Contemplate how much more pleasant your afternoon will be if you arrive at your home rested and refreshed, instead of worn and tired from a hot, dusty walk.''

His persistence irritated Katherine.

''Surely you are not nervous about driving with me?'' Knowlton flashed her an injured look. ''I would understand your hesitation if I was inviting you into a closed carriage, but I hardly think you are in much danger from me in the curricle.''

As her reluctance stemmed precisely from her apprehensions about the earl, Katherine was at a loss for a civil reply. Why would he not leave her alone?

Knowlton shook his head sadly. ''I see that I have misjudged you, Mrs. Mayfield. I thought you were the type of lady who would not judge another merely on the basis of hearsay. How can you be so certain that I am not a suitable companion?''

''You mean to suggest otherwise?'' she asked dryly. She could not resist the temptation to bandy words with him. Words, after all, were perfectly safe.

He flung a hand to his breast. ''You wound me, my lady. You impugn my honor.''

The rakehell *had* no honor, she thought, amused nonetheless by his protestations of injured innocence.

''You can rely on my complete trustworthiness,'' he promised, pleading for her capitulation.

''I thank you for your concern, Lord Knowlton,'' she said coolly. ''But I much prefer to walk. Good day, my lord.'' After bobbing a slight curtsy, Katherine turned and resumed her steps down the lane.

Despite his disappointment, Knowlton's admiration rose a notch. This was to be no easy conquest. He picked up the reins and urged his horses into a slow walk. Mrs. Mayfield would find that he was not readily discouraged.

''You have not yet asked me what drew me into town this afternoon.'' His voice held a slightly mocking tone.

Katherine kept her eyes facing forward, grateful that her bonnet hid most of her face. She would not give him the satisfaction of seeing her reluctant curiosity. ''Do tell.''

''I was visiting with the vicar.''

She resisted the urge to laugh. Did he really think to impress her with such a ridiculous tale? ''I see.''

"You sound rather doubtful."

Katherine glanced with undisguised skepticism at the earl. "Pardon me for seeming so, but in all the tales I have heard of you, my lord, not one has mentioned your propensity for the religious."

"Did I not tell you it is unwise to listen to idle gossip?" Knowlton looked at her, his face full of wounded vanity. "I always make it a point to attend services when I am in residence at Warrenton. I feel it is my obligation to set an example for the lower orders."

Katherine's eyes held a challenge. "Then I shall look forward to seeing you this Sunday," she replied, thinking to trap him with his outlandish boasts.

"I certainly hope so!" Knowlton smiled at his success in finally gaining a reaction from her. "I was speaking with the vicar about that very matter. I feel it incumbent upon me to visit him whenever I return, to remind him that I am now here and he can no longer get away with the boring drivel he spews from the pulpit during my absences."

Katherine's lips twitched in suppressed amusement. "How do you know it is so dreadful if you are not here?"

"I have my sources," he said with a mysterious air. "The vicar knows that he dare not bore me, for whatever good example my attendance sets would be dashed to pieces if I fell asleep in the process."

"I am certain the vicar appreciates the challenge."

"I daresay he does."

All too soon, to Knowlton's mind, they reached the gate of the Rose Cottage. How he would have liked to continue this conversation for another hour—preferably with Mrs. Mayfield in his carriage, not walking alongside it. But he congratulated himself on the progress he had made this day, and determined not to be too greedy for success. He must allay her apprehensions first.

"Perhaps next time you will not be so reluctant to accept my offer of transportation," he said, watching her face carefully to see how she reacted to his suggestion. "Now that I have demonstrated my respectability to you."

It would take more than a few boastful remarks about a visit to the vicar to overcome *his* reputation, Katherine thought. "We shall see," she said noncommittally. "Once again, I bid you good day."

Knowlton watched as she walked down the flagstone path to the cottage door. He resisted the impulse to laugh aloud. She was such a skittish thing, terrified of his reputation as a man no lady could feel safe with. Which was highly untrue. He knew any number of women who had never been forced to fend off an unwelcome advance from him.

Of course, they were outnumbered entirely by those who had accepted the advance, or even begged for it, but that was not the point. He needed to convince Mrs. Mayfield she was perfectly safe with him. The fact that this was a total untruth did not bother him one whit. With a wide grin he urged the horses homeward. The pursuit of Mrs. Mayfield was already proving to be a delicious antidote to boredom.

Katherine set her basket down with a thunk on the kitchen table and struggled to untie the ribbons of her bonnet, which had become hopelessly tangled.

Drat that man. She had sensed the danger from him at their first meeting, and he had done nothing to dispel that image today. Oh, he had been as polite as could be, but she knew that behind that facade lurked a man who only ached to get his hands on her. He was just like all the others. She should have ignored him completely, instead of trading sallies. Why had she been so foolish?

Because you wanted to be, a small voice said. *Because despite the danger, you are intrigued by the man. And secretly flattered that he finds you attractive.*

Katherine shut her eyes. It did not help in the least that Knowlton was a devastatingly handsome man. He had looked every inch the lord today in his polished Hessians, form-hugging pantaloons, and expertly tailored coat; quite a contrast to the muddy and disheveled man who had graced her parlor only a few days ago. But the look in those expressive gray eyes had not changed. The admiring gleam she saw there did nothing to dispel her apprehension.

The years since Robert's death had taught her to be increasingly wary of men. She had grown adept at politely fending off their advances. If a situation grew too intolerable, she moved. Now, she feared she was in the midst of her worst situation yet. It had been easy to turn up her nose at bumbling squires and lewd old lords. Now, for the first time, she found her pursuer dangerously attractive. And that would never do. She reminded herself she had a son to raise now, and there was no time for dreams. She must make it quite clear to Lord Knowlton that she held him in disinterest.

She only hoped he would not see that for the lie it was.

4

O, what a tangled web we weave,
When first we practice, to deceive.

—Scott, *Marmion*

If Katherine found herself looking forward to the Sunday service with more than an ordinary interest, she assured herself it was mere curiosity over how the vicar would respond to Knowlton's charge to improve his sermons. She told herself she was quite content not to see the earl again.

After leading Robbie to an empty pew, Katherine noticed with a mixed twinge of disappointment and satisfaction that the earl was not in his box. All his talk of a public display of piety had been just that—talk. As she had suspected. Then she grew aware of the sudden hushed silence of the congregation. Trying to dismiss the small thrill that raced through her, she slowly returned her gaze to the earl's box. There he stood, surveying the assembly with an amused smile at the stir his presence created. He caught Katherine's eye and gave her an ostentatious wink. She abruptly dropped her gaze to the hymnal in her hands, wishing she could hide her flaming cheeks. Drat that man!

The service seemed to last for an interminable time. Katherine was unable to appreciate whether Knowlton's talk had had any effect on the vicar, for her attention and her eyes kept straying to the lone man in the Beauchamp family box. She knew she could not allow the earl to disconcert her so, yet she felt powerless to control her thoughts. Even here in church, when her mind should be on holy matters, she was more aware of his clean, pure baritone singing "A Mighty Fortress Is Our God" than she was of the words of praise.

When at last the congregation was dismissed, Katherine grabbed Robbie and nearly raced out of the church. She did not want to risk another encounter with the earl while her thoughts were so disordered. But Robbie darted from her side the moment they reached the steps, and she was forced to wait.

"A most edifying sermon, I do declare." Knowlton stepped up behind her, pitching his voice low so only she could hear. "Did you not find it so, Mrs. Mayfield?"

Whirling to face him, Katherine did not miss the wicked twinkle in the earl's eye.

"Most edifying, my lord," she replied, primly lowering her gaze.

"I must say, I thought the vicar's sermon incorporated a highly instructive lesson." Knowlton smiled at her discomfort. She was not half so reluctant to be in his presence as she pretended, he knew. It provoked a desire to see how far he could push her. "It shall be a rare pleasure to listen to the next sermon if he continues in this manner."

"Perhaps the repeated exposure to such edifying thoughts will do you good," she retorted, turning away abruptly. How dare he express his interest in her by blatantly striking up a conversation in full view of everyone in the parish? If her name ever became linked with Knowlton's, her reputation would be in tatters. No single woman was deemed safe with him. Spotting the vicar and his wife at the church steps, Katherine hastened to join them.

Knowlton determined not to allow Mrs. Mayfield to get the better of him this time. With quick steps he once again stood at her side.

"Robbie has made a decided improvement in his Latin, Mrs. Mayfield," the vicar said to Katherine. "I may make a scholar of him yet."

"He has been working very hard," Katherine acknowledged, uncomfortably aware of Knowlton's presence again.

"Excellent sermon, vicar," Knowlton interjected with an approving nod.

The vicar beamed at the compliment. "Thank you, my lord. It is a pleasure to have you with us again."

"I think you will have that pleasure often," Knowlton said, with a pointed glance at Katherine. "I have a mind to remain at Warrenton for some time. I find I am learning to enjoy the simpler pleasures of country life."

Katherine frantically glanced about, looking for her son. She could not leave without him, yet every moment she spent in the earl's presence was torture. She nearly collapsed with relief when she heard Robbie's voice. "I will tell him you are pleased at his progress, vicar. If you will excuse me . . ." She executed a brief curtsy and hurried toward her son.

"I want to play with Sam," Robbie announced.

"You can see Sam another day," Katherine said, hastening him toward the lane. "There are chores to be done at home. And I want you to gather blackberries for me today."

"But I wanted to—"

"You will do as I say," she snapped, and then instantly regretted her harsh words. It was not Robbie's fault that the earl disconcerted her so. She would have to take greater care to avoid him next time. In a conciliatory tone she added, "If you pick berries for me as soon as we arrive home, you may have the rest of the afternoon free."

"All right," he said grudgingly. He had secretly nourished hopes of being able to catch a ride in the earl's curricle today. At least there would be time to walk over to Warrenton and maybe talk Knowlton or his groom into another ride in the paddock.

The following morning, Knowlton stretched lazily in his bed, leaning back against the soft pillows. Country living was having a decidedly harmful influence on him—he felt downright slothful having slept so late. If he was not careful, he would soon be rising at farmer's hours. And that would never do.

With a resigned sigh he tossed back the covers and swung his legs over the edge of the bed. As if on cue, Rigsby, his valet, entered. Without a word he picked up Knowlton's blue brocade robe and helped his master into it, then stood aside as Knowlton padded across the thickly carpeted floor into the bath chamber.

It was the only improvement he had installed here at Warrenton, and was worth every penny, the earl thought. The bathing tub itself, fashioned from Italian marble, was large enough for two, as he had proved to his satisfaction more than once. However, it was not the tub itself but the newly installed shower bath of which Knowlton was most fond. The craftily arranged cistern in the attic, combined with the warming stove, provided ample hot water at his command. And there was something very refreshing about drenching oneself in water rather than soaking in it like a stewed chicken.

A discreet knock came at the door while Knowlton toweled himself dry.

"Young Robert is here, my lord," Rigsby announced.

"Has he been to the stables yet?"

"I think not, my lord."

"Have him wait in the morning room, then," said Knowlton, reaching for the clothing Rigsby had laid out on the bed. Smiling to himself as he dressed, Knowlton anticipated Robbie's reaction to the new pony in the stable. He only hoped that Mrs. Mayfield would not cut up too strongly when she discovered the gift. He suspected she was not comfortable with her impecunious status, and would resent anything which she would consider charity. He would have to tread carefully to avoid alienating her.

Knowlton dressed quickly in buckskin breeches and Hessians. Disdaining the formality of a cravat, he tied a simple Belcher scarf around his neck and shrugged himself into his chocolate-colored riding coat.

He exited his room and hastened down the stairs, eager to see the young lad's response to the surprise that awaited him. It would make up for the abominably boring afternoon Knowlton had spent yesterday at Squire Moreton's acquiring the animal.

"Good morning, Robbie," Knowlton greeted, with a laughing glance at the plate of crumbs on the boy's lap. "Breakfast?"

Robbie rose to his feet, his face flushing. He gestured at the tea tray. "They brought this in . . ."

"Excellent idea," Knowlton agreed, taking a large bite of one of the spiced buns. He poured himself a cup of tea and took a seat facing Robbie. "I surmise you are here to continue your riding lessons."

Robbie vigorously nodded his head.

"Did you finish your Latin this morning?"

"Yes, sir. I did five whole pages."

"Admirable, admirable." Knowlton nodded, privately thinking it a miserable task to set before an adventurous boy.

It was a measure of Robbie's respect for his mother that he had complied. Knowlton never would have.

The earl quickly drained his cup, snatched another bun from the tray, and rose from his chair.

"I had a slightly different plan today," he explained to Robbie as they walked across the yard to the stables. "Alecto is not the perfect horse for one just learning to ride, so I thought—"

"I know I will do better today," Robbie interjected. "It is only . . . well, it was so high up and she'd never moved so fast before."

"And you performed with creditable skill. I am not taking you off her as punishment, Robbie." Knowlton smiled gently. "I only thought a more suitable mount would speed your progress. Do not fear, I have no more a liking for slugs than you."

He paused before the stable entrance, peering into the darkened corridor.

"Shall I bring the new 'un out?" Frank asked.

Knowlton nodded. "But not saddled or bridled. The lad needs to learn that task as well."

Robbie's eyes grew wide as Frank reappeared with a horse that looked every bit as lively as Alecto but a great deal smaller.

"Does he have a name?"

"He has none," Knowlton replied. "I thought you would perhaps wish to name him."

"Should it be Greek or Latin?" Robbie asked, tentatively reaching out to stroke the chestnut pony's nose.

Knowlton shrugged. "I always believe the master should name his own horse."

"He is mine?" Robbie's eyes widened in wonderment.

The earl grinned. "Now, what use would I have for a horse this size? Granted, he has a good deal of spirit and I daresay he could hold his own with nearly any mount in the stable. But I fear it would be a comical sight with my legs dangling near the ground."

"Really mine?"

"Really."

The sunny look that had brightened Robbie's face suddenly faded. "But . . . but Mama will not approve, my lord. I know we cannot afford to keep a horse. Thank you very much, anyway.''

"Now, would I make a gift of something and expect you to pay for it?" Knowlton chided his young guest. "As long as he resides in my stable, he is entitled to my hospitality.''

"Mama will still say no," Robbie reiterated. "She does not wish me to join the cavalry.''

"Not every lad who rides joins the cavalry," Knowlton explained. He hesitated over his next words. "I think, Robbie, there is no need for your mother to know about this present. She really would not understand, would she?''

Robbie grinned at the earl's conspiratorial tone. He understood what a deuced bother mamas could be at times. "I think that is a capital idea.''

"I will expect you to take charge of the creature," Knowlton explained. "Frank here will tend to his feed and watering, but it shall be your job to saddle and bridle him for riding, and to cool him down and groom him after every ride.''

"I will be glad to do that," Robbie said. "Can I start now?''

At Knowlton's nod, Frank took the bridle and gave Robbie a quick demonstration on how to put it on the horse. Even if the animal was a pony, he was still tall enough that Robbie needed the mounting block to fasten the strap behind the ears. The same procedure was followed with the saddling, as Knowlton himself checked the tightness of the girth. Robbie beamed with pride when the earl congratulated him for a job well done.

Knowlton remained in the paddock for an hour, gently instructing Robbie in the finer points of horsemanship. With his natural seat, combined with the fearlessness of youth, the lad would soon make up for his lack of earlier training, and be a bruising rider within a year's time.

As he watched Robbie's wide grins of delight, Knowlton realized he took genuine pleasure in pleasing the lad. He felt a twinge of guilt, knowing he had first sponsored the connection as a method of ingratiating himself with Mrs. Mayfield, but he found he quite liked Robbie for his own sake. Robbie still carried the wide-eyed wonder of childhood, the fascination with the world that Knowlton had lost so long ago. Maybe Robbie could show him how to see the world through those eyes again, if only briefly.

At last relinquishing Robbie's tutelage to Frank, Knowlton saddled his own mount and headed out across the estate for his own belated morning ride. The ripe heads of grain were close to bursting with their seeds. Harvest would start in a few short weeks. It was a project involving skilled teamwork, a joy to watch as well as participate in.

And once the last shock was tied, the last load hauled to the granary for threshing, there was the celebration. Knowlton looked forward to it with eager anticipation. It was one of the few times of the year that the aristocrats and gentry rubbed elbows with the laborers, as class barriers tumbled down with foaming mugs of ale and the riotous contests of strength, skill, and speed that made up the annual Warrenton Harvest Home. And perhaps during the evening there would be the opportunity for a dance with the lovely Mrs. Mayfield. He really needed to accelerate his attempts to undermine her resistance. The harvest festival was the perfect setting. He made a mental note to remind the musicians to play lots of waltzes. He intended to dance them all with her.

Katherine fought against her concern at Robbie's lengthy absences from home. She suspected he and his crony Sam were up to the usual boyish pursuits—fishing or some such activity— and she did not want to smother Robbie with too much mothering. It was a constant effort to fight against her need to keep him close. Robbie had bloomed over the summer, rapidly losing some of the boyishness within him. It momentarily saddened her to see her baby beginning to show signs of the man he would grow into. But it was the lot of every mother to experience that bittersweet sense of pride and loss.

She reached again for her sewing. There had been time, at least, for her to start making Robbie some new shirts for the winter. With any luck she would have his wardrobe in good order before the rush of sewing for the fall and winter assemblies began. It was peaceful to sit in the sunlit yard in back of the cottage and do her own work, for a change.

Katherine looked up in pleased surprise when she heard the rear gate thud shut. "Hello, Robbie."

He started guiltily.

"Did you have an entertaining afternoon?" Katherine asked.

"Yes," was his faint reply.

Katherine patted the bench next to her. "Tell me about your fun," she said invitingly.

Robbie's face took on a reluctant expression. "Let me wash up first," he said.

His response aroused her suspicions. Robbie never liked to wash unless he was reminded.

"Oh, no, come talk now," she said pleasantly.

Warily he took his place at her side.

Once in the closer confines of the garden bench, it was obvious to both her eyes and nose that Robbie had been up to some amazing mischief.

"You smell decidedly of horse," she observed.

"Oh, well, we were walking and . . . um . . . we stopped and petted this horse that was in the field."

She frowned. "Do you wish to try again?"

He looked at his toes. "No, ma'am."

"Robert Mayfield, I want to know where you went and whom you were with."

Still staring at his feet, he mumbled, "At Warrenton."

"You were at Warrenton?"

"The earl said I could visit there anytime I wanted," he said defensively. "Remember?"

"I am certain the earl was only being polite when he issued that invitation," she said. "He has more important concerns than to be pestered by ten-year-old boys."

"But he does not mind," Robbie protested. "He says he likes my visits." And when he is busy, Frank is there to help me with my po . . ."

"Your what?"

Robbie clamped his mouth shut.

Katherine closed her eyes, willing herself to retain her temper. "Robbie, what exactly goes on when you visit Warrenton?"

He stood silent, his eyes wary and defiant.

"Robbie, if you do not tell me this instant what is going on, I will forbid you to leave this house again."

"Lord Knowlton is teaching me to ride," he admitted.

Katherine bit down on her lip to restrain her anger. "You did not think to ask my permission for embarking on this project?"

"I thought you would say no."

Katherine sighed. Robbie was right, she probably would have. That was no longer the point. Robbie had been lying to her about his whereabouts for several weeks now.

"I am disappointed that you could not see your way clear to telling me what you have been doing—and that you have lied to me."

Robbie frowned. "I did not want to lie, Mama. But it is so wonderful to ride! Knowlton says I have a natural seat and it will not be long before anyone is unable to tell I have not been riding since I was little."

As the enthusiastic words tumbled out and his eyes lit with excitement, he reminded Katherine of his father. Robert had always responded with the same animation when he was excited. She knew what he would say if he was standing here beside her now. That she was coddling the boy. That Robbie was ten and needed to spend less time with his mother and more time with boys his own age—and other grown-ups as well. And that he should learn how to ride.

Katherine sighed, knowing that to say no now would cause more harm than good. "You should have spoken to me about this earlier," she said, attempting to look stern.

"Yes, ma'am." Robbie looked at her with apprehension. "Will I . . . will you still let me learn?"

Katherine nodded, then found herself nearly knocked off the bench as Robbie flew at her, grabbing her in a grateful hug.

"Oh, thank you," he gasped. "I promise I will be very, very careful. That is why Knowlton bought the pony—because the other horses were all so big, he said even if I did fall off it would not be such a long way to the ground, and—"

His words finally registered. "Lord Knowlton bought you a pony?"

Robbie reddened at his untimely revelation.

"Robbie?"

"Just a small one," he whispered.

Katherine's control snapped. This was outside of enough. Knowlton must have known that she would not be pleased with Robbie's riding lessons. But to actually buy him his own horse to ride . . . Tears of anger and humiliation stung at her eyes. She took a deep breath.

"Robbie, I should like you to go and wash up now. Dinner will be ready soon."

As soon as Robbie entered the house, she gave vent to her anger with an elaborate oath. Damn Knowlton and his charity. She was well aware she could not afford to provide Robbie with the usual possessions of a young boy of his class. But that did not give the earl the right to do it for her. Her cheeks burned with humiliation. Why was it that every time she thought she had reached an accommodation with her current status, something like this came along to remind her of all the things that were no longer possible?

She clenched her hands in an attempt to still her rage. This life had been her choice, she reminded herself. She had known at the outset that there would be times like these, when the poverty she had sentenced them to would grate on her soul. But there were worse things in this life than poverty. She and Robbie were still together, and that was more important than all the ponies in the world.

Robbie would be unhappy with her, she knew, when she informed Lord Knowlton that her son could not accept such a present from him. But she could not allow her love for Robbie to overcome her scruples. Tomorrow she would tell Lord Knowlton exactly what she thought of his gift.

5

Virtue, how frail it is!
Friendship how rare!

—Shelley, *Mutability*

Katherine's fingers trembled slightly as she struggled to fasten the tiny buttons on the back of her gown. A night's sleep had not lessened her anger with the earl. He had no right to involve himself so deeply in Robbie's life, teaching her son how to ride and presenting him with a pony. Such arrogance! She would put an end to it once and for all. Robbie would be disappointed, but this was something she simply could not tolerate.

She was almost grateful to the earl, in a way, for precipitating this crisis. For now she truly had a reason to be angry with him. At every encounter, Katherine had found it more and more difficult to retain her firm barrier against his immeasurable charm, despite the danger he represented. Today, after such a provocation, it would be easier to keep him at arm's length.

Anxiously, she surveyed her appearance in the cracked glass above her dressing table. In her Sunday best gown of dove-gray silk, a survivor from her days of mourning for Robert, she made a respectable sight. There would be no flour smudges to amuse the earl today. And with her outrageous hair tucked under her bonnet, she would present the very image of a responsible, concerned, and efficient lady. A lady whose words would be heard and heeded.

Hastening down the stairs, she gathered her cloak and bonnet and moved into the dining parlor to use the sideboard mirror to ensure she had tied her ribbons just so. Satisfied at last with her presentation, she grabbed up her reticule and stepped outside.

Despite the bright sky, there was a fall chill in the air and she was glad to have her cloak about her shoulders. With businesslike strides she set out for Warrenton. The lion would be bearded in his den.

"Excuse me, my lord, but there is a Mrs. Mayfield here to see you."

Knowlton started with surprise at the butler's announcement, and he stepped from behind his desk. He could barely believe his good fortune. He had been trying to think of a reasonable excuse to invite her to Warrenton, and now she appeared as if in answer to his wish.

"Please escort the lady in, Hutchins. And have a tea tray sent up."

From the moment she had stepped over the threshold of Warrenton, Katherine's courage had begun to desert her. As she followed the butler up the stairs, she suspected there were few country homes that matched the splendor and opulence of this house. Katherine found it odd to have a rakish bachelor in possession of such worldly magnificence. She fleetingly longed to turn tail and run; then she mentally shook herself. It was she who had a grievance, not the earl. It was she who dealt from a position of strength. He was the one who had acted in error.

Knowlton's lips curved into a welcoming smile as she entered his study.

"Good day, Mrs. Mayfield. How delightful to have you visit me at last." He nodded to Hutchins to withdraw and bring the tray. "Allow me to take your bonnet and cloak."

"That will not be necessary—"

He cut her off with a peremptory wave of his hand. "No, I insist. You must stay for tea and whatever else Hutchins brings from the kitchen." He reached out an imperious hand for her outer clothing.

Katherine ignored his outstretched hand, clutching her reticule tightly in her nervousness. She felt all her confidence draining and she strove to regain control of the situation. She was here with a complaint, and she would not let his honeyed words soothe her into forgetting her purpose.

"I am not here for a social call, Lord Knowlton," she began, fixing him with a stern look. "I have come because I was very upset to discover that not only have you been teaching my son to ride but also you have purchased a mount for him with all the attendant accoutrements. I simply cannot allow such a thing.''

"And pray tell why not?'' Knowlton kept his expression blank.

"You have no right to present my son with expensive gifts.''

Knowlton suppressed the urge to grin at the indignant look on her face. He did not think she would appreciate humor at the moment. "You find it improper? I would agree with you—had I given *you* a gift. But I hardly think it wrong for me to present Robbie with a token of my friendship.''

"A horse is hardly a 'token of friendship,' '' she retorted angrily.

"It is also a gift not worthy of such anger.'' He knew his deliberate calmness would ruffle her further.

"Certainly, you are aware that I have no means to maintain a horse for Robbie. Why else do you think a ten-year-old boy raised in the country does not ride?''

"Robbie's horse may reside in my stable. That was my intention when I purchased it for him.''

"And for how long?'' Katherine lifted her chin indignantly. "At some point in time, responsibility for its care will devolve upon me.'' Her expression turned bitter as she acknowledged the truth of her situation. "I cannot afford it. It is better that he should never have access to an animal, for he then will not know what he is lacking.''

"He will be a poor cavalry officer if he cannot ride.'' Knowlton could not hide his mocking smile.

"I have no intention of allowing Robbie to join the military.''

He watched her stiffen into a prim position, so in contrast to that distracting hair that peeked teasingly from under her outmoded bonnet. His hands itched to free it.

"Oh, come now, Mrs. Mayfield. Your own husband was an officer in the cavalry.'' He smiled more benignly now, his head tilted to one side. "It is an honorable career.''

"It is a highly unsuitable one for a young man of little means,'' she retorted. "It is a air-castle dream without any foundation in reality. If there is no money to maintain a horse, there is even less to purchase a commission.''

Knowlton hesitated, wishing to choose his words carefully. He could easily lose whatever advantage he had gained if he misspoke. ''I realize, Mrs. Mayfield, that your financial situation is precarious and I respect the economies it forces you to follow. I fail to see where the gift to your son of something you are not capable of purchasing yourself can be such a problem.''

''Perhaps because you have always been able to buy everything you want,'' she said heatedly. ''When have you ever had to measure out your pennies and make the choice between a serviceable pair of shoes or a sack of flour?''

''I am aware that I live a fortunate life.'' He flashed her a self-deprecating smile. ''But if I can afford to give a horse to your son, what is your objection?''

''It is far too expensive a gift for him to accept. Had I known of it from the beginning, I would have instructed him to refuse it.''

''To what purpose? Should Robbie suffer because your pride is wounded?'' He gestured to his booted foot. ''Do you have any idea what one of these boots cost, Mrs. Mayfield? More than I paid for the horse, saddle, bridle, and a year's worth of feed. And I have a closet full of boots like these.''

He continued speaking in a softer tone. ''I know it is galling to want to provide the best for one you love, and not be able to. If a friend is willing to present a gift, it is only churlish to refuse. It gave me great pleasure to present the pony to Robbie. Do not sacrifice Robbie's happiness on the altar of your pride, Mrs. Mayfield. Do you honestly think you will achieve anything noble with your stubbornness?''

Katherine considered the wisdom of his words. He was right in saying Robbie would suffer because of her inability to accept what was in effect charity. Tears stinging her eyes, she shook her head.

''Then we will consider the matter settled. Robbie may keep his pony. And I promise I will consult you before I make any more purchases on his behalf. Agreed?''

Katherine nodded slowly. "Agreed, my lord."

Knowlton flashed her a warm smile. "That was not so difficult, was it? Now, please, Mrs. Mayfield, take off your bonnet and cloak and we can sit and enjoy the refreshments that should be arriving momentarily. I do not want your enmity. Can we not be friends?"

She stood silently, wavering in her resolve. Despite his air of wounded innocence, she still sensed that danger lurked in a "friendship" with Lord Knowlton. His reputation precluded the idea of an innocuous friendship with a woman.

"Come now, Mrs. Mayfield, I will not bite. Despite the lurid stories I am certain you have heard, I am not in the habit of seducing ladies in my study. At least, not unless they are willing. Stay and have some tea." He again extended his hand for her bonnet and cloak.

Surprised at how little shocked she was by his bold manner, Katherine had a sinking feeling that she had somehow lost the fight as she untied her bonnet ribbons. She did not want to be at her ease with this man. She was angry—nay, furious—with him. Yet his friendly smile was most disarming.

"I had hoped you would grace Warrenton with a visit one day." The earl smiled as he guided her to a chair. "We are beginning to think of Robbie as another member of the household. It is only fitting that his mother should be a familiar face as well."

Katherine opened her mouth to speak but closed it again as Hutchins came in with the tea tray. For the next few minutes she busied herself with the tea and filling her plate with the dainty cakes Knowlton insisted on pressing upon her.

"My weakness," he confessed as he popped one of the richly buttered delicacies into his mouth. "It is fortunate I allow my cook to prepare them only once a week or I would be as fat as a prince in no time."

She raised an eyebrow at his sly dig at the Regent.

"So tell me, Mrs. Mayfield, why did you and Robbie decide to settle in Lincolnshire? Do you not have family elsewhere?"

Katherine stiffened slightly at the polite interrogative. "The lease terms on the cottage are very generous," she replied evasively.

He sighed imperceptibly, knowing he would get no more information out of her. There was a slight air of mystery about Robbie's mother that intrigued him. For a brief moment he wondered if she really was a widow—perhaps she had merely been the mistress of that dashing cavalry officer. It would explain her straitened financial circumstances. Yet would a cavalry officer have left his sword to his mistress? It was a puzzle.

"I understand Robbie is taking lessons with the vicar," he said, trying to hit on a conversational topic that would elicit a positive response from her.

"He is. I fear Robbie fell behind in his studies this last year when we were in the process of moving. I tried to keep him caught up, but he is well beyond my limited abilities in Greek and Latin."

"He will be ready for school one of these days, then."

She flushed. "Perhaps."

Knowlton berated himself for such a stupid remark. School was very likely just the type of luxury that Mrs. Mayfield could not afford. He felt a fleeting twinge of anger at that unknown cavalry officer for leaving his widow in such precarious financial circumstances.

Katherine busied herself with refilling her cup. She hated Knowlton's solicitous concern. She had deliberately chosen her path; if she was beginning to have doubts that she had made the right decision, she was still unconvinced that it was a disaster either. It was much easier to forget her situation without his subtle references to her poverty.

"Harvest will start next week," Knowlton said, attempting to ease the awkwardness in the air. "It is traditional that the lord of Warrenton throw a party for his tenants and laborers at its completion. It has developed into a rather ostentatious affair, I am afraid," he said with a self-deprecating grin. "Footraces and pie-eating contests for the lads, more brawny competitions for the men, while the ladies display their talents in the culinary and domestic arts. I fully expect you and young Robbie to attend."

"I do not think—"

"Consider it an order," he said sternly. "From your land-lord."

"Put that way, how can I refuse?" She flashed him a withering glance.

Ignoring her irritation, Knowlton allowed a slow, sensual smile to light his face. "Your presence will make it a memorable event."

Katherine concentrated on sipping her tea. What a provoking man! He expended considerable effort to disarm her concerns about Robbie and the horse, then reawakened all her fears with his broad hints of interest and that wicked smile. What kind of a devilish game was he playing?

After Mrs. Mayfield's departure, Knowlton sat back in his worn leather chair with a self-satisfied smirk. The victory over Robbie's pony pleased him. Whatever else came between him and Mrs. Mayfield, he did not want to see Robbie hurt. He must keep his relationships with the lovely widow and her son separate. He knew that now, and felt a twinge of guilt for ever thinking he could use Robbie to ingratiate himself with his mother. It simply would not do.

There were other methods of conquering Mrs. Mayfield's fortress. His face broke into a broad grin as he remembered how her emotions had swung from one end of the pendulum to the other and back during their conversation. He meant to keep her off balance, so she would not be able to readily marshal her defenses. Let her wonder just what his game was. As long as he did not rush his fences, it might be just the proper strategy to take.

He did not know when the pursuit of a woman had so enter-tained him. Perhaps that had been the source of so much of his boredom in London—there had been no need of pursuit. From the diamonds of the demimonde to the leaders of the *ton*, they had pursued *him*. His only problem had been in deciding where to bestow his favors among the many offers. No wonder he had grown jaded. The pursuit of Mrs. Mayfield was just the thing he needed to restore his enthusiasm.

Despite her present poverty, he suspected she had known

much better times. It would certainly account for her stubborn refusal to accept assistance. Her adamant attitude only showed how much she resented her current situation. That was something he could easily rectify.

She would not be as skilled a lover as he was accustomed to, but that was no matter. Technique could easily be taught, if the pupil was willing. And with that flaming hair, he had no doubt of her suitability. It would be only one more delightful advantage to the situation—the opportunity to awaken a less-experienced woman to her sensual nature. Although he had been often pleased, satisfied, and sometimes even a little amazed at the skills of his many bed partners, there was something to be said for molding a partner to suit his own particular preferences. It would be a most pleasurable task.

The anticipation of the prize—for he held no doubts of his ultimate success with Mrs. Mayfield—began to have a decided effect. Briefly, he contemplated a minor dalliance to take the edge off his growing hunger. There were several delectable prospects within easy riding distance of Warrenton. But no, he decided. It was all part of the game. His enforced celibacy would only heighten his pleasure at the pent-up release. He would await Mrs. Mayfield's capitulation with growing eagerness.

It was time, however, that he did take steps to further his aims. He must move quickly to solidify the gains made today. With the Harvest Home less than two weeks away, if the weather held and the crops were brought in on time, he had a perfect goal to aim for. He would slowly reel Mrs. Mayfield into his net, then pounce when he judged her sufficiently entangled.

Knowlton shifted in his chair, his mind caught in a reverie that involved removing every last hairpin from Mrs. Mayfield's upswept tresses, allowing that flaming mass to swirl about her shoulders. Then, with a shrug at such precipitate thinking, he cleared his mind of her. He would never admit to being *bored* at Warrenton, but he did concede he would not mind some company. That matter could easily be remedied; the shooting would be excellent in a few weeks and he knew there would be no lack of takers for any invitations he tendered.

Seb Cole would come—if he was not already committed to a rendezvous at some other house with whatever new flirt he had acquired. And he really should ask Hartford, and Drummond—and Pelham was never averse to a convivial gathering. And of course, Wentworth.

At that name, he paused. He thought Somers would come, but now that he was married, with a fat, drooling little daughter ensconced in his nursery, he might not wish to. Marriage had a way of changing a man. Knowlton would never criticize his closest friend for marrying, although that event had shocked Knowlton to the core. It was too close for comfort.

Knowlton had nothing against marriage, actually. It was a useful institution—for some. He had a deep certainty, though, that it was not for him. Constancy was not a part of his nature, and no woman had ever captured his interest long enough for him to doubt that supposition. He preferred matters as they were—even if his last mistress had driven him to boredom in less than a month. Knowlton shrugged. He would take care to choose more carefully in the future. He suspected Mrs. Mayfield would not begin to bore him for a long, long time. That thought set off another reverie, this one involving the creamy white shoulders that he knew must lie beneath Mrs. Mayfield's high-necked gowns.

Katherine was not surprised to find Robbie waiting in the parlor when she returned to the cottage. She saw how he struggled with his desire to know what had transpired at Warrenton, and his very real fear that she had put an end to his riding.

"I talked with Lord Knowlton," she said, knowing she must put his fears to rest at once. "And we both decided that for now, you may keep the pony and continue your riding lessons."

"I can?"

"You may."

Robbie hurtled across the room and embraced her in a breathless hug. "Thank you, Mama."

"I want you to continue to be very polite to the earl," she continued. "He is very generous, and I want to make certain that he knows how well you appreciate his efforts."

"Oh, I will," Robbie said. "Can I go up to Warrenton now? Atlas will need his exercise."

She smiled lovingly at his eagerness. "Yes, you may go. Be careful, now."

"I will," Robbie called back over his shoulder as he raced out the door.

Katherine sat down with a sigh. He was growing and changing so before her eyes. It would not be so long before he was a young man, and what then? She was going to have to do some very serious thinking about Robbie's future. Knowlton's innocent remark had only reminded her of the difficulties ahead.

Her mind drifted back to her talk with the earl. The man was most exasperating, and she suspected he acted so deliberately to goad her into some unladylike reaction. Yet his interest in Robbie seemed sincere and she could not honestly say that she minded. Robbie had so little contact with adult men; the vicar was the only other alternative. And although she was quite aware that Knowlton was not a stand-in for a father, she did appreciate the time and trouble he took with Robbie. It was difficult for a lad to be without a father, particularly one as enthusiastic and adventurous as Robbie. Knowlton did not seem to be dismayed by the boyish high spirits that often threatened to overwhelm her. It was only one more example of how much Robert's death, and her own actions afterward, had affected them.

For Robbie's sake, at least, she would try to maintain an amiable relationship with the earl. She did not need to have much contact with him, which she thought was all to the good. His presence made her uneasy, as if he could see through all her carefully built defenses to the woman inside. The very part of her that she did not want him, of all people to see. It would only encourage him.

She half-believed, after his protestations of friendship today, that they could meet in amiability, without her having to fear any untoward behavior on his part. And she was forced to acknowledge that he had not overtly done anything to cause her alarm. He had jokingly talked of his reputation as a rake, implying that the rumors were overblown, and always assuring her that he would never act against her will. But it was the unuttered aspects of his communication that most disturbed her, the knowing grins, coolly appreciative glances, and appraising looks that caused her the most distress. That man could say more with a glance than with all the words in Christendom. And none of it proper.

6

When we arise all in the morn,
For to sound our harvest horn.
We will sing to the full jubilee, jubilee;
We will sing to the full jubilee.

—Nineteenth-century harvest song

Knowlton's valet awakened him in the cool hours before dawn on the first morning of harvest. Shivering at the chill in the room, Knowlton quickly donned his well-worn breeches and gratefully pulled a warm woolen coat over his shirt. Once the sun rose, the coat would be quickly discarded, but at this moment it was a welcome bar against the predawn air.

The rest of the house was beginning to stir as Knowlton made his way to the kitchen for a hasty breakfast of bread and cheese. He simply could not stomach the massive harvest breakfast that was presented to the laborers at the granary. He would take a more substantial repast at the noontime dinner. Knowlton was filled with an eagerness to be off to the fields.

Ever since he could remember, he had loved the harvesttime. Beginning in June with the first hay cut, harvest continued in one way or another until October, when the last of the fruits had been pulled from the trees. But it was the corn harvests of late August that really defined harvest for him. The glorious golden fields were at their peak, the stalks of grain drooping under the weight of their ripe heads. Even the smallest breeze sent rippling waves across the land, like the waves radiating from a stone tossed in a pond. In less than a week it would be gone, the fields reduced to bare stalks of stubble. It was a massive undertaking, a true test of teamwork and organization, a symbol of man's mastery over nature.

He had watched the workers in his youth, sneaking out of the house before dawn and not returning until the men had stopped for the night. His father could not understand his fascination with the harvest. Corn was money, and the previous Earl of Knowlton had had no opposition to that. However, he cared little for the process by which it was earned, as long as everything went well and his coffers were filled. But to his son, there was something elemental in watching the men with their razor-sharp sickles moving down the rows like a giant tide, felling everything that stood in their path. As he grew older, he became more and more involved in the process, bringing beer and ale to the workers in the fields, taking the sickles to the smith for sharpening in the evening. Then, in that glorious summer when he was sixteen, he had been given his own sickle by the indulgent bailiff and let loose on the fields.

The men had not laughed at him, though he could not cut at nearly the same rate as the more experienced laborers. His hands had been bleeding and blistered by the end of the day, and he could barely straighten his back, but he doggedly, if foolishly, kept coming every day until the last stalk had been cut. And in the process, he had earned the grudging respect of the workers, who looked upon the young lord in a new light. Many of those same men, or their sons, still worked for him, and the bonds forged during the yearly weeks in the fields had lasted through the years. Knowlton treated his tenants well, and they knew it was due to personal interest, not self-serving obligation.

Most of the workers had finished their breakfast and already gathered at the foot of the first field when Knowlton arrived. He greeted the men with a wave or nod or a friendly call of a name. He saw Robbie Mayfield standing beside the fence, looking a bit awed and forlorn. Knowlton guided his horse to him and dismounted. It would increase Robbie's status to be seen with him.

"Excited?" Knowlton asked.

Robbie nodded. "I hardly slept a wink last night," he confided.

"That will not be the case tonight, I'd wager," said Knowlton, suspecting the boy would be ready to drop with exhaustion by midafternoon. He would learn. "Is your mama to be here today?"

"She will be here to help the parish ladies serve dinner," Robbie said.

"The men are ready, my lord," Taggert, the bailiff, called to Knowlton.

The earl clapped Robbie on the shoulder. "Do not try to do everything today," he cautioned. "Harvest lasts many days and we do not want to lose you too soon."

Knowlton stripped off his coat and poured himself a foaming tankard of ale from the barrel at the edge of the field. Raising it in salute to the workers, he took a large swallow of the strong brew, then gestured for the work crew to take their own sample. It was customary, this first tasting of the harvest beer. As the day wore on and their throats choked with dust and chaff, they would not appreciate the taste, but only the moisture. When all had sampled the brew, Knowlton took the sickle handed him by Taggert and raised it above his head as a signal to the workers to form their staggered line. Behind the men stood the women and children, who would bundle the cut stalks into sheaves. Stepping to the edge of the field, Knowlton bent to cut the first swath. Harvest had begun.

At the sound of the dinner horn, Knowlton straightened cautiously. After stooping for hours, his back ached horribly, if the truth were told, but he would never complain aloud. He no longer worked the entire harvest; it was an indulgence that he could not justify when he knew there were men more skilled than he, who could accomplish the task with greater ease. But Knowlton persisted in cutting on the first day, and the last, to remind his workers that their lord was not too proud to toil alongside them, and to remind himself of the value of the land that was the source of his family's wealth.

He pulled off his sweat-soaked shirt and wiped his face. God, it was hot today. The thought of cool water, wet beer, and the noonday meal quickened his steps across the stubbled ruin that marked the workers' path.

Katherine had arrived at the field an hour ago, curious to see this ritual labor and willing to lend her hand in the feeding of the workers. She hoped Robbie had fared well. It had been thoughtful of Lord Knowlton to invite him to participate.

"Mama, Mama." Robbie raced up to her, his face flushed with excitement. "Is it not wonderful?"

She smiled at his enthusiasm. In truth, there had been little for her to see, for the workers had moved an impressive distance down the field. After the meal, perhaps she would stay and watch for a while.

Robbie danced at her side as they followed the wagon hauling the food and drink to the workers. The sheer quantity of food provided by the earl impressed her. Knowlton did not stint his workers. There were cold meat and pies, bread, cheese, puddings and, of course, the ubiquitous beer and ale. She wondered dryly how the workers could even stand at the end of a harvest day with the quantity of beer that they drank. Eight quarts was a prodigious amount for anyone to consume.

She could see the workers now as the laden food wagon rolled to a stop. They stood in small groups, laughing and joking while they traded gibes about each other's prowess with the sickle. A few men stood about the water barrels on the wagon, eager to wash the grit and dust of the field from their bodies before the noonday meal. Katherine turned to speak to Robbie, when she caught sight of the earl.

He was standing beside the wagon, his hand curled about the ladle he dipped into the barrel of fresh, cool water. Katherine could not tear her eyes away from him. The form-fitting breeches, riding low over his narrow hips, only emphasized the hard, muscled plane of his abdomen. As he turned, she nearly gasped at the sight of the dark, curling hairs that trailed down his belly, disappearing into the waistband of his breeches. It was an all-too-clear reminder of what lay lower, and Katherine was stunned to have such thoughts enter her mind. She quickly raised her eyes, but the sight of his upper torso did little to settle her equilibrium. She watched in fascination as he poured water over his upper body and arms, her eyes following each rivulet as it traced its path down his bronzed skin.

As if sensing her gaze, Knowlton turned slowly. His gray eyes met hers and a lazy smile creased his face. Katherine's cheeks flamed, but she did not turn away quickly enough to miss the ostentatious wink he directed at her. She wanted to take to her heels and not stop until she was safely back at the cottage, with every door and window bolted against him. But she knew that would be no protection against the traitorous thoughts that danced through her mind.

"How nice of you to offer your help with the harvest, Mrs. Mayfield."

Knowlton's words caused Katherine to freeze, afraid of what her eyes would reveal if she faced him. Yet she would look foolish beyond belief if she tried to converse with him with her back turned.

Turning toward him, she took care to keep her eyes averted. "I think I will find it an interesting experience."

Katherine realized her mistake instantly. There was no relief in keeping her gaze lowered, for it directed her glance to that thatch of dark, curling hair that swept up across his abdomen from the edge of his breeches. Katherine hastily raised her eyes to meet Knowlton's knowing gaze.

"Poor Mrs. Mayfield," he teased. "She cannot decide what is worse—a half-naked man's chest or his face." Deliberately he began to towel the droplets of water off his chest with his crumpled shirt.

Katherine's cheeks flamed. "If you had any decency, you would not be parading around in such a state of undress," she said through clenched teeth.

"If I had any decency, Mrs. Mayfield, you would not even think twice about the situation." He grinned wickedly. "Why, if Mr. Ashe removed his shirt, I doubt you would have any reaction at all."

She had a strong urge to slap that silly smirk off his face. He did this on purpose, she knew, but his aim puzzled her. If anything was guaranteed to cause her to draw away in alarm, it was his outrageous behavior. He took such pains to deny his rakish reputation, yet now he rashly dispelled his protestations with his actions. What was he trying to accomplish—beyond leaving her inarticulate with irritation?

He pulled his damp shirt over his head, covering himself, but for Katherine the damage had been done. The image of that muscled chest, the dark hairs swirling into patterned whorls, was emblazoned on her mind.

Knowlton casually took her elbow and led her to the other side of the cart.

"I am hungry," he said. "And it is your job to feed me." He thrust a plate into her hands.

Katherine fumed silently, filling the plate to overflowing with every bit of food she could. Watching him from the corner of her eye as he leaned casually against the wagon side, his arms folded over that now-hidden chest, she again rued the day she had decided not to quit the neighborhood. She busied herself with the food, studiously avoiding the earl until she shoved the heaping plate into his grasp.

"Oh, good," he said, eyeing the pile of food with feigned enthusiasm. "I am starved. And thirsty. Some ale, if you please, Mrs. Mayfield?"

Her hands itched to dump the foaming mug over the top of his aristocratic head. But she somehow knew that if she did, it would be his victory and not hers. She contented herself with ignoring him for the remainder of the work break.

Knowlton grinned inwardly every time he caught a glimpse of her bustling about the food wagon. He knew she avoided him intentionally, and reckoned that a triumph. Mrs. Mayfield must be closer to surrender than he had thought, if the sight of his half-naked body could inflame her so. There had been time to catch a glimpse of the look in her eyes before she turned from him. He recognized admiration—and desire—when he saw it. He could not have planned things better if he tried. He was almost tempted to remain with the harvesters for the duration, if it would quicken the outcome of the campaign.

But fruits too often displayed might pale with familiarity. Far better that she have time to think on and remember what she had seen today during the next week. It would make the last day of the harvest all the sweeter. He was becoming a master at controlling his anticipation, and if it had half the effect on Mrs. Mayfield that it had on him, she would be a quivering blob of jelly by next week. The thought cheered him as he picked up the sickle. His muscles were already beginning to stiffen, and if he did not get back to the field, he doubted he would be able to continue for much longer.

* * *

Robbie could barely keep his eyes open when Katherine finally dragged him home. The men were still cutting when she left the field, but there was no point in Robbie exhausting himself the first day. Katherine stood over him while he scrubbed his arms and face, then tucked him into bed. She was certain he was asleep before she reached his door.

She smiled at his enjoyment of the day. He had been so eager to help. Harvest was a fascinating process; she had been glad to participate herself. If working at the harvest meant she and Robbie could eat with the workers and avoid the expense of a week's meals, all the better.

Today, trading gossip with the other women, Katherine for the first time felt a part of the community. At first she had been surprised to learn the vicar's wife and daughters always attended harvest, but they explained it had long been a tradition in the parish. The earl's household prepared the food, and the parish ladies served. It made harvest go faster, and by freeing up the laborer's wives to help in the field, it put a few extra pennies in the farmers' coffers. And since the earl held the living, it was only thoughtful on their part to help him with the harvest.

They had also told her more about the Harvest Home, the premier celebration in the neighborhood each year. Knowlton intended it for the tenantry and villagers, but Mrs. Ashe said the gentry came from miles around as well. It was the only festivity at Warrenton that the mothers felt comfortable sending their daughters to, she confided. Not that she wished to speak ill of the earl, for he was a good man. But there had been more than one party at the house with women that no God-fearing member of the parish would wish to associate with. Mrs. Ashe did give the earl credit for keeping his hands off the local lasses. He had done nothing to earn the enmity of the neighborhood.

Unbidden, the image of Knowlton, with rivulets of water rolling down his torso, rose again in Katherine's mind. She shook her head as if to rid her brain of the mental picture. He was even more audaciously attractive than Robert, she realized with a start, shocked that such a comparison came to her. Knowlton knew the power of his attraction, and used it with a skill she was forced to admire. Those expressive gray eyes, which could change in an instant from cool cynicism to smoky warmth, haunted her thoughts.

Her pure, physical reaction to Knowlton shook her more than she cared to admit. It stirred up emotions and passions that she had struggled to subdue during the six long years of her widowhood, for passion was a luxury she could not afford. At best, it was a transient emotion, and at worst, it could bring disaster. But today the earl had shown her just how close to the surface those feelings lay, and how easily they could spring back to life.

It was foolish in the extreme, for there was no respectable outcome to any passing fancy he might entertain of her. She had no illusions whatsoever about her status in his eyes— dalliance perhaps, but nothing more. She knew his reputation as a womanizer, and he had done nothing to dispel that notion from the day they met. On the contrary, he had done everything to confirm it. If she had not been a fool, she would have packed up their belongings and hustled herself and Robbie into the next county within hours of that first meeting.

Yet she had not, and it became apparent to her that she was being drawn deeper and deeper into his web, losing her will to resist his blatant charm. She was lonely; she did want for companionship, and the earl would only be too eager to provide it. She simply could not let him disturb her so. She would have to keep her own emotions firmly in check during her dealings with him. From now on, she would be immune to his wiles and tricks. Buoyed by her new confidence, she picked up the lamp and made her way up the stairs to bed. As long as she remained steadfast in her resistance, she was safe.

So why did that thought depress her?

7

The Mellow Autumn came, and with it came
The promised party, to enjoy its sweets.

—Byron, *Don Juan*

The day of Warrenton's Harvest Home dawned clear and sunny. Knowlton hummed a bawdy ditty as he wrapped the intricate starched length of cravat around his neck, weaving it into an impeccable knot *à la Warrenton*. It was deucedly foolish to dress so formally for an outdoor party, but the tenantry expected their lord to look like, well, a lord. He could only be grateful they did not expect him to appear in white satin knee breeches with a *chapeau bras* under his arm. Ah, well, by the early evening he would have discarded most of this tomfoolery. He stuck a fine ruby stickpin in his neckcloth, fastened two fobs to his chain, and looked to Rigsby for assistance in donning his skin-hugging coat.

Taking the back stairs, Knowlton quickly made his way to the kitchen. That room was full of bustling servants, with Cook up to her elbows in flour as she prepared the last-minute dainties for the feast. Knowlton grabbed a piece of sugared apple out from under her nose, earning himself a scowl, which he returned with a laugh. He exited the house and circled around to the front, noting with approval that the long tables were already set out on the south lawn. His staff bustled about, laying out the tablecloths and setting up the serving dishes. Across the drive, the livestock pens awaited their customers. Satisfied that all was going according to custom, Knowlton strolled back into the house through the terrace doors.

The large drawing-room table was piled high with wrapped packages, cups of silver, and beribboned medallions. He smiled. It gave him great pleasure to hand out the various prizes and awards. The trinkets were not much, but they were treasured and valued by their winners. He knew many a farmhouse that still displayed prizes won during his grandfather's day. It cost him little, yet cemented his tenants' loyalty.

He circled the room, glancing in dismay at the mantel clock. The guests would not be arriving for at least an hour, and there was no way of knowing when *she* would arrive. He had no particular plans for dealing with Mrs. Mayfield today, preferring to wait and see what opportunities developed. But he was quite certain that he would have made significant progress in his pursuit by the end of the evening. He had let the anticipation build for long enough. It was time to reap the fruits of his sacrifice.

"Now, Robbie, promise you will not eat too many sweets." Katherine could see the tables groaning under the weight of the food upon them. The earl's party promised to be as lavish a display as rumor held. "And be careful of your clothes. I do not think those breeches will stand for another patching."

"Yes, Mama," Robbie replied absently, his mind on the delights ahead. Sam had said there would be more food than he could imagine, and games and races. He wished there had been some pony races, for then he could ride Atlas. But Knowlton said there were too few lads in the district with ponies and they would have to race on foot instead.

Edging away from his mama's watchful eye, Robbie desperately hoped he would win some contest, for then he could receive his prize from Lord Knowlton. Sam had said the earl always gave out the prizes. And after the prizes they could eat their fill and watch the grown-ups as they danced and sang. Sam said it could get pretty entertaining later in the evening, when most of the men were in their cups. The party would grow loud and boisterous and no one would care what the younger boys did. Robbie did not think his mama would allow him to stay that long, but he hoped he could stay out of her way long enough to have fun.

Katherine looked about her with growing interest. Across the drive, makeshift pens filled with farm animals covered one section of the lawn. She saw Robbie and Sam reaching over one barrier to pet the enclosed sheep.

She deliberately tried to avoid spotting the earl, averting her gaze whenever she saw a man who looked to be dressed remotely as she thought Knowlton might be. Yet when she had not seen him after a half-hour, she grew anxious. He was here today, was he not? Perhaps he only made his appearance in the evening, after the dining. In which case all her silly posturing to avoid him had been most foolish and—

"Good day, Mrs. Mayfield." Knowlton was suddenly in front of her, sweeping an elegant bow.

Katherine started. Had she conjured up the man out of thin air?

He gently clasped her elbow. "Shall we stroll about the grounds? I believe you have not seen the gardens yet?"

"I do not think—"

" 'Tis a pity. I appreciate a beautiful woman who can think."

"I see it is to be a day of flummery from you, sir," she said, but made no move to free herself. She could firmly control the situation. "Can you afford to ignore the rest of your guests in such a cavalier manner?"

"They have already seen the gardens," he said with a wicked grin. " 'Twould be only a dull procession for them."

"While I shall be filled with transports of delight?"

"Undoubtedly," he replied. "My gardeners do their work well."

They crossed the gravel drive, following the flagged path that led around the house to the rear terrace and the gardens spread below.

"I have yet to thank you for allowing Robbie to help with the harvest. He enjoyed himself immensely." She offered him a grateful smile.

It was such a rare reward that he nearly caught his breath. How he would like to have that dazzling smile bestowed upon himself more often. In reward for other achievements. He patted her hand. "Harvest was my favorite time of year when I was his age," he said.

"And now?"

He looked at her quizzingly.

"Do you still enjoy harvest above all?"

A flicker of amusement danced in his eyes. "No," he said

slowly, his voice low and seductive. "There are other pursuits I find more enjoyable now."

Katherine quickly averted her gaze. Fool, she chided herself. She had walked straight into that one.

Knowlton smiled and took her hand in his, leading her down the terrace steps as if nothing had been said. Knowing he needed to quickly redeem himself ere she fled, he calmly pointed out the organization of the garden as if he were unaware of the attractiveness of the woman at his side.

"I should like you to see it in high summer, when the blooms are at their fullest," he said as they strolled back toward the house. "Or in spring, when the first color appears. I shall have the gardeners send you some bulbs for the cottage."

"That is kind of you, my lord," Katherine replied with a wary look.

He laughed aloud. "Kindness is rarely the virtue ascribed to me. There are those who would say that even the simple gift of some flowers to a delectable widow is only a sign of my baser intentions."

"Is it?" Katherine stopped and calmly surveyed him. It was what she herself believed. Would he have the honesty to admit it?

"You wound me with your suspicions." Knowlton placed a hand over his heart. "Here I have behaved with the utmost circumspection for at least ten minutes, yet you still doubt my intentions? Have I given you any cause to question my actions?"

Katherine had to admit he had not. Overtly. But she knew he was watching her, wanting her, seducing her with his eyes and his wickedly innocent—and not-so-innocent—words. Yet to accuse him on such grounds would make her look a fool.

"I thought not." He tucked her hand in the crook of his arm again and led her back toward the front lawns. "I think, for that slur, Mrs. Mayfield, that you owe me a boon."

"What did you have in mind, my lord?"

He eyed her with amusement. She knew perfectly well what he had in mind, the saucy witch. It was all part of this game that they played, the verbal sparring, the penetrating glances, the averted gaze when he had crossed the line. He thrust, she parried in as excellent display of swordsmanship as he had seen in a long time. But he would slip past her guard eventually and his lance would hit home.

"A simple dance, my lady. An unexceptionable request."

Nothing he did was unexceptionable, thought Katherine suspiciously. Still, it was only a dance. There could be little danger in that.

"I will grant you a dance, my lord. But nothing more."

"Knowlton," he responded. "Certainly, Mrs. Mayfield, after an acquaintance of our duration, you can find it within yourself to call me by my name, at least. No one would find it the least bit forward."

She frowned. He was doing it again, teasing her and skirting around the edge of a blatant flirtation.

"Very well, *Knowlton*."

He flashed her a grin of triumph before they were once again enveloped by the gathering on the front lawn. He deftly instigated a polite conversation with the vicar, drew Katherine into it, then drifted off as if that brief interlude in the garden had never happened.

Katherine wished it had not. Every moment spent in his company was a moment closer to disaster. He could disarm her with a word, and despite the fact she knew exactly what game he played, she was powerless to withdraw from it. Had it not been the nineteenth century, she would have accused him of witchcraft.

She drew herself up with a start. This was ridiculous. She was perfectly able to deal with Knowlton. Her reluctance stemmed only from her foolish desire to fill the void left in her life after the death of Robert. Six years was a long time to be alone, with only her son for company. But Knowlton was no answer to that problem. His presence in her life would be only temporary, and she had no wish for that.

"I believe this is my dance?"

Knowlton stood before her, his face as eager as any little boy's. He had doffed his jacket at some point during the evening, his cravat had vanished from his neck, and only his elegantly embroidered waistcoat hinted at his aristocratic veneer. In the wavering lantern lights, he had a slightly raffish air.

"I am not certain . . ." Katherine began.

"You promised." Even in the dim light she could see the challenge in his eyes.

That put too fine a point on a simple agreement, but Katherine nodded her acquiescence. She had seen him earlier, joking with the squires and farmers as they hoisted mugs of foaming ale, and she suspected Knowlton had drunk his share. Pray he was not foxed enough to make a spectacle. Guests parted to allow him to lead her out into the middle of the dancing platform, and the musicians struck up another tune.

"A waltz," she said as he pulled her into his arms. "I should have guessed."

Knowlton grinned. "I like to waltz, Mrs. Mayfield. And it is very obvious that you are at least acquainted with the dance."

She nodded, allowing the magic of the music to take hold as she twirled in his arms. There was something dreadfully disconcerting about waltzing with a man in shirtsleeves. Her fingers sought only the lightest contact with the soft linen of his shirt, but it was all too easy to feel the heat from the skin below. She wished she had worn her gloves—but Mrs. Ashe had said few ladies bothered for this party. With Knowlton half-undressed, they were rapidly becoming a necessity.

"Has it been an enjoyable day for you?" Knowlton asked as the pattern of the dance brought them together again.

"Yes," she said. "I have never been to such an event and it is . . ."

"Marvelous?" He eagerly fished for the compliment.

"Fascinating," she continued, smiling softly. "The entire neighborhood is here, and all the barriers are down for a day."

"Are your barriers down, Mrs. Mayfield?"

She looked guiltily into those deceptively calm gray eyes. Sometimes it was as if he could read her mind. "I believe I have not forgotten that I am a lady."

"Neither have I," he replied, and subtly tightened his hold on her waist.

"I believe you are holding me too close, my lord," she said in protest.

"I do not think such a thing is possible," he replied, his eyes twinkling. "After all, this is a waltz, the most scandalous of dances, precisely because it allows one to hold one's partner close.''

His slow, seductive smile mesmerized her. He was not completely sober, yet he was as lithe and agile on his feet as if he had abstained the entire evening. But there was a new gleam of appreciation in his eyes when he looked at her that made her uneasy. Before, he had teased her with words, which could easily be deflected. Now those eyes . . . Without leaving her face, she knew his gaze was raking her frame, mentally stripping her. She *felt* naked as he circled her around in the motions of the dance, the warmth from their bodies radiating whenever they drew together in the intimate movements. She was almost tempted to pull free and flee, before it was too late.

Katherine uttered up a grateful prayer when the music ended at last. Knowlton lightly held her arm and led her to the side of the platform. He stopped and said a word to a man here, teased a lady there, and before Katherine quite knew what had happened, they were very alone in the empty garden he had shown her earlier in the day. Discreetly placed lanterns lent just enough light to the scene.

"My lord," she began in protest.

"Knowlton," he corrected softly. "Or even Edward. I answer to both."

"It is highly improper—"

"Not unless you wish it to be so," he replied with a husky rasp to his voice.

Katherine moved to walk away, but he grabbed her wrist and drew her to him.

"Stay for a few moments," he pleaded. "I would like to hear my name just once from those rosy lips."

"You are being ridiculous," she snapped, but he drew her even closer until it was all she could do to keep their bodies from touching.

"It is not such a bad name," he whispered. "It has been borne by kings and dukes."

"And rakes who tempt women in the dark."

"Tempt?" He laughed. "Do not say you can be tempted, Mrs. Mayfield? Or may I have leave to call you Katherine?"

"No."

He nodded agreement. "You are right. Katherine does not quite suit. Kate is better. Although you are not the least bit shrewish."

"My lord, you are foxed," she said, her alarm growing. How could she have been so incautious as to have allowed herself to be alone with him?

"Edward."

"*Edward*, you are foxed." She tried to pull away from his grasp, but the hand on her wrist tightened.

"No, just a trifle elevated," he insisted. "It is the nearness of you, not the ale, that flummoxes my senses and leaves my brain in such a state of disarray." He lifted her imprisoned hand to his mouth, pressing a gentle kiss on the palm before folding her fingers over it. He planted another kiss upon the bent digits before his lips traced a searing path down her thumb to her wrist.

"Enough!" she cried when the pleasure-pain became more than she could bear. "You know that I am not inclined toward a dalliance with you."

He eyed her with amusement. "Why, my dear Kate, how interesting that you should hint of such a thing. The thought had not crossed my mind."

"And pigs have wings," she muttered.

"One kiss. 'Tis all I ask. Surely not an overly demanding request?"

She opened her mouth to protest, knowing already that he had won. Because she did not want to say no. She wanted to kiss him, to feel the lips that had traced such fire across her hand. Would their touch be so potent when pressed against her own?

"One," she said shakily. "And then you will escort me back to the front lawn."

"Assuredly," he agreed.

He made no move to take his boon, but merely looked into her face with his now-familiar amused grin. Then he pulled her close, crushing her against his body as his strong arms wrapped around her. His mouth lowered to hers, softly touching, caressing, brushing her lips with the faintest of pressure until her reluctance faded. His tongue teased against her mouth, begging, pleading for entry until she granted him that favor too.

Katherine nearly jumped from the shock of the gentle invasion, relishing the sensation, yet afraid of the intimacy she had allowed him. She felt herself relaxing in his embrace, her arms creeping up to wrap themselves around his neck, pulling his head farther down as she responded to his demanding mouth. She refused to listen to her doubts, her fears, instead giving herself up to the sheer exquisite pleasure of his nearness. Katherine nearly cried aloud when he finally tore his mouth away.

He held her clasped against him; she felt his thudding heart beneath her ear and heard his labored breathing mingled with her own.

"We should go back," she whispered when she could take air to speak again.

"I fear it will be a short while before I can escort you back into polite company," he said slowly. "Perhaps we can take another turn around the garden?"

Katherine's gaze flew to his face and she saw the smoldering desire that lurked within his eyes, frightening in its intensity. It was that which returned her to her senses at last. She stepped away from his embrace.

"I shall see myself back," she said hastily, turning toward the house.

Knowlton watched her go with a mixture of regret and hope. He had cast down the gauntlet this evening; the next days would tell whether she would pick it up or not. Drawing in a deep breath of cool night air, he smiled at the darkened garden. He would take it as an encouraging sign if she did not commence packing on the morrow.

On one matter he had been right: Katherine Mayfield was as passionate as her red hair indicated. It was going to be a delightful experience to unleash the full force of her desire.

8

Folly is an endless maze,
Tangled roots perplex her ways.
How many have fallen there!
             —Blake, *The Voice of the Ancient Bard*

Sleep did not come easily to Katherine that night. After the kiss in the garden, she had wished to flee immediately from the party, only to recollect that she needed to wait for a ride home with the vicar and his wife. So she stayed close to Mrs. Ashe until it was time to depart. Katherine caught no further sight of Knowlton, for which she was grateful.

What must he think of her after her wanton response to his kiss? She should never have allowed him to kiss her so, should have drawn back at the first sign that it was to be more than an innocent brush of his lips. Instead, she had allowed him an intimacy that frightened her.

She dreaded their next encounter, fearing that the naked desire she had seen in his eyes that evening would be there always now, when he looked at her. She must make it very clear to him that her behavior had been an aberration, a foolishness born of the hour and the circumstances. He must not think he could ever dare such a thing again.

Her first impression of him had been correct: he was dangerous. He had pierced her armor as easily as if she were an innocent child, rather than an experienced widow who had grown adept at fending off improper advances from all manner of men. Yet Knowlton had the power to disarm her at a glance. No, Katherine could never allow him to get so close to her in the future.

If she had an ounce of sense, she would pack up her own and Robbie's meager belongings and find another cottage, in another county, where she would never have to worry about seeing the earl. Yet she was reluctant to do so. She liked it here in Lincolnshire; she had made friendships in the short time she had lived here. And she hated the thought of wrenching Robbie away from another home.

Ironically, it was Robbie who made their departure difficult, precisely because of his fondness for the earl. Robbie idolized the man. Katherine should have anticipated that sooner and cut the connection earlier, when she had the chance. Now it was too late; Robbie would be hurt and resentful if she refused any further contact.

Still, it would not be a bad thing to try to ease Robbie away from the man. She suspected Knowlton's interest in her son was more of a whim of the moment, one that would fade over time. They could not expect the earl to remain indefinitely in the neighborhood; he would be returning to the excitement of London ere long, and Robbie would be bereft. It would be best to prepare him now for the eventual disappointment.

As for the earl and herself . . . She would inform him quite succinctly that she was determined to keep him at arm's length in the future. His attentions might be good for Robbie, but they were nothing but troublesome for her.

By Sunday, Katherine seethed with frustration. She had agonized over what she would say, how she would react when she saw the earl next. Yet there had been no opportunity for an encounter over the last four days. She had not been able to greet him in the coolly correct manner she planned, to indicate to him that whatever madness had seized her in the garden had faded upon reflection. Robbie finally divulged the news that the earl had left Warrenton for a brief trip to Nottingham. The truth left her strangely deflated.

So now she would be forced to confront him at church, with all the neighborhood in attendance. She would not put it past him to make some sort of embarrassing scene, just to cause her discomfort. She simply did not trust him to behave anymore, whether in public or in private. Her stomach churned with apprehension as she and Robbie traced the lane toward the village.

Katherine spotted Knowlton the moment she entered the church, lounging in solitary splendor in the family box. His face bore a trace of resigned boredom, which changed when his eyes lit upon her. He smiled, inclining his head a fraction in greeting. Katherine nodded politely in turn and turned her attention to Robbie.

The service lasted for an excruciating passage of time, the vicar's words no more than an endless drone in Katherine's ears. Every time she tried to concentrate on the service, Knowlton's presence distracted her. One could not look toward the vicar without seeing the earl. In desperation, she cast her gaze onto her hymnal, but before long her eyes were drawn toward the front once again.

She wanted to escape to the safety of the cottage the moment the service ended, her resolve draining away with each passing moment. But she had to talk with him, in order to put an end to this foolishness once and for all. Katherine forced her steps to slow as she took Robbie's hand and led him down the aisle. The earl was behind her, she knew, taking his time as he stopped and greeted nearly ever member of the congregation, as if he knew how it would only increase her agitation. Stepping into the warm sunshine, she had half a mind to dish out the same treatment, and strike out for home without confronting him, but Robbie had already vanished somewhere with Sam, and she needed to wait for his return.

She watched with growing apprehension as Knowlton finally appeared in the church door, deep in conversation with Mr. Ashe. If he put on this facade of piousness to impress her, he was failing miserably. Knowlton looked up for a moment and caught her gaze. A slow smile lit his face. He mumbled something to the vicar and slowly ambled toward her.

"Good morning, Mrs. Mayfield." He doffed his hat.

"Good morning, my lord," she replied coolly.

"Young Robbie has abandoned you already?" He lifted one mocking brow.

She nodded. "He and Samuel Trent are up to some mischief, I am certain."

"It is fortunate, for there is a matter I wished to speak with you, without Robbie present."

"Yes?" She strove to remain cool. What would he dare now?

He smiled in his most disarming manner. "I have invited some friends for a small shooting party next week. I wished to ask you—beforehand this time—if you will permit Robbie to accompany us.''

She stared at him as if she had not heard. He wanted to speak about Robbie joining a shooting party? He was going to stand here and pretend that nothing had happened that night in his darkened garden?

''I thought he could help with the game bags or carry the shot,'' Knowlton continued, a smile teasing at the corner of his lips. ''I assure you, he will not be allowed near any of the guns.''

Katherine quickly gathered her wits. It was a heaven-sent opportunity to put one part of her plan into effect.

''It is kind of you to ask,'' she said slowly, ''but I think it would be best if Robbie did not participate. He is about to resume his studies with the vicar, and a little extra preparation would not be amiss.''

''I see,'' Knowlton said.

Katherine was certain she was mistaken. That could not be disappointment she saw in his eyes.

''Robbie has had a most enjoyable summer,'' she rattled on, ''but it is high time he settled down again. And truly, my lord, I do not think your guests will wish to be bothered with a ten-year-old pest.''

''Perhaps you are right, ma'am. I trust the lad will still be coming to Warrenton to ride?''

She hesitated. ''Perhaps for the duration of your party, it would be best if he stayed away.''

He frowned. ''Are you taking out your anger with me on your son? If so, it will not do.''

''Anger?'' she asked in some surprise.

''I believe I behaved with less than circumspection the last time we spoke.''

His eyes lit with a teasing laughter that belied his apologetic words. Katherine's irritation rose.

''The only anger I felt over that incident was with myself, my lord, for allowing such an untoward situation to occur. Who could blame you for taking advantage of such a foolish soul?''

''Who, indeed?'' he asked, and there was a hint of that wicked gleam in his eyes.

Katherine did not avert her gaze. "I am concerned more about Robbie," she explained. "He adores your company, and I am most grateful for the attention you have lavished upon him. But I know that the situation cannot continue. You have your own interests, and we can hardly expect you to remain here in the country forever. This will allow Robbie to see that matters will change as the year wears on."

"A good point," he said, although he had yet thought little of leaving Warrenton. "But I hate to deprive the lad of his horse while the lesson is learned. I meant it sincerely when I said the animal was a gift to your son. If you do not wish Robbie at Warrenton, perhaps I can make some other arrangements for the stabling of the beast."

"There is the small shed at the rear of the cottage garden . . ."

"Of course. 'Twill be just the thing. Robbie is adept at caring for him now, and I can have Frank amble over from time to time to make certain he is carrying out his duties properly."

"Then it is arranged."

"I will take care of matters this week, then." Knowlton took her gloved hand and bowed over it in departure. "Oh, there is one more thing, Mrs. Mayfield."

"Yes?"

A roguish twinkle lit his eyes. "It was a very lovely kiss."

Katherine's cheeks flamed as he took his leave, a broad grin upon his face. He had done it again—disarmed her completely, then struck with lightning speed. Drat the man!

Knowlton's grin lingered for most of the ride home. How he loved to bring the color to her cheeks. She blushed more prettily than any woman he knew. He had noticed her studied casualness in her treatment of him, knew she was remembering their last encounter the entire time he nattered on about Robbie and the pony. He had not been able to resist that little reminder, just to make certain she knew he had not forgotten it either.

Lord, he was glad he had availed himself of that bouncy barmaid in Nottingham. There were limits to what one man could endure, and he had reached it long ago. That simple kiss in the garden had shaken him more than he could ever have imagined. He was quite certain he had the delectable Kate Mayfield wavering, but a precipitate move on his part could still scare her into flight. With his hunger assuaged, he could now behave with a modicum of restraint until he had her willing acquiescence.

He honestly did regret her refusal to allow Robbie to participate in the shooting party. He genuinely liked the lad. Yet he agreed with Mrs. Mayfield's concerns: he had no intention of staying forever at Warrenton, and Robbie would have to realize that eventually. Knowlton had noticed with growing dismay the worshipful way Robbie regarded him. It was flattering and frightening at the same time. His gradual withdrawal from the boy's life would be the best thing. But how was he to reconcile that with his pursuit of the mother?

Quite simply, Robbie needed to be out of the way. He was old enough for school, and it would do him good to be with more lads of his own age and class. Samuel Trent was a spirited lad, but a farmer's son was not the best companion for Robbie. He came from gentry stock at the least, and in spite of their poverty, he should be consorting with those of his own kind.

Knowlton was certain, however, that Mrs. Mayfield did not have the funds to send Robbie away to school. That would be the problem he must tackle. He knew her pride would not allow him to finance such an endeavor—even if it was not uncommon for a noble to finance several charity students at the premier schools. Somehow, he would have to find a way to provide her with the means to purchase the lad's education without letting her know it came from him.

Then, with Robbie away, he could avail himself of the widow's charms without restraint. The Rose Cottage would make an admirable love nest. Cheered by the thought that his designs might yet succeed, he broke into most ignoble whistling.

Katherine watched Robbie with sympathy as he moped about the house. He had deeply resented her order that he stay away from Warrenton while Knowlton entertained his shooting party. Even moving his pony to the makeshift stall in the shed had not improved his disposition. It worried her, for it showed that he had grown as attached to the earl as she had feared. And that would never do.

"Why don't you see if there are any late apples left on the trees?" she suggested helpfully. "I could bake a pie for dinner."

"They are probably all gone," he grumbled.

"We will not know for certain until you look," she reminded him. "Put on your coat and take the basket. And do not get yourself dirty!"

She watched his reluctant form as he ambled down the walk. Once again, she was filled with regret—and doubt. Had she chosen the life that was best for him? As he grew older, she grew less certain. Their lack of funds grew more critical the older he became. Lessons with the vicar would suffice for only so long. How much easier it would be for the both of them if she had the money to pay for Robbie's schooling. She had heard the tales of the horror of scholarship life, the boys no better than unpaid slaves to the other students. Katherine did not want a life like that for Robbie. She determined that there would be no Eton or Harrow for him under those circumstances.

But the price that would be exacted for the money to send him off properly had been too much for her to pay six years ago, and she still thought it was too heavy a burden now. She could delay a final decision for a few more years. Perhaps there would be some miracle in the intervening time . . .

She shook her head wistfully. Her father would have reprimanded her for thinking of so worldly a miracle as money to send a young boy to school. But she did not think the miracles of holy angels would be of much use to her. There were other schools, with endowed openings, that would put Robbie on the same standing as the paying students. It was time she began to investigate these matters.

At least with Robbie out of the house today, she could finish with her fall cleaning. There were only the upstairs bedrooms to finish, and the cottage would be gleaming from top to bottom. Then she would have to devise some other project to occupy her time. There was little extra sewing at this time of the year, and matters would not improve for another month. Yet it was a glorious relief not to have to sew more lace and trimmings on the elegant gowns that she could never afford for herself.

She had just succeeded in turning the mattress in Robbie's room, noticing the increasing lumps in the matting feathers and knowing she did not have the funds to purchase a new one, when a strange male voice hailed her from below.

"Mrs. Mayfield?"

She came down the stairs warily. A disheveled but expensively clad man stood in the front hall.

"Mrs. Mayfield?"

She nodded.

"Lord Knowlton sent me, from Warrenton. We were out shooting and there has been an accident. Your son—"

"Robbie?" she gasped, a wave of dizziness sweeping over her. "Shot?"

"Oh, good God." The man scowled. "I am making a mull of this. Your son has a broken leg, ma'am, from falling off his horse. Knowlton took him up to the house, sent for the doctor, and dispatched me to bring you to Warrenton."

"I will come at once," she said rapidly, tearing off her mobcap and darting into the kitchen to grab her cloak.

By sheer force of will, Katherine forced down her panic. Robbie would be all right, she told herself as she followed Knowlton's guest to the waiting curricle. It was only a broken leg. Boys broke their legs all the time and suffered no lasting harm. But the calming words had minimal impact.

She sat quietly on the rapid carriage ride to Warrenton, only her firmly clenched hands betraying her anxiety. She was grateful the man beside her was disinclined to speak. Katherine did not think she could have carried on a conversation if her life had depended upon it.

She was poised to leap from the carriage before it came to a clattering halt at the bottom of Warrenton's steps. Throwing a grateful thank-you over her shoulder, she jumped from the coach and raced up the stone steps. Knowlton's imperious butler awaited her at the front door and ushered her quickly up the stairs.

Robbie looked so small in the massive canopied bed, eyes closed, long streaks marking the path of his tears across his dirty face. Knowlton sat beside him, Robbie's small hand clutched protectively in his.

"Robbie." Her voice came out as a choked whisper.

"Mama?"

Knowlton stood up, motioning her to take his place and placing Robbie's hand in hers. "The doctor should be here at any moment," he said quietly, then retreated to the far side of the room.

Katherine reached out and brushed back the hair from Robbie's forehead. "You are being a very brave boy," she said. "I know it must hurt dreadfully."

He nodded. "I cried, a little," he confessed, and those very words brought the tears back to his eyes. "I'm sorry, Mama."

"Hush," she said. "Do not worry about anything now. Is it only your leg that hurts?"

"My head hurts a bit too," he said. "And my side."

She felt under his hair, flinching when he winced at her touch. There was a nasty bump.

"What happened?"

"Atlas heard the shooting and he got scared and started to run and I . . . I fell off."

"And were you not told to stay away from Warrenton while there was shooting?" the earl asked sternly.

Robbie nodded.

"We will talk about that later," Katherine said, surprised that the earl chastised Robbie. Did he fear she would hold him at fault?

"The doctor is here," Knowlton announced after looking out the window. "I will bring him up."

An hour later, Katherine again sat next to Robbie, his small hand curled securely in hers, while she watched him sleep. As soon as the preliminary examination was finished, the doctor had given him laudanum to deaden the pain of splinting his leg. Now Robbie lay with his leg straight and bandaged. The bump on his head was little more than that, and his ribs were only bruised. He had been very fortunate, if "fortunate" could describe the plight of an active ten-year-old who was to be confined to his bed for several weeks. It would not be difficult at first, but as he convalesced and the pain eased, Katherine knew it would be a taxing experience, for both her and Robbie. He would grow to loathe his small room at the cottage, and she knew her days would be an endless succession of trips up and down the stairs as she sought to do her own work while she kept Robbie entertained.

"Is he asleep?" Knowlton's voice was soft as he slipped quietly into the room.

She nodded. "The doctor said he will probably not awaken until tonight. He wishes to keep him dosed with laudanum for a day or two until the pain subsides."

"He was a brave little boy," Knowlton said.

"How did you find him?"

"Purely by chance. We had achieved little success in the upper field and were heading toward the corner when Somers— Lord Wentworth, the man who brought you here—noticed Atlas wandering about."

"I feared something like this would happen if he began riding."

"You cannot protect him from everything, Katherine. I do feel at fault, for I had not thought that blasted pony would be so skittish. I never would have wished Robbie harm."

"I know," she replied, and gave him a comforting smile.

"Are you comfortable? I can have a tea tray sent up."

"Thank you, that would be nice. Would it be a dreadful imposition for me to beg the use of your carriage to take Robbie home? I thought he would be easier moved after his next dose—"

"Absolutely not," he said sternly. "I talked with the doctor and he made it very clear that Robbie was not to be moved about."

"But I must take him home," she said. "We cannot stay here. You have done enough, for which I am grateful."

Their eyes met and he saw the apprehension in hers. Damn! Did she think he would dare to take advantage of the situation?

"I will take care of matters," he said noncommittally, then rose from his chair. "The tray will be sent up."

Katherine nodded and looked back to the pain-etched face of her sleeping son. How lucky they had been. She brushed his tousled hair back from his forehead.

Knowlton's sincere concern for Robbie's welfare touched her. She remembered all his past kindnesses to her son, and her often ungrateful responses. She might justifiably question Knowlton's interest in her, but they both seemed to be of the same mind regarding Robbie. And as her knowledge of Knowlton increased, her power to resist him weakened. Katherine rightly feared the close proximity remaining in his house would entail. It was well, then, that she would be taking her son home tonight.

9

What is virtue but a calculation of the consequences
of our actions?
                    —Mary Hays, *Memoirs of Emma Courtney*

After arranging for tea and some food to be sent up to Mrs.
Mayfield, Knowlton went in search of Lord Wentworth, finding
him alone in the study. The other guests were still tramping
through the fields.

"Is there any chance your lovely lady would be willing to
join you here, Somers?" Knowlton asked, his voice light. "The
doctor has recommended that the lad not be moved until the
leg heals, yet it is a highly improper situation for his mother
to remain in a bachelor household. She is determined they leave,
and I cannot help but feel it would not be good for the lad."

"Elizabeth would come in a moment—if she can bring Caro."

Knowlton winced. "I suppose it is too much to hope that your
lovely daughter is one of those quiet children who never exercise
their lungs?"

Somers laughed. "The vain hopes of a confirmed bachelor.
I shall let you in on a secret, my friend. The main reason to
have one of these monstrously large houses is that you can tuck
the infants into a far corner. Out of sight, out of hearing.
Distance works wonders."

Knowlton sighed. "I will allow the chit, only on the condition
that word of her presence does not leak out. Too many ladies
would see it as a sign of hope."

"Little do they know that there is nothing better to encourage
a man in his bachelorhood than exposure to a small child."

"That bad?" Knowlton lifted a sympathetic brow.

Somers shook his head. "I am afraid to say I was captivated
from the first moment I saw her. You cannot know the feeling,
to hold your own child in your arms, to know that you had a

hand in her creation. It is an awe-inspiring experience." He clapped Knowlton lightly on the shoulder. "We shall have to get you married off one of these days, so you can discover it firsthand."

"Spare me that joy." Knowlton gave a mock shudder.

Somers laughed. "I will write to Elizabeth."

"I shall dispatch a groom today." He eyed his friend hopefully. "Do you think she can be here within a week?"

"Of a certainty. She was rather put out at my leaving in the first place, so I am assured she will be willing of an early reconciliation."

"Under the cat's paw already?"

Somers raised a knowing brow. "Someday, my friend, I hope you will understand," he said enigmatically, and seated himself at the desk to pen his letter.

Knowlton stared out the window while Somers prepared his missive. Marriage had wrought a change in his friend, and he could not say whether it was for good or ill. Still, Somers was barely two years into his marriage, and the thrill of new fatherhood had yet to wear off. What tune would Somers sing five years hence?

As soon as the letter was finished, Knowlton rang for a footman and ordered its delivery. Now, if Lady Wentworth cooperated, he only had to protect Kate's reputation for a week. Knowlton realized he should ride to the vicar's and see if Mrs. Ashe would be willing to play duenna.

What a laughable situation. He had been scheming for weeks to get Kate into his arms, and his bed. And now here he was, presented with a perfect opportunity, with her son's sickroom a hairbreadth away from his, and he felt obligated to treat her with all the honor and respect he would pay any noble guest. It would be intolerably funny if it was not going to be so damn difficult.

Mrs. Ashe was perfectly willing to settle for a time at Warrenton, agreeing with Knowlton that the boy should remain where he was. Knowlton returned home with a lighter heart, knowing he could forestall Kate's every argument. Robbie's recovery was of the utmost importance. He was certain he and Kate could adjust to the awkward situation. Besides, she would be preoccupied with her son and he had his own guests to entertain. They would see little of each other.

"Everything is arranged," he announced as he slipped into the room. Robbie still slept his drugged sleep.

"Thank you, my lord." Katherine smiled gratefully. "I appreciate your efforts. I shall let you know when I give Robbie his next dose. He should be ready to travel within half an hour of that."

"Mrs. Ashe will be arriving within the hour to play propriety for you, Mrs. Mayfield. There is no need for you to disturb your son. You may stay as long as the doctor thinks is necessary for Robbie's leg to heal properly."

Katherine surveyed him with dismay. "Is it not rather presumptuous of you to have arranged such a thing?"

"I am doing what is best for Robbie, which is what we both desire. If you take him home, apart from the danger of the journey and the struggle to get him into his room, have you thought about the effect it will have on you? To play nursemaid for him as well as perform all your other duties at home?" Knowlton struggled to rein in his real anger. "Here you need to do nothing beyond sit with him for as long as you like. Your meals will be prepared for you, your laundry will be washed, your every whim accommodated. I think you would be a fool to leave."

"You would." Her blue eyes filled with anger.

Knowlton walked over to the window, his arms folded across his chest. He looked out over the lawn for some time in silence, then turned and leaned against the sill. He had created this awkward situation between them, and however much he regretted the need, he knew he must reassure her.

"I wish you to know that I will remain out of your way," he stated. The promise pained him, but he knew it was the only way he could convince her to stay. "You need not fear that I will be anything but a gracious host."

She studied him for a moment. Could she trust him? Better yet, could she trust herself to remain under the same roof and not fall further under his spell? It was a risky proposition. But with Robbie's health uppermost in her mind, it was a chance she would have to take. "Thank you," she said at last.

"Then it is agreed? You and Robbie will stay?" He cringed at the eagerness in his voice.

"We will stay," she agreed. "But I shall need to return home, to pack some things."

"I will take you now. My housekeeper can sit with Robbie until you return."

Katherine was grateful that Knowlton remained in the curricle while she raced about the cottage, gathering up the clothing and items she and Robbie would need for an extended stay at Warrenton. She was still apprehensive about the matter, not completely trusting Knowlton to behave himself, nor completely trusting herself to be in such close proximity to him for any length of time. She had already learned how easily he could overcome her defenses, and she would have to take great care to stay as far from him as possible. Fortunately, since she would be busy with Robbie, that would not prove too difficult. She hoped.

"Lord Wentworth has written to his lady, to ask her to come and stay," Knowlton told her on the drive back to Warrenton. "I think you will enjoy her company. She will be busy with her young daughter, but I imagine you will have some time to talk together. You are very close in age, I believe."

"We are ruining your shooting party," she said with dismay.

He shrugged. " 'Twill not be much disruption. I fully intend to ignore the presence of you ladies until the evening meal. Does that set your mind at rest?"

She smiled. "It does, my lord. Although I hope Lady Wentworth does not mind having to come."

"Somers assures me she will not. He claims that as long as she can dote on her daughter without interference, she will be content in any location."

She could not stifle her laugh.

"Yes?" He arched a brow.

"It will undoubtedly be an interesting experience for you, I am certain, to have your house overrun with children."

"I hardly think one lad in a splint and a toddling child will have much power to disrupt my household," he said.

"We shall see."

* * *

The first week at Warrenton sped by with rapidity. Katherine and Mrs. Ashe sat together in Robbie's room, sewing and talking quietly while he lay abed. Knowlton, despite his plan to ignore both Robbie and his mother, dropped by several times each day to ascertain that they were managing well. Both Katherine and Mrs. Ashe preferred to eat with Robbie, and they saw little of Knowlton's guests.

By the end of the week, after several days of unwanted rain put a damper on the hunting, matters changed. Lord Wentworth was the first to pop his head into the room.

"Thought I would see how the lad is getting along," he said. "Bored to flinders yet, Robbie?"

Robbie glanced at his mother, as if wondering what she wished him to say. She nodded in encouragement.

"Only a bit, sir. Mama and Mrs. Ashe are doing all they can to engage my interest."

"But it is not enough for a lively lad stuck in bed, is it? Do you play chess?"

Robbie shook his head.

"Then I shall teach you," Lord Wentworth assured him. "Knowlton must have a set around here somewhere. If you do not mind, Mrs. Mayfield?"

"Goodness, no," Katherine replied, pleased that Robbie would have the opportunity.

Yet it was Knowlton who appeared half an hour later, carrying not a chess set, but a backgammon game.

"I know there is a chess set somewhere in the house," he said by way of apology, "but it will take a bit longer to locate it. We will start with backgammon."

Katherine smiled uneasily. This was precisely the situation she had wished to avoid during their enforced stay at Warrenton. But her dismay was replaced by gratitude as Knowlton studiously ignored her. He patiently taught Robbie the rules of the game, and played with him for over an hour, until it became obvious Robbie was tiring.

Katherine walked Knowlton to the corridor. "Thank you so much for entertaining Robbie."

"He is a bright lad," he said. "When I find that blasted chess set, I am certain he will learn as quickly."

"And what will come next?" she asked in a teasing voice. "Whist?"

"A capital idea!" Knowlton returned her teasing. "Drummond lived for a time on his skill with the cards. He will prove a most instructive teacher."

Katherine shuddered in mock horror. "I hate to think what other skills your guests are qualified to teach."

"Only those suitable to a ten-year-old," Knowlton promised.

"He will enjoy the company," Katherine admitted. "He has already grown bored with my efforts, I fear."

"We will soon chase away his boredom," Knowlton promised. He caught her gaze, his eyes twinkling. "But whatever shall we do to relieve your boredom, Mrs. Mayfield? A stroll in the garden, perhaps?"

Katherine paused. She had hoped that this sojourn at Warrenton would pass in an unexceptional manner. Knowlton would keep to his friends; she would tend to Robbie in the isolation of his room. As long as they were not forced into close contact, she could deal with Knowlton. But his words, his nearness, brought back in a rush all the memories of the feel of his body pressed close to hers as they exchanged kisses in the garden. She saw his gray eyes coolly watching her, as if he could discern her thoughts, and her cheeks grew redder. Knowlton was becoming far, far too dangerous for her to deal with. Precisely because she was losing her will to fight against him. Avoidance was her only defense.

"I shall suggest that to Mrs. Ashe," she said, consciously stiffening. "Perhaps this afternoon we shall act upon your suggestion."

Knowlton bowed graciously, but Katherine saw the flicker of disappointment that crossed his eyes. She must keep firm in her resolve.

The elusive chess set was finally unearthed and the following day Lord Wentworth began teaching the game to Robbie. His visit was soon followed by appearances by the other men of the party: the flirtatious Seb Cole, who struck Katherine as a rogue of Knowlton's ilk, the rakish, widowed Duke of Hartford, who talked proudly of his own son away at school, and the rather aloof Viscount Drummond, who managed to look cynical and sad at the same time. Katherine marveled at their patience as they taught Robbie chess and whist, regaled him with stories of valor and glory at Waterloo, and generally inspired hero worship to rival Robbie's feelings for Knowlton. And they never once made her uncomfortable with unwanted attentions.

Lady Wentworth arrived in due time, in a carriage Knowlton laughingly insisted was crammed to the roof with baby para- phernalia. He did not miss the eagerness with which Somers leapt to his feet at the announcement of her arrival. Knowlton shook his head in dismay. Somers was well and truly caught.

Despite all Knowlton's intentions, the presence of Lady Went- worth altered the nature of the previously idyllic bachelor retreat. Whereas Kate and the vicar's wife had remained up- stairs, Lady Wentworth joined the men for dinner most nights. That forced the gentlemen to be on their better behavior, and the easygoing bachelor life of their first week in residence reformed itself into a more restrained atmosphere. Lady Went- worth graciously stayed out of the way as much as possible, but the mere fact of her existence disrupted the household. Knowlton was not surprised when the duke cornered him in the library one morning.

"I cannot say that it was not entertaining, Knowlton, but it is time to be gone." Hartford extended his hand.

"Ladies driving you away, eh?"

"More a reminder of what is waiting back in London," the duke replied. "One of the most delectable morsels I have had in years. Good thing you were here in the country when she made her debut, else you would have tried to snap her up."

"You can only be glad I was here," Knowlton replied. "Else she would not have taken a second glance at you."

"But I am a duke," Hartford protested loftily.

"But I am Knowlton."

They both burst into laughter.

"Take care, Hart, on the journey home. And I promise that the spring shoot will be more convivial."

Knowlton sighed as his friend left the room. Hart gone today; Cole and Drummond would not be far behind. He was now struck with entertaining the Wentworths, whose cozy domesticity was rapidly growing tiresome. Knowlton had been more than startled by Somers' defection from the bachelor ranks, but this new role of blissfully besotted husband shook Knowlton to the core. Somers, with whom he had drunk, gamed, and wenched for years, was becoming an unknown quantity. Knowlton could not help but harbor a bit of resentment against Lady Wentworth. She was an admirable lady, strikingly lovely, intelligent, and witty, yet she had brought his closest friend to such a pass.

One thing for certain, he was going to have to drag Kate out of her seclusion and into the drawing room. The thought of spending the evening in the sole company of the Wentworths while they made calf's eyes at each other, was more than he could stomach. If Kate joined them, they could at least play cards or drum up some other diversionary program.

Besides, he looked forward to spending more time in her company. He had remained studiously circumspect these last two weeks, playing the correct host and never overstepping the bounds of propriety. With three other bachelors in the house, he dared not do else. Now that only Somers and his lady were left, he could lower his guard a bit. There would be no word of gossip from the Wentworths. While he would not take full advantage of Kate's presence in his home, it would take more of a saint than he to continue to ignore her. He had come too far not to press for her final capitulation. Despite that trip to Nottingham, he found his body ached for her as much as ever.

Knowlton set about advancing his scheme on the very morning his other guests departed, bounding up the stairs to the invalid's room as soon as the last carriage cleared the drive. Robbie, his recuperation far enough along that he was back working on the dreaded Latin, was frowning over his books while his mother sat near the window, reading.

"If you will excuse your mother, Robbie, I have a matter I should like to discuss with her."

Robbie nodded glumly. It made no difference whether his mother was in the room or not; he would have to finish his Latin.

"I hope you do not want to ring a peal over me for driving all your guests away," Katherine said when she joined him in the hall. "I am truly sorry."

He waved a dismissive hand. "They rarely stay longer than this. Too many other amusements to draw their attention."

"Are we keeping you from your diversions as well?"

Not for long, he hoped. "I fear there has been a sad want of requests for my presence this fall," he said with a rueful expression. "I had planned to stay here at least until the start of the new year, so you have not overset my plans."

"I am glad."

"I am certain you have grown tired of your confinement in that room," he continued. "Now that there are no debauched males lurking in the hallways, I wish you would make yourself at home in the house."

"I fear your guests were so gracious at entertaining Robbie that he will be suffering from increased fits of boredom if I do not keep him close company."

"Nonsense. He is a sensible lad and knows he cannot rely on you for constant amusement. I think it is high time that you began to act as a proper guest."

She eyed him cautiously. "And how does a proper guest act?"

"She joins her host in the drawing room in the evening, for conversation and companionship," he said. "And allows herself to be taken for a tour of the house. You have been here for over a fortnight and have yet to see more than a fraction of Warrenton. It is enough to make a more sensitive man take offense."

Katherine could not resist him when he was determined to be charming. She told herself she would be safe with him; she had his promise that he would not misbehave while she was under his roof. He had behaved admirably up until now; there was no reason to think he would alter his behavior.

"I would very much like to see your home," she said.

He took her hand in his and led her along the corridor to the wide, curving staircase that rose from the ground floor. "From the cellars to the attic, or from highest to lowest?"

"I hardly think I need to peruse the attics *or* the cellars," Katherine replied.

He shrugged. "Do not complain, then, that I gave you less than a thorough inspection."

Knowlton rushed Katherine through most rooms, giving her an almost self-deprecating tour, as if he felt embarrassed at being the owner of such a magnificent estate. She stopped him occasionally to linger over a fine piece of furniture or a collection of curios, but she mostly let him have his way until they reached the portrait gallery. There she forced him to slow and explain each and every painting.

"I do not know who half these people are," he protested.

"Then you should," she retorted. "Show me the family, at least."

He led her past an endless array of portraits, starting, inexplicably, with his grandfather, the seventh earl.

"Gambler," Knowlton explained. "Lost and won the family fortune several times over."

"I trust he was on the winning side when he passed on."

"Most assuredly. He'd just won ten thousand pounds at a game, stood up from the table, and dropped dead. My grandmother always claimed it was by the grace of God or he would have lost it all the next night."

Katherine gave him a sidelong look.

"Now, this rogue," he continued, pointing to a man with the long curls of Charles II's age, "was a crony of Lord Rochester's."

"Who was he?"

Knowlton stifled a smile. "One of the minor poets."

"He must be *very* minor; I have heard naught of him."

"He was not prolific," Knowlton admitted. "And his poems were mostly circulated privately."

Katherine could only guess at what scurrilous scribbling his ancestor's friend had prepared. "Were any of your ancestors respectable?"

Knowlton laughed. "I doubt it. There seems to be a streak of misbehavior that runs from father to son."

"Where is the portrait of your father?"

"I had it removed."

Katherine busied herself with studying the next portrait. Another clue to the mystery that made up Knowlton. For despite his reputation, Katherine was beginning to understand that there was a far more complex man lurking behind the rakish facade than he let on. That was the man she wanted to know.

"What of the women in your family?" she asked loftily. "Whatever possessed them to align their lives with such a packet of rapscallions?"

"Need you ask?" His gray eyes twinkled mischievously. Knowlton took her hand in his, rubbing his thumb across her upstretched fingers. "We Beauchamps are decidedly impossible to resist."

"Are you so certain of that, my lord?"

An amused smile flitted across his lips. "Would you care to put the matter to a test?" His fingers tightened on hers.

Katherine looked into his eyes, trying to capture a glimpse of what he really thought. Did he truly believe he was irresistible to any woman? Or did he only think she was less than firm in her resistance? Had he sensed the doubts and longings that plagued her?

They stood for long minutes, their gazes locked together, without moving and barely breathing. Katherine knew that one step forward would take her into his arms, and her will wavered. But still she stood her ground.

Knowlton brought her hand to his lips, brushing them softly against her fingers, while his eyes never left hers. His expression was enigmatic; Katherine saw neither desire nor pleading there. Only curiosity.

A voice echoed down the long, paneled corridor and broke their concentration.

"Shall we call it a draw—for now?" Knowlton asked, a knowing smile spreading across his face.

Katherine nodded silently. He placed her hand on his arm and led her from the room.

10

And for marriage I have neither the talent
  nor the inclination.

—Byron

If Katherine had been honest with herself, she would have taken
Robbie that very day and fled not from the mansion, but from
the entire neighborhood, without a backward glance. She knew
she was playing with fire, but like the moth drawn to the flame,
she could not tear herself away.

So instead of quietly remaining in Robbie's room in the
evening, she allowed herself to be drawn into the convivial
atmosphere of the drawing room, playing whist or other card
games with Knowlton and the Wentworths. Often Katherine
remained with Knowlton after the others retired for the night.
He made no overt physical approach toward her, but his mere
presence in the room was enough; she was acutely aware of
his every move and look. She often caught him watching her
with a knowing smile on his lips, which brought a flush to her
cheeks.

And if his presence discomfited her, it also lured her into more
and more intimate discussions. More than once they talked long
into the night, Knowlton almost eagerly revealing more and
more of himself to her.

"I am no saint," he said to her one evening.

"I would not have thought to label you such," she replied
dryly. "But why veer so far in the opposite direction? You are
not an evil person."

"Why?" He shrugged. "I think it is much easier to lead a
life of debauchery than to walk the straight and narrow. And
it is infinitely more entertaining."

"Does it not bother you to have such a dreadful reputation?"

"I have found that there is nothing more alluring to the ladies than a dreadful reputation." Knowlton's face creased in a self-satisfied smile.

"I do not understand the reasoning behind that. Why would any woman be interested in a man who she knows will treat her only as a casual interest?"

"Perhaps because that is all they wish from him."

She sighed. She had hoped to gain some insight into her own attraction to the earl, but his explanations did not enlighten her. Casual dalliance was not a thing she favored. "I am afraid that I simply do not understand the *ton*."

"You are operating under a severe handicap," he explained with an amused smirk. "You were one of those rare creatures who actually had a marriage based on love. Many couples do not, and therefore think little of casting their vows aside for a bit of fun."

She knew he taunted her with his flippant remarks, knew also that he was hiding behind them as well. Could she goad him into an unexpected revelation? "I refuse to believe that the entire world is like that. Look at Somers and Elizabeth."

"A very rare exception," he murmured, shifting in his chair. "Look at Hartford, a doting father, but he rivals me for the numbers of mistresses he has kept"

"But he was once married, so he must have formed some regard for a woman."

"To his great regret."

"Truly?" Katherine's eyes grew wide.

"He discovered quite shortly after the wedding how eminently unsuitable they were. When it was far too late."

"And you, of course, will never allow such a thing to happen." The bitterness in her voice surprised Katherine. Why should she expect Knowlton to behave any differently than his rakish reputation allowed?

"Precisely. What need have I of a wife when I can have nearly every woman I wish in my bed?"

Katherine was long past having the shocking nature of Knowlton's conversation disturb her. What did bother her was Knowlton's callous dismissal of the possibility of love and happiness with another. She pitied him more than anything. It strengthened her to know that she had more experience and wisdom in one area, at least.

"I have shocked you," he said. "I am sorry."

"No, it is not that." Katherine self-consciously twisted her fingers. "I find that it is I who am sorry for you. You cut yourself off from the possibility of ever finding lasting happiness."

" 'Tis an impossible dream," he replied, the sarcasm heavy in his voice. "I will wager in five years' time Somers and Elizabeth will appear as any other bored couple."

"I do not believe so."

"You sound as if you desire a wager."

"Do not be foolish," Katherine snapped. "How cruel to actually wish unhappiness on someone, if only to be proved right in a silly wager."

"I am not wishing unhappiness upon them," Knowlton protested. "I am merely stating the unlikelihood of their besotted state continuing much longer." He leaned forward, the intensity of his look startling Katherine. "Good Lord, they have been wedded for nearly two years now. I have seen newly married couples less in each other's pockets."

"I think it speaks well of Lord Wentworth that he holds his wife in such esteem," Katherine said archly.

"And did Captain Mayfield live in your pocket in such a way?"

Katherine paled, averting her eyes. "He was not at home long enough."

Knowlton set down his glass and took her hands in his. "I am sorry, Katherine. My damnable tongue. I am certain the captain was an admirable husband; you are too fond of the married state for it to have been otherwise."

She offered him a wan smile, captivated by the warmth in his voice. If only he knew just how much he tempted her to cast caution to the winds, to once again act on her impulses and not her wisdom. Particularly when he looked at her in the way he did now, his eyes pleading for forgiveness. She glanced down at their joined hands, then raised her eyes to meet his gaze, nearly recoiling at the new expression she saw there.

His expression of pleading had changed to one far more deadly. There was pure, naked desire in the look he gave her now. He was doing nothing to hide it, showing her blatantly how much he wanted her. She felt a long-remembered thrill race through her and she could not tear her eyes away from his penetrating gaze. Those cynical gray eyes made silent love to her, causing the heat to rise within her at the very thought. The power in his look was almost hypnotic, and Katherine did not think she could glance away even if she wished. His thumb rubbed a sensuous pattern along her palm, and every nerve in her body tingled with growing anticipation and apprehension. She swayed slightly as the struggle raged within her.

"Katherine," he whispered hoarsely.

The sound of his voice jolted her back to her senses and she wrenched her gaze away. Her breathing was fast, her pulse racing. He had totally, utterly seduced her with only a look.

"I think it is time I said good night" she said a trifle breathlessly.

"Must you?" His thumb kept stroking suggestively along her palm. "There is so much more we could discuss."

Katherine snatched her hand away and jumped to her feet. She had to get away. Now. "Good night, my lord."

"Edward," he corrected as he politely rose.

"Edward," she whispered as she fled through the doorway.

Knowlton sank back into his chair, his mind and body disordered. Yes, she had fled from him, but not before he had clearly seen how she reacted to his advance. He had watched her breathing quicken, watched the soft rise and fall of her breasts increase as her awareness grew. She had responded to him physically, and he knew he had made progress. After all her talk of love and marriage, she had not been averse to his invitation.

She had declined it, to be sure, but not with any note of ringing finality. She had been interested, of that he was certain. The passionate nature she had shown him during that long-ago kiss in the garden still lurked within her, barely hidden under the surface. It would not be a torturous struggle to bring it to the forefront again. A few more *tête-à-tête* evenings like this, a glass or two of warmed brandy, and she would be falling into his arms and bed like a ripe plum from a tree. And once he had fully awakened her to the pleasures to be found there, he could look forward to a very satisfying relationship. Very satisfying. He had great hopes for Kate. She would not be a boring companion.

Katherine avoided Knowlton the next day, her thoughts still too jumbled from what had transpired the previous evening. She knew that a firmly worded set-down would cool Knowlton's ardor; he was too much a gentleman to press forward where he was not wanted. But she could not bring herself to say the words that would free her from his attentions.

Knowlton was an enigmatic man. He was, without a doubt, one of the most blatant rakes she had ever met; at the same time, he was a responsible landlord and a thoughtful and caring gentleman. She was beginning to learn about the man under the flippant facade, the Knowlton that few people ever saw. The Knowlton who could buy a little boy a pony and spend endless hours teaching him the finer points of horsemanship. The Knowlton who would cut hay alongside his workers, then entertain them with all the pomp and hospitality a royal guest would receive. The man who would allow his hunting party to be broken up and his home invaded by women and children, just to ensure that a young boy's broken leg healed properly. There was more depth to him than most people imagined.

She wanted to probe those depths, to bring out the hidden Knowlton who possessed tenderness and consideration. She wanted him to openly acknowledge that side of himself; the side he was afraid to face. He disclaimed interest in marriage, yet he had the patience of a doting parent when he dealt with Robbie. He would make a marvelous father, Katherine decided, and it was sad to think that he would not allow himself the joy of that relationship. Why was he so dreadfully opposed to admitting to his feelings?

She refused to accept that he was as satisfied with his libertine existence as he claimed. Surely there were times when he must wish for something as simple as companionship, a woman who was there for more than just the pleasure of her body. Abruptly, Katherine recalled the sensual gaze that had held her transfixed last evening, rekindling the very real attraction she felt for him. He almost could make her believe that a physical relationship would be enough, almost convince her that the pleasure would be worth whatever it cost.

Almost. But she had paid dearly for her hard-won widow's respectability. Knowlton would take all that from her, leaving nothing in return. If only she could reach his heart . . .

"I find the idea of a dinner party wholly ridiculous," Katherine complained to Lady Wentworth as they sat in the drawing room the next evening after dinner.

"Humor the man. He is dying here in the country without the social diversions of the city."

"Then why does he not go back to London?" Katherine restlessly prowled the room. "He insists he is perfectly happy rusticating away here."

Elizabeth shrugged, calmly setting another stitch in her embroidery. "Sometimes I think Knowlton does not know his own mind. But if he wishes to have a neighborhood dinner party, who are we, as his guests, to gainsay him?"

"I never said he could not have a dinner. I merely said I think it is foolish to expect me to attend."

"Nonsense." Elizabeth smiled. "It would be good for you. We are all getting a little too familiar with our enforced company. It will be a welcome respite to swap gossip with some new faces."

"Think how it will appear if I am at dinner!" Katherine whirled to face her new friend. It was one thing for her to remain at Warrenton as nurse for her son. To be a guest at a formal dinner would put her on a much different footing. It was a sharp reminder of how she could move in Knowlton's world—if she chose.

"Katherine, the entire neighborhood knows you are staying here. And they know that I am here as well and that the situation is entirely proper."

"But to appear at the dinner table like I am an honored guest? It will engender untold gossip."

"It would inspire worse gossip if you did *not* appear at the table."

Katherine sighed at the thought. She had not realized it before, but what Elizabeth said was true. "You are right, I believe that would look worse." She thought for a moment. "But whatever shall I wear?"

Elizabeth laughed, recognizing the battle had been won. "Show me your wardrobe. I imagine we can contrive something."

· There was no question it would have to be Katherine's gray silk, years out of date and much the worse for wear. With new trimming it would be passably acceptable, she thought, though nothing could transform it into the quality suitable for a formal dinner at an earl's table. Yet she had little choice. A new gown for such a singular occurrence was out of the question. A trip to the village with Elizabeth produced some new lace, which Katherine quickly stitched to the drab dress. It would have to do.

By the time she had finished the alteration, Katherine actually looked forward to Knowlton's party, after a fashion. The doctor had decreed that Robbie would probably be released from his enforced leisure by then and could return home. Katherine decided they would depart the day following the dinner. So the party would be a farewell of sorts—to Warrenton, Knowlton, and the leisurely life she had led here. It had been lovely to be so free of duties and responsibility, spending a few weeks living the life she had turned her back on before even knowing its delights. If she felt the tiniest regret for that decision, she pushed her qualms to the back of her mind. She dared not look back.

Katherine stretched carelessly and shifted in her chair. She had deliberately remained with Robbie this morning. It would not be long until they returned to the cottage, and she must begin to accustom herself to not being in the earl's presence each day.

"Katherine, darling, would you be a dear and rescue Knowlton?" Elizabeth stood in the doorway to Robbie's room. "I left Caro with him in the drawing room and I am afraid he will take fright and run at the least provocation."

"Certainly," said Katherine, smiling in anticipation of the earl's discomfort.

"I will not be above ten minutes," Elizabeth replied. "Caro

tore my lace and she is sure to destroy the rest of the gown if I do not get it out of her reach.''

Katherine set down her book, glancing over to Robbie. He was absorbed in his own reading. "I will be back when Elizabeth has repaired her dress," she said to him. "Unless you would like me to bring Caro up here to keep you company."

Robbie wrinkled his nose. "I do not want any babies in my room."

The drawing-room door stood ajar and Katherine was able to look into the room without attracting Knowlton's attention. She brought her hand to her lips to smother a laugh. There he sat, Caro perched gingerly on his lap while he tried to keep her active hands off his neatly tied cravat.

"Here, now," he said in dismay as she managed to grab one of the ends. He disentangled her pudgy fingers, but the moment he released her hand, she grabbed again.

Katherine could hear Caro's gurgle of delight. The look of panicked frustration on Knowlton's face was priceless.

"Stop that, Lady Caroline," Knowlton said, his face mirroring his helplessness. "Men do not like ladies who destroy their cravats for no good reason." He fumbled at his waistcoat and pulled out a gold pocket watch. He dangled it in front of the quickly enraptured girl, who followed every motion with her bright eyes.

"That is a watch, my lady. Can you say 'watch'?" Knowlton half-laughed. "Of course you cannot. You can barely lisp 'mama.' ''

"Mama?"

"Oh, the devil take it," Knowlton mumbled. "Try to say 'Knowlton.' 'Knowl-ton.' ''

"No-ton," Caro parroted.

"Very good. You are a smart girl." He allowed her to grab hold of the watch. "A watch is for telling time. A very important thing you will learn when you get older. If you do not know what time it is, how can you ever contrive to arrive fashionably late at a ball?" He leaned closer and whispered in a conspiratorial tone, "That is as important as learning how to pick out the most expensive item in a shop. Your papa will be paying for your things for a very long time, so you must learn at an early age to ask for the best. Papa would never say no to his girl.'' Knowlton's face broke into a wicked smile. "You must insist on having the nicest bonnet and the fanciest lace for your dresses. How else is your papa to show you he loves you?''

Katherine was almost tempted to interrupt his outrageous advice, but she knew Caro did not understand a word of it. Yet his words gave her pause. Did he think all women were like that?

"Oh, Elizabeth, where are you?'' he sang in mild despair as Caro fixed her attention and her hands on his cravat again. "This female seems to be impervious to my charms. How can you insult me so, dear lady?''

Caro answered with a chortling laugh.

"Now you try to flirt with me, you saucy baggage.'' He grinned and tapped her cheek with his finger. "You are going to lead your papa on a merry dance when you get older, I will wager. He will find his hall littered with your admirers. But none of them will be good enough for his precious baby, will they?'' He wrinkled his nose at her and she did the same in return.

A new sensation, not laughter, but something more like astonishment, swept over Katherine. She had seen how patient Knowlton was with Robbie, but had taken that for granted. Most men did well with boys his age. But watching him now with Caro, she saw that it was not just older boys, but also baby girls who brought out the hidden side of him. He had been ill-at-ease initially, but the longer she watched, the more relaxed he became.

He would be a marvelous father, she realized. Patient and understanding with his sons, teasing and loving with his daughters. A mixture of sadness and longing swept over her. He protested so vehemently against marriage, yet by turning his back on it, he was rejecting this experience as well. Would he ever admit, deep down inside, that he might like to bounce his own daughter upon his knee? Want to be cajoled by sweet smiles and demanding pouts into buying her the most expensive bonnet in the shop? Katherine knew if she asked him, he would deny such thoughts. But she would call him a liar.

Caro rapidly lost interest in the ruined folds of Knowlton's cravat and slid off his lap, landing with a plop on her well-padded bottom. She grinned up at him.

"What, leaving so soon?" He peered down at her clear blue eyes. "I cannot believe I am such a failure with a lady. Perhaps you would rather take a stroll, Lady Caroline? Shall we take a walk through our domain?" He stood up, reaching down to pull her to her still-unsteady feet.

"Now, if what your doting papa says is true, you can march like a trooper." Knowlton stood behind her, holding her tiny hands in his fingers. "Shall we make a circuit of the ballroom, my lady?" He shuffled behind her awkward, high-stepping gait. "Look, there is Lady Barnham. Isn't she wearing the most dreadful head ornament? And look at Lady Welmore! Such a shocking display. You will have to remember to tell your papa you wish to patronize the same modiste. That will keep the lads interested. Oh ho," he said, reaching down to catch her as she stumbled. He swept her up into the air. "Shall we waltz instead, my lady? I know we have not been properly introduced, but I assure you that I am the very model of good manners and restraint. Just ask your papa."

Holding Caro in his arms, Knowlton whirled her about the room at a dizzying pace, the girl's delighted laughter goading him to ever greater speed.

Katherine stepped back in alarm when they came in her direction, but she was too slow.

Knowlton spotted her as he twirled past the door, and was flooded with chagrin to have such a witness to his foolishness. He stopped and looked at her quizzically for a moment; then he turned his head to Caro. "Uh-oh. It is that mean dragon of a chaperon, come to take you away from me."

Katherine stepped into the room. "Why, I would not dream of such a thing. You two make such an adorable couple." She was delighted to see the faint traces of color cross Knowlton's cheeks.

"It is true," he said, setting Caro down carefully. "I seem to be notoriously irresistible to the ladies." He flashed her a wry grin. "Except for one."

"Ah, we are a fickle lot," Katherine said airily, kneeling

down to give Caro a hug. "Why, I daresay if her papa came into the room, she would bolt from you like a shot."

"No," he said in mock disbelief. "Lady Caroline would do no such thing. Would you, my dear?"

"Bapa?"

"Bapa is off somewhere, Caro. But I can take you to your mother now." Katherine grinned in delight at Knowlton's bedraggled cravat. "You seem to have decidedly adverse effects on people's clothing," she scolded the girl. "Look what you have done to Lord Knowlton's cravat."

"Oh, do not scold her for that," said Knowlton, a wicked gleam lighting his eyes. "I have never yet objected to a lady removing my cravat. Or any other article of clothing, for that matter."

Katherine planted a noisy kiss on Caro's cheek to avoid a reply. "Shall we find Mama?"

"Outright rejection from two ladies." Knowlton placed his hand over his heart. "Ladies can be so cruel, but do not despair. I know one day I will recover from the wound to my vanity."

"Do not listen to your Uncle Knowlton when he is being so silly," Katherine warned Caro.

"Uncle Knowlton?" His eyes mirrored his disgust.

Katherine flashed him an impish smile. "But assuredly. You performed an excellent rendition of the doting uncle. I cannot wait to tell Elizabeth and Somers of your achievement."

"Kate . . ." he said warningly.

She quickly sidestepped him and headed for the stairs.

11

Take heed of loving me,
At least remember, I forbade it thee
                              —John Donne, *The Prohibition*

Katherine was eager to talk with Knowlton about what she had seen and heard while he entertained Caro. Surely, confronted with such irrefutable evidence, he would acknowledge that he was not completely averse to family life. As if coming to her aid, Somers and Elizabeth had retired early again—ostensibly because Elizabeth was fatigued. The knowing glance the two exchanged before leaving made it clear to Katherine the real purpose of their departure. She gave a longing sigh at the marked sign of their affection and, picking up her sewing again, edged her chair infinitely closer to the candles.

"I begin to wonder if I have unknowingly committed some grievous offense," Knowlton said while he refilled his brandy glass from the decanter on the table. "They flee from me with such ease."

"I rather think they prefer to be alone with each other," Katherine said.

Knowlton frowned and leaned negligently against the mantel. "They remind me of someone newly converted to Methodism, with their superior attitude and smug smiles." He tossed back his head for a long swallow of brandy.

Katherine stuck her needle into the cloth and looked at him with a quizzical expression. "Why do you make mock of their happiness?"

Because I know it will not last," he said curtly.

Katherine picked up her needle again, forcing herself to concentrate on taking neat, even stitches. Knowlton hated the evidence that Somers had a heart. Was it because he feared to discover that he had one of his own? Or was he envious because he had none?

"My father once said that one should never question the strength of another's love," she said quietly. "For the answer was more often a reflection of the questioner's own desires, rather than a true measure of the other's."

"But there is nothing at stake for me in this matter," Knowlton said, his gray eyes darkening.

"Are you so certain?" she asked quietly. "Perhaps it is envy that causes your irritation. You covet what Somers has."

Knowlton glared at her oddly. "Are you implying that I desire Elizabeth?"

Katherine shook her head. "Of course not. I meant what they have together, a settled marriage, with a family."

"What would I do with a collection of brats?" He grimaced. "Noisy, loathsome creatures that only cut up your peace, spend enormous sums of money, and then run off with unsuitable partners."

"Your protestations are weak, Edward." Katherine was determined to draw him out, to force him into an explanation or at least an admission of his antipathies. "I have seen how you deal so patiently with Robbie. And after this morning, Caro worships you. All she could say after I restored her to Elizabeth was 'No-ton, No-ton.' "

"I do have a way with the ladies," he replied with a smug smile.

"Why are there so many?" she persisted. "Is not the admiration of one woman enough for you?"

"But how could I be so cruel as to confine my attentions to only one?" he said in feigned indignation. "When there are so many others who would welcome it as well? It would hardly be the gentlemanly thing to do."

Katherine sighed in exasperation. "There has not yet been one lady who captured your heart?"

"You are looking at an anatomical miracle—I have no such organ. Or so it has been claimed." Knowlton presented a front of calm indifference as he strolled to the table and refilled his glass. Kate's piercing questions made him edgy. He had not wanted an inquisition this evening, he only wished to pass the time amiably with a woman whose company he enjoyed. Kate seemed determined to spoil all that.

"Besides, by bestowing my interests in several directions, I perform a valuable service," he said, turning back toward Kate. "For who else would listen as disappointed wives tell their troubles? And only think of all the young ladies who would be forced into the streets if deprived of my generous subscriptions. I could not be so unfeeling."

"You are quite the philanthropist," she said dryly.

"Let us talk of you for a change," said Knowlton, eager to deflect her attention. "For someone who is so eager to trumpet the joys of the married state, you set a poor example. Alone for six long years . . ."

"There are not many who would offer for an impoverished widow with a son," she said.

"Have there been any?".

"No offers I would deign to accept," she said quickly, focusing her gaze on her sewing so he would not see her heightened color. Oh, she had received offers aplenty. But none of them respectable.

"Of course, the prim-and-proper Kate Mayfield would not listen to an improper offer." Knowlton stepped closer, reaching out his hand to stroke his fingers lightly across her cheek. He had caught a glimpse of the passion that lay beneath her surface calm. Could she really be content to remain alone forever? "Sometimes I wonder about the woman who hides behind that facade. She must long to come out at times. I wager she would enjoy herself very much if she did."

Katherine's skin burned under his touch, his nearness making it difficult to collect her thoughts. He came so close to the truth. And each moment she spent with him made it harder to hide her yearnings. But as he remained closed to her, she must remain the same to him.

"Perhaps not every woman is susceptible to your entreaties," she said quickly, fighting against the distracting feel of his fingers as they caressed her neck.

"I have never yet met a woman who was indifferent to me," he said in a seductive whisper. "Are you so certain you can be?"

No, she thought. She was no more impervious than any other

of his conquests. But she still had the strength to resist him. Barely. "Yes."

"I think otherwise," he said, withdrawing his hand from where it rested on her neck.

"Only a fool would express interest in a man with a self-proclaimed lack of heart."

"Perhaps no one has ever wished me to possess one," he said lightly, taking a step away from her chair.

His comment jolted Katherine. Could it be that no other woman had desired or demanded his love? A wave of sympathy rushed over her. No wonder he protested so vehemently against that which he had never known. Yet it also stirred hope within her—for it was possible that he would one day acknowledge that he could care.

Knowlton gazed at Katherine, wanting to reach out and touch her fiery curls, the reflected firelight streaking them with gold. The brandy, the warm room, and Kate's nearness wreaked havoc with his senses. It had been so very long since that kiss in the garden. His self-imposed restraint grew more difficult with each passing moment in her presence.

Looking at him, Katherine saw the desire in his eyes and she was afraid. Not of him, but of herself. She grew less certain of her willingness to say him no.

"I fear the hour grows late," she said, folding up her sewing and gathering her threads.

"Tarry awhile longer," he urged. "If our discussion bores you, we could play cards."

"Thank you, but I should be to bed. Robbie will waken early."

He nodded, accepting her departure with regret. He saw her to the door, pressed a swift kiss on her hand, and watched her walk up the stairs. Returning to the room, he sank down into the chair she had only recently moved from.

Was it possible that Somers and Elizabeth would continue to live for years in their besotted state, as Kate seemed to think? The possibility sent a cold chill through his heart. For if Somers, the laughing, teasing, amatory expert he had known so long, was snared by love, it meant that at last there was a barrier between them that could never be breached.

For Knowlton held no illusions about his ability to love. He could no more confine himself to one woman for any length of time than he could avoid eating, or breathing. It was variety that had always been the siren call in his life. Endless variety, sampled with an appetite bordering on voracious. He had been fonder of some than others, he was willing to grant, but no more than that.

And, admittedly, he was fond of Kate. She had intrigued him from the first, generating a mixture of lust and need that surprised him with its intensity. After his disturbing *ennui* in London, it was comforting to know he could still desire a woman as deeply as he desired Kate.

Yet there was more than sheer lust guiding his dealings with her. He had never danced attendance on a woman for such a length of time without slaking his physical need. But it was possible, in the middle of a drawing room conversation, or a walk through the garden, to forget for a moment how much he wanted her and to simply enjoy her company.

It was the novelty of the situation, surely, that made it so enjoyable. He had never lived in such a domestic situation with another woman. It was, he thought wryly, something like having a wife. They took breakfast together at times, shared a luncheon now and again, and were always together for dinner. After he and Somers enjoyed a companionable glass, they then joined the ladies for a quiet evening. And Knowlton found it all eminently enjoyable. Particularly when the Wentworths departed and he had Kate to himself.

He grinned in rueful amusement. If he was not careful, Kate would have him half-believing that it was possible to be content with only one partner. *Perhaps* it was possible for Somers. But not for him. Kate might hold him for longer than any other woman had. But "forever" was a word used only by poets and dreamers. It had no basis in reality—for him.

The next afternoon, Katherine noted with surprise the large box resting on her bed. It had not been there when she went down to lunch. Puzzled, she lifted the cover, unwrapped the paper, then drew back her hand in stunned surprise. It was a dress, of a deep, rich plum hue. The bodice and sleeves were ornamented with ribbons and lace of a shimmering silver. Her hand trembling, Katherine drew the gown from its wrappings. With its high waist and deeply flounced hem, it was of the first stare of fashion and the most exquisitely beautiful dress she had ever seen. She had looked at enough of Elizabeth's fashion books over the last weeks to recognize that.

Tears of humiliation stung her eyes. Elizabeth knew she did not have a proper dinner dress and had purchased this for her. It was a generous gesture, but hateful just the same. Katherine knew she should be filled with gratitude, but her pride would not allow her. How hateful it was to be poor.

"Katherine, have you seen . . . ? Oh, what a beautiful creation!" Elizabeth stepped through the door. "You decided on a new dess after all! I like it so much better than the gray silk."

Katherine turned toward her, a bemused expression on her face. "It is not from you?" she asked in confusion. "It was here on my bed."

"Had it been mine, I never would have given it away," sighed Elizabeth, running her hand over the silky fabric. "Did you think that I . . . ?"

Katherine nodded.

Elizbeth smiled. "I had thought to do such a thing, but I feared you would say no if I asked. Obviously the giver did not bother to ascertain your desires."

Katherine instantly knew from whom the dress had come. "I will be back," she said, dashing from the room.

Knowlton was in the library, his head bent over a pile of papers. His face lit with a warm smile as Katherine entered.

"Did you order that dress?" she demanded angrily.

Knowlton leaned back in his chair, his arms crossed over his chest. "We are direct and to the point, are we not? No time spent in idle chatchat or greetings for Kate Mayfield. We must immediately reach the heart of the matter." The smile never left his face as he capped the inkwell and folded his hands upon the desk. "Now, my dear, what dress is it that you refer to?"

For a minute Kate's assurance faltered. Yet if not he, then who? "There was a dress upstairs, on my bed. A very elegant, fashionable, and expensive dress."

"Oh, that one. You came in here with such a flurry, I was afraid I might have switched it with the one that arrived for the housekeeper. That certainly would have been an error."

Katherine trembled with her anger. "How can you possibly think I could accept such a gift from you?"

"Now, Katherine, you are not going to get on your high ropes and throw out all those loathsome remarks filled with pride and injured vanity and such things?" Knowlton's smile took on a mocking cast. "I am having a dinner party. You are an invited guest without a suitable garment to wear. Therefore, I have provided you with one. I found it to be a rather simple solution."

"It is highly improper." Katherine glared at Knowlton. "You cannot buy clothing for me as if I were your . . . your . . ."

"Mistress? *Chère amie*?" His smile widened. "I assure you, I am quite aware that you hold no such position in my life." He uttered a long, regretful sigh. "Since you do not, what does it matter?"

"What will the other guests think?"

"I highly doubt, unless you wear a neatly lettered placard stating, 'This dress purchased by Lord Knowlton,' that anyone will have the foggiest notion that the dress did not come from your own closet."

"Everyone knows I could not afford such an elegant gown." Humiliation began to war with her anger.

"Then let on that you borrowed it from Lady Wentworth. I understand it is not unheard-of for ladies to share their clothes."

"But I will know!"

"And it bothers you greatly, doesn't it?" Knowlton tilted his head to one side and examined her closely. "Kate, Kate, Kate. When are you going to learn how to be a gracious recipient? Were you never taught that it is always polite to say thank you for a gift, even if the present you receive is not one that you particularly want? Lord knows, I have been accused of all manner of rudeness, but I am still able to remember that particular rule."

She wrung her hands in frustration. "It is not that I object to the gift, Edward, but what it represents."

"And what does it represent?" he asked, his voice light and teasing.

"That . . . that there is more than friendship between us."

"Is there?" He arched a querying brow.

"We are merely *friends*," she insisted hastily. "Friends do not exchange such intimate gifts."

Knowlton laughed. "I would hardly call a dress 'intimate.' Now, had I given you a chemise, or stockings, or garters, you might have cause for complaint."

He sat silently for a moment, as if appraising her thoughts. "I know! It is the color to which you are averse. I had thought to consult with you on the subject, but I knew we would have a tiresome argument along these lines, so I thought to trust my own judgment. I *knew* I should have ordered the green."

"You simply do not care a whit about my feelings on this matter, do you?" She made no attempt to hide the anger in her voice.

"No, I do not." Knowlton grew exasperated with her obstinate refusal to accept his gift. "You are being stubborn to the point of stupidity. You were given a gift—take it graciously and leave off with this argument." He stood and took a menacing step forward. "I assure you, Kate Mayfield, that if you do not wear that dress to dinner tomorrow, I will announce that fact in front of the entire company and bring down worse embarrassment than you could ever imagine upon your head. You can toss the thing in the rag bag the next day, for all I care, but you will wear that damned dress to dinner!"

Katherine scowled angrily. Could he not see that his persistence only caused her further humiliation? "How can you continue to offer help to me when you know I do not wish it? First Robbie's pony, then your invitation to remain here, and now this."

"I interfere because I want to," he said, his gray eyes softening. "I know this will be difficult to believe, but I have a great weakness for ladies in distress. They bring out whatever vestiges of respectability are still left within me. It would be immodest of me to recount some of the good works I have performed, but I assure you, there are several ladies in the kingdom who have me to thank for rescued lovers, restored incomes, and salvaged brothers.''

"So now I am your current charity project? That is almost a worse insult.''

"I assure you, Kate, I am not acting out of charity." His eyes darkened to a smoky gray. "If I told you that I desire you more than I have ever desired any other woman, and long to see that rich fabric draped over your soft curves so that I may further admire them, would you then consent to wear it?''

Katherine clenched her fists. "You are impossible!''

"I agree," he said, his eyes twinkling at her discomfort. "But since you are so opposed to 'charity,' I thought lust might make a more appealing motive.''

The ridiculousness of the whole situation suddenly struck her. He was impossible. Impossible and irresistible. She laughed. "You could talk an angel into marrying the devil if you set your mind to it.''

"What a mocking thought! I would never do such thing.'' Knowlton's eyes danced with merriment. "Now, I might talk her into becoming his mistress . . .''

Katherine shook her head and turned toward the door.

"I will think on it,'' she said, and hastily quit the room. Not ready for the confining walls of the house, she sought out her cloak, and then stepped out into the gardens again. Here she would be free to think.

Knowlton's candid acknowledgment of his desire for her grew more and more disturbing. And she had only herself to blame. Their talks had outstepped the bounds of propriety long ago, yet she had never stopped him. Each time they talked, he grew more and more bold, as if trying to see just how far he could take matters before she objected. And she truly could not imagine what he could say that would accomplish that. It was flattering to know that he wanted her. If only she did not want him equally as much. She could deal with his desire. Her own wants were the problem.

It was foolish beyond extremes. She would never be more than a casual dalliance to him, she knew that. It was not what she wanted from life. However rash the manner of her marriage to Robert had been, she did not regret it, or the closeness that came to a couple only through the bond of matrimony. She would never know that with Knowlton.

But she had no doubts that he would be a skillful and exciting lover. Once her maidenly hesitation and ignorance had been overcome, she had quite enjoyed that aspect of married life. Those feelings had lain dormant since Robert's death, but Knowlton had awakened them until they burned hotter than ever. Katherine reddened to find her thoughts straying in such a wanton direction, but she could not help herself. After all, it was what Knowlton wanted of her. He knew the allure of the prize he offered.

It was frighteningly tempting. All she had to give up was her conscience. And her dream of finding love again. But it was not the initial step that threw fear into her heart, it was the eventual parting that chilled her. For she knew that if she allowed herself to succumb to Knowlton, she was lost. Now, knowing only part of the man, she could almost convince herself that her feelings for him were formed from gratitude and friendship and nothing more. It was merely his bold, suggestive remarks that made her skin grow warm and her face grow heated whenever they were together. It was only her physical desire, not anything more lasting. She had to fight it. She could not love a man who offered her so little.

Love? The idea was patently absurd. She was certainly not hen-witted enough to fall in love with a man who neither wanted nor would return such affection. Yet she had. How could she feel so strongly about the worst possible sort of man? She knew full well what he was: a womanizer, a connoisseur of the fair sex, who looked at women as bedmates. One who offered her a temporary future at best, to be followed by a lifetime of longing and regret. It was madness.

As Katherine walked past the fading roses, she could almost laugh at her folly. Here she was, at eight-and-twenty, behaving as rashly as she had at seventeen, when she had fallen top-over-tails for the dashing Robert Mayfield, ignoring the disapproval of his family and hers. At least then she had the excuse of youth to explain her actions. She had no such convenient explanation for her present predicament. It was as if her very determination to resist Knowlton had led her in the opposite direction. And now she was foolishly, futilely in love with a man who would not be flattered by that declaration.

How she wished she could reach his heart. For despite his protestations, she knew he had one. She saw it in his patience with Robbie and in that teasing time he had spent with little Caro. And she thought, too, that he must feel some affection for her. Despite her earlier anger, the gift of the dress had been a generous gesture. It would make her feel more at ease in the glittering company, would make her look as if she belonged to their society. And why would he do such a thing if he did not have a care for her?

As she thought further, her smile deepened. He wanted to see her dressed in finery, looking like a lady of the *ton*. It was churlish of her to refuse to wear such an honorably intentioned gift. It would please him to see her in the dress, and she was suddenly deeply eager to please him.

Katherine briefly closed her eyes, dizzy with excitement and anticipation. If only she could get him to admit he cared. Once past that monumental wall, anything was possible. Even capturing the heart of a self-proclaimed heartless man.

12

One Kiss, dear Maid! I said and sigh'd—
Your scorn the little boon denied.
Ah why refuse the blameless bliss?
Can Danger lurk within a kiss?

—Coleridge, *The Kiss*

Katherine's stomach churned with nervous anticipation as she put the finishing touches on her toilette. She could scarce believe the elegant lady reflected in the pier glass was herself. It was not merely the fashionable dress; everything about the woman in the mirror looked unfamiliar: the hair that Elizabeth's maid had coaxed into an elegant concoction of braids, curls, and ringlets, the cheeks, with their faint application of color, or the eyelashes she had allowed Elizabeth to darken. Even the simple jewelry—a filigree silver necklace and ear bobs, brought from Spain by Robert—looked dazzling on this stranger.

Katherine deliberated about waiting for Elizabeth and her husband before she went downstairs, but then shrugged off her cowardice. It was best to get the matter over with quickly. She resolved to enjoy this last night at Warrenton and not allow nervousness to rule her actions. After six weeks in Knowlton's company, it would be foolish to develop apprehensions at this late date. She had elected to wear his dress, and therefore he was entitled to see it. Gathering up her gloves and the shawl lent to her by Lady Wentworth, Katherine proceeded down the stairs to the drawing room.

Knowlton was already there, waiting. He stood with his back to the door, staring into the flickering flames of the fire. Katherine could not help but admire the picture he presented: his pantaloons set off his nicely formed legs; the tight-fitting coat revealed his narrow waist and muscled shoulders. Unbidden, in her mind rose the image of Knowlton at harvest, naked to the waist, with the mingled droplets of water and sweat sparkling on his chest. She took a deep breath to still her pounding heart.

Sensing her presence, Knowlton turned, but the greeting he had been prepared to utter stuck in his throat.

She was, by far, one of the most beautiful women he had known. He had recognized that at their first meeting, despite her severe coiffure, cap, and dowdy gown. Dressed now as a lady of the *ton*, she truly took his breath away.

It was not entirely the dress—although that daring neckline, skimming low over the swell of her creamy breasts, was enough to set his blood pumping. Her decision to wear it pleased him. He was not even certain he liked her hair fashioned in such an upswept style. It was something more indefinable that made her look different. It came out in her carriage, her bearing. Katherine walked and stood as if she had finally realized just how alluring she was, and found security instead of fear in that knowledge.

He hastened to her side.

"You look exquisitely lovely tonight, Mrs. Mayfield." His gray eyes raked her with frank admiration.

"Thank you, my lord," she replied with a faint smile. "You look quite handsome yourself."

"All for you," he whispered, raising her gloved hand to his lips.

God, how he wanted her. She was quickly driving him mad with need and desire. Not for the first time he damned his noble promise not to take full advantage of her presence under his roof. He had not known then what a sweet temptress she would be. Her skittishness, her modest blushes, only served to inflame his desire. The dress he had forced upon her had been pure folly, for it set off her curves in maddening detail. His hands and lips ached to cover those breasts . . .

He felt the slight tremor in her hand and realized just how intently he stared at her. Lifting his eyes to her face, he felt a thrill of satisfaction as she met his gaze without flinching. His mouth widened into a broad, sensual smile.

"Your gown fits . . . nicely." His smile grew broader as she modestly looked away. "One would think—"

"Thank goodness, we are not late." Somers' voice caused Knowlton and Katherine to step back from one another with a start. "Elizabeth insisted on tying my cravat, and I fear she is sadly out of practice."

His wife shot him a knowing smile.

"The other guests should be arriving momentarily," Knowlton said, half-relieved that the Wentworths had arrived when they had. He was afraid he might have sadly crumpled Katherine's gown if they had been left alone much longer. "A glass of wine?"

Elizabeth drew Katherine aside while the men sauntered to the side table. "You look marvelous."

"Thank you," Katherine replied.

"Nervous?"

Katherine nodded. "A little. I feel as if I am in the middle of a masquerade; I barely recognized the woman in the mirror. I am grateful it is only the neighbors here tonight. I do not think I could face strangers in this new guise."

Elizabeth gave her a reassuring squeeze of the hand as they turned to greet the newly announced visitors.

Knowlton had kept the party small—the vicar and his wife, Squire Moreton, his wife and two daughters, and Sir Richard and Lady Court. It was a "duty" dinner, designed to maintain amiable relationships in the neighborhood. Not that Knowlton ever looked down upon or disdained the other residents of the county. If they were not frequent quests at Warrenton, it was more because the usual entertainments there were unsuitable for family attendance. Tonight he made every effort to demonstrate just how respectable the present situation was.

The vicar and his wife were the first to arrive, and immediately greeted Katherine.

"And how is young Robbie doing?" the vicar asked.

"Quite well," replied Katherine. "Bored beyond belief. But the doctor says the splints may come off tomorrow and we shall be able to return home." She directed a smile at Knowlton. "It has been most gracious of Lord Knowlton to extend his hospitality to us for so long."

Katherine turned back to the vicar. "Robbie has done an admirable job of keeping up on his studies. I shall have to wait for the doctor's advice, of course, but I think he will be able to resume his work with you soon.''

"It will be good to see the lad again," Mr. Ashe replied. "Although I expect he may prove more rambunctious than usual this fall after such a long period of forced inactivity.'' They all laughed.

The other guests soon arrived in a flurry of greetings.

"It is a surprise to see you here, Mrs. Mayfield.'' The voice of the squire's wife held a slightly condemning tone. "I would have thought your son's leg healed by now.''

"I anticipate the doctor will say we can return home when he visits tomorrow,'' Katherine said politely, choking back her irritation.

"There is nothing quite like being in your own home,'' Mrs. Ashe sympathized. "And you must call on me, my dear, if you need any assistance. I know how exhausting Robbie can be.''

"That is such a lovely dress,'' the squire's wife commented, drawing attention back to Katherine. "Surely it is not sewn by Mrs. Gorton's hands? Did you make it yourself? I hear you do such exquisite work.''

Katherine stiffened, knowing that she had stitched the lace on the very gown Mrs. Moreton wore, and that lady was probably aware of it as well. "Lady Wentworth was gracious enough to share her wardrobe,'' she lied smoothly.

"Interesting,'' murmured the lady, casting a sly glance at Elizabeth.

Katherine was relieved when Hutchins entered and announced dinner.

Knowlton chose to seat Katherine partway down the table rather than next to him. To have seated her in the place of honor would only have raised troublesome questions about her status in the house. He knew how grindingly respectable the situation was, but the Wentworths were an unknown entity in this part of the county. Unfortunately, his neighbors were all too familiar with the typical cut of guests he entertained. He must do all in his power to ensure no harm would come to Katherine's name.

The slight distance had the added advantage of making it easier to watch Katherine unobserved. He looked with interest while she chatted amiably with the vicar while waiting to be served, then alternated her attention between him and the squire's younger daughter during the soup course.

"Mrs. Mayfield," the squire's wife began as the soup was removed, "I understand your late husband served during the Peninsular campaign?"

"That is correct," Katherine replied with a trace of wariness.

"My own eldest was there also, as you know, although fortunately he returned to us. What regiment did your husband serve in?"

The next course, of stuffed pheasant, was set before her and Katherine took advantage of the slight pause to calm her thoughts. "He was in the 18th Hussars."

"The Hussars, you say?" Squire Moreton looked at her curiously. "That's a mighty difficult regiment to join."

Katherine did not miss the implication. The Hussars were notoriously selective. Why had she not claimed a less-exalted regiment?

"Regimental commissions are such a strange thing," Knowlton interjected, noting Katherine's discomfort. "One tries for ages to buy one without success, then one day there is suddenly an opening and at a bargain besides." He smiled warmly at her. "I am certain Captain Mayfield was pleased with his luck."

"Yes, he was," Katherine said, grateful for Knowlton's rescue. It had been purely family influence that eased Robert into the Hussars, but she did not want to admit that. It would lead to too many other questions.

"I understand your son has received a new posting?" Knowlton turned the conversation and the attention back to Mrs. Moreton, who he knew could rattle on for hours about her son. But his mind pondered Katherine's surprising revelation. The mysterious Captain Mayfield had purchased a commission in the Eighteenth Hussars. A rather intriguing story, one that implied a certain family background. Someday he must question her more thoroughly about it.

Katherine still appeared at ease, Knowlton noted with relief when he dared to glance her direction again. He had not wished this party to make her uncomfortable, and for a moment he feared it would have that result. The squire's wife was a gossipy worm.

But as he watched, he observed Katherine talk and smile and look as unconcerned as if this type of entertainment were a daily occurrence in her life. She looked very much as if she belonged at the table. With the possible exception of Elizabeth, Katherine outshone every lady there in grace and manners, let alone beauty. In that, she was unparalleled. The golden glow from the candles gave her hair a fiery luminescence that constantly drew his eye. How he wished she had worn her hair down so that it floated in soft waves about her shoulders. He ached to bury his hands in its silky softness.

Knowlton clenched his fingers to control his burning desire. How was he going to allow her to leave tomorrow? He had grown accustomed to her presence, the knowledge that he could seek out her company at any time during the day, that they would dine together in the evening, and talk long into the night. And despite the torture it inflicted on his body, he loved to sit and savor the sight of her.

"May we count on your support, my lord?"

The vicar's voice broke into Knowlton's distracted thoughts. "Certainly," he mumbled. Seeing Katherine's amused smile, he wondered what he had committed himself to. Repairing the church organ? The Christmas Fund? He dared not ask.

"Perhaps Mrs. Mayfield would be willing to assist with the new altar cloths," Mrs. Moreton suggested.

"I am not certain I shall have the time," Katherine protested.

"Oh, but you do such beautiful work," the squire's wife said with a sly smile.

Katherine fought down her anger at Mrs. Moreton's deliberate taunting. Remembering the long hours spent in her mother's parlor, sewing every manner of altar cloth imaginable, Katherine never wished to see one again. She no longer had the luxury of sewing for free. The squire's wife knew perfectly well that she needed to devote her time to the paid sewing given her by the seamstress.

"Perhaps your lovely daughter would be willing to lend her talent," Knowlton said, smiling in an avuncular manner at the young lady seated at his right. He did not know if the chit could even thread a needle, but it grew apparent that Mrs. Moreton was determined to discomfort Katherine this evening. He offered up a prayer of relief when the next course arrived.

"We sponsor a school in our district for the local girls," Elizabeth offered. "Sewing is one of the skills they are taught. Perhaps you could establish a similar program here, and thus have many willing hands for your cloths."

"Capital idea," said Knowlton, looking pointedly at the vicar. "Perhaps we could discuss such a thing next week?"

"Will your son be going to school soon, now that his leg is better?" Mrs. Moreton pressed on with her inquisition, disregarding the efforts of the others to turn the conversation. "Our youngest is presently at Eton."

"Robbie is doing quite well with Mr. Ashe, at present," Katherine replied.

"It is never too early to plan ahead for these things," Mrs. Moreton continued. "Particularly if Robbie is to attend on a scholarship."

Knowlton winced at the tactless reference to Katherine's lack of funds.

"Not all schools are as expensive as Eton," Katherine replied coolly. "And based on my husband's experiences, Eton is the last place I would choose to send Robbie."

"Quite right," Knowlton interrupted, cutting off Mrs. Moreton before she could open her mouth. "I detested Eton myself."

"Hartford sent his son to an interesting school," Elizabeth interjected, and launched into a lengthy description of that place.

Knowlton inclined his head to listen absentmindedly to Elizabeth and the squire's wife, but his attention remained on Kate. She had revealed another clue about her late husband—he had attended Eton. That knowledge only added to the mystery surrounding her current circumstances. Circumstances he hoped to change soon.

Once or twice her eyes strayed to his, and he reveled in the intimacy of their shared look. He watched the gentle rise and fall of her chest, noticing her quickened breathing when she became aware of his gaze. Her cheeks colored with that maddeningly enticing rosy glow when their eyes met again.

Damn propriety. He was going to have to find a way of furthering their relationship in such a way that no attention was drawn to them. But he was damned if he was going to let much more time pass before he pursued her in earnest. He had promised to remain a gentleman while she was under his roof, but tomorrow she repaired to her own house. The constraints on his behavior would be gone and he intended to make every use of the opportunity. He would waste no more time before he learned if she was as passionate in bed as her hair would indicate. Modest blushes or no, he had no doubts that she would be.

Knowlton was relieved that he had included a chilled dessert on the menu. He needed the cool ice to dampen the fire in his body. That brief interlude in Nottingham seemed centuries ago. He belatedly jumped to his feet when he realized the ladies were taking their leave.

He endured the remainder of the evening with growing impatience. Knowlton called the private gathering of the men to a close in an indecently short interval, and did nothing to promote a lengthy evening entertainment. Lady Wentworth was prevailed upon to play the pianoforte, which she did with consummate skill, but Knowlton only wished that everyone would go home so he could have Kate to himself for a time.

She thwarted him in that endeavor, for when the vicar and his wife took their leave, she pleaded the need to check on her son and fled the drawing room before Knowlton could protest. The other guests rapidly departed as well, Somers and Elizabeth retreated to their rooms, and he was left quite alone in front of the dying fire with an unwanted glass of brandy in his hands. Whatever hopes he had held for the evening, he had not envisioned a scenario like this. He might as well seek his bed; perhaps he could find a moment alone with Kate on the morrow.

As he reluctantly passed down the corridor, he noticed that the door to Robbie's room was slightly ajar, and Knowlton could not resist the temptation to peek inside. Kate was probably safely in her own bed by now. But as he quietly pushed open the door, he saw she had not yet retired. He stood silently in the shadows, watching her as she stood in front of the window. With the curtains thrown open, the blue-white light of the moon cast her corner of the room into almost daylike brightness. She was looking out onto the moon-drenched grounds of the estate, her arms loosely clasped about her. She still wore her dinner gown, although she had taken down her hair and its soft curls fell in flaming clouds about her shoulders. She looked so fragile and delicate. He clenched his fingers. If he retreated quietly, she would never know he had come . . .

He silently crossed the carpeted room.

"Robbie has dropped off at last, I see," he whispered softly as he came up behind her.

Startled by his presence, Katherine turned to face him.

"It was a long battle," she confessed, then returned her gaze to the moonlit scene outside. Her skin prickled in the knowledge of his nearness.

He rested his hands lightly on her shoulders. "I hope you enjoyed tonight."

She smiled warmly at the night. "I am glad you persuaded me to attend. I did enjoy myself."

"Your presence certainly made the evening more enjoyable for me," he whispered softly, brushing back her hair to expose one creamy white shoulder. "I scarcely noted what I ate. It was too difficult to tear my eyes away from your beauty."

She laughed nervously. "Of a certainty, my lord."

"Set off to great advantage by the lovely dress you are wearing," he said, stroking his fingers across the bare skin of her shoulder, then tangling them in her fiery curls." I have been longing to bury my hands in your flames all evening."

"Edward, I—"

"Shh," he said quickly, turning her so she faced him. They stared at one another for an eternity of silence; then with a slow, seductive smile he cupped her chin in his hand and covered her lips with his before she could protest further. Feeling her initial hesitation, he kept his kisses light, feathering them across her lips until he felt her relax. He drew away, looking into her face for her acquiescence before he went further. Her blue eyes were wide with surprise, yet he saw a flicker of desire there that encouraged him.

Dropping his hands to her waist, he gently pulled her against him, bringing their mouths together once more. This time, she responded, and his kisses grew more demanding, more posses-sive. His senses reeled in a way he had not thought possible from a few mere kisses. He softly flicked his tongue over her lips, teasing, pleading until they parted beneath his and he could probe the warm moistness of her mouth.

Katherine almost jumped at that all-too-obvious invasion of her body, yet she did not resist Knowlton's bold advances. She would regret her weakness later, but for now she did not want to think coherently, only wanted to give herself up to the sensations coursing through her veins. Deliberately ignoring all the warning voices in her head, she raised her arms and curled her fingers in the hair at his nape.

Cold shivers ran up Knowlton's spine at her touch. She was a redheaded witch, casting a spell of sensual pleasure over him that he was powerless to resist. He buried his fingers in her hair, drawing her even closer. His other hand, pressed in the small of her back, held her pinioned in an embrace that scorched along the length of their touching bodies.

Katherine trembled as she willingly pressed her body against his. She leaned her head back, closing her eyes against the warm sensations of his lips, her breath catching as he trailed kisses down her neck, pausing to nibble her ear before he once again claimed her mouth. She burned with fire; she was filled with an all-consuming need and want that overcame all rational consciousness.

Knowlton grew bolder, kissing her with growing urgency, his tongue twining with hers as his hands roamed over her body.

"Kate, Kate," he whispered as his hand sought the softness of her breast. Through the thin silk of her gown he felt the nipple go taut beneath his seeking fingers, matching the growing tightness in his groin. Dear God, it had been so long . . . She was like a drug, sapping his mind, his thoughts. He was burning with a fire that only she could quench.

A low moan issued from the shadowed corner of the room. Instantly, Katherine wrenched herself from Knowlton's arms and quickly crossed to her son's bed.

Knowlton berated his stupidity for choosing such a poor location for his lovemaking. But he had not intended such a thing when he had paused at the slightly open door—or had he?

"He is asleep." Her whisper broke into his thoughts.

Knowlton hesitated. The spell had been weakened, but not broken. Then slowly he brought her hand to his lips, kissing first her curled fingers, then pressing his mouth to her palm.

"I apologize for my inopportune choice of place," he said quickly, willing his rapid breathing to slow. Kate stood there silently; in the shadowy light it was difficult to read the expression on her face. He exhaled slowly. "These rooms connect with mine, you will recall. We could be more private there."

She knew what he asked, what he wanted. And knew that she half-wanted it as well. But she still held on to the last vestiges of her resolve. If only she could hear the words she wanted from his lips. "It is late," she demurred.

He accepted his dismissal with grace. "Then I shall bid you good night, my fair Kate." Knowlton pressed another kiss on her fingers, exiting silently into the corridor.

Katherine stood in the middle of the room, unmoving, staring at the door. She had nearly lost all her control this time. If Robbie had not stirred . . . She had no doubt that she would have found herself in the earl's bed. And she truly was not certain which outcome to the evening disturbed her more.

With only the shadowy moonlight lighting his bedchamber, Knowlton stripped off his neckcloth and tossed it onto the dresser. Every nerve in his body still flamed with the memory of Kate's shape pressed close to his. She had been so close to capitulation. Only his incredibly stupid move of attempting a seduction within feet of Robbie's bed had cost him his prize. And tomorrow Kate would be gone from his roof.

Unbuttoning his shirt, Knowlton considered. He grew tired of this clever game they played; he advanced, she parried, but they progressed toward the goal nevertheless. After tonight, there was no point in disguising his aim. She knew exactly what he wanted of her. And, he felt confident, she wanted the same of him. Kate had been just as passionate as her red hair indicated. He smiled quickly. Once again, his judgment had not failed him. Kate Mayfield was as delectable a morsel as he had desired in an age, and would be every bit as delicious as he hoped. His anticipation grew as he divested himself of the rest of his clothing and crawled beneath the covers of his solitary bed. Tomorrow he would finalize matters.

13

Come live with me and be my love,
And we will some new pleasures prove
                              —John Donne, *The Bait*

Knowlton awoke the next morning and stretched lazily beneath the covers, a smug smile of satisfaction crossing his face at the memory of Kate's heated embrace. He had to have her, had to possess her.

He had never before taken a mistress without first sampling her talents, but he held no fears that Kate would be a disappointment. He had seen and heard and felt enough last night to have no worries in that area. Whatever skills she lacked could be easily taught, and the pleasure would be in the teaching. His imagination stirred at the thought.

He experienced a momentary doubt over Kate's willingness to become his mistress, but quickly set it aside. With her straitened circumstances, it should be easy to work out a satisfactory arrangement. He knew how her poverty grated upon her. His offer would put an end to all that. And if gowns and jewels and money were not enough, there was always Robbie's future to consider. Knowlton felt a twinge of apprehension at using the boy again to further his own interests, but quickly ignored it. It would benefit everyone if he paid for Robbie's schooling. And if it meant that the lad would be away for a good part of the year, giving Knowlton uninterrupted access to Kate, all the better.

With a low chuckle, Knowlton threw back the covers and padded across the room to the bell rope. He must plan his strategy carefully. He was determined to win the prize at last.

Katherine looked up in trepidation when Knowlton entered the room. She was afraid to face him this morning, uncertain how she should react after her wanton behavior the night before. He would never believe her protestations now.

She owned she had been more than a trifle surprised at her reactions to his lovemaking. Granted, Knowlton was a skilled practioner of the art, and it was to be expected that he would know all manner of tricks to get a lady to respond. But she had responded with all the pent-up yearnings of the last six years. And now she must face the ramifications of her recklessness.

Knowlton was pleased to find Katherine at Robbie's bedside when he entered the room. "Good morning, Mrs. Mayfield. Robbie."

Katherine did not turn her head. "Good morning, my lord."

Knowlton sat down next to Robbie on the bed. "Ready to do battle with grammar again this morning?"

Robbie made a disgusted face.

Knowlton laughed. "Cheer up. I promise I will come up to play you a game of chess later, before the doctor comes."

Robbie turned an apprehensive gaze toward Knowlton. "Will we . . . will we be able to play chess again after I go home?"

"Certainly," Knowlton reassured him. "That is, if your mama does not object."

Katherine shook her head, knowing future contact with the earl would only further her folly. "You have done more than enough for us, Lord Knowlton," she protested weakly.

"But not nearly as much as I wish," he said in a low voice.

Katherine turned away. It took only a look from him to set her pulses racing. Last night had been madness. How could she have allowed herself to do such a thing?

Knowlton rose, pleased at her discomfort. It meant she was as affected by his presence as he was by hers. For a brief moment, seeing her averted gaze, he feared the morning would be full of recriminations. But Katherine Mayfield did not look like a woman filled with anger. On the contrary, she looked like a woman who very much needed to be kissed, again and again. He could not wait for the next opportunity.

However, it was as if events conspired against him. Whenever he thought to draw Kate away and discuss his plans for her, some other matter always intervened. He seethed with frustration. Once the doctor gave permission for Robbie to go home, Kate would be gone before Knowlton had the opportunity to talk with her.

When he finally freed himself from the latest minor crisis, he raced to Robbie's room, only to discover Kate was elsewhere. He searched the drawing room and library before realizing she was probably in her favorite haunt—the garden. He quickly slipped outdoors. Relief flooded his face when he spotted her, and he hastened to her side.

"I had hoped to find you here."

Katherine turned away slowly from her contemplation of the last brave roses scattering their color across the landscape. She could not keep the soft smile from her lips. "And why is that, my lord?"

Taking her hand and placing it upon his arm, Knowlton led her along the graveled path. He prayed she would accept his offer. She would be a fool not to. Even he acknowledged that the terms he proposed were more than generous. He doubted there was another lady in the kingdom who had been offered as much. Yet he knew that the idea of becoming his mistress might be difficult for her to accept. She had been a properly married lady once, and throwing off the mantle of respectability, no matter how carefully he disguised their relationship to others, would give her some pause. He wished there had been more time to entice her with the pleasures of the flesh. Had they not been interrupted in such an untimely manner last night, he was certain the evening would have ended in his bed.

But it had not, and now it was up to him to convince her that was where she belonged.

Katherine walked nervously by his side, but did not draw away from him. They had but a few short hours more together. She wanted only to revel in his presence this one last time. She wanted to store away all the memories of him that she could, to warm herself with on those long, lonely winter nights.

"My bed was such a cold and solitary place last night," Knowlton said at last, a wistful smile creasing his face. "I kept thinking how much more pleasurable it would be with a lovely lady to keep me warm."

Kate closed her eyes for a brief moment. He was not going to let her forget last night, after all.

Knowlton stopped abruptly and turned toward her. Cupping her face in his hands, he brushed her lips briefly with his, then kissed her with a searing intensity that brought back all the passion of the previous night. Katherine swayed against him, helpless to stem the sensations rising within her. To deny him now would take more strength than she would ever have.

"I know what I want, Kate," he said when he released her, his breathing erratic. "And last night proved beyond a doubt that I want you very badly."

He flashed her that wickedly seductive smile that sent a tingle of anticipation through her body. Her heart leapt at his words. He wanted her. He *cared* for her.

Knowlton took her hands in his, his gaze caressing her face. "I should like to take you under my protection. Know that I do not make the offer with any intention of causing you insult, Katherine, for I mean it as the highest compliment. I realize there are some . . . uh . . . different circumstances here than I usually deal with. I am quite willing to make arrangements for Robbie as well. For you, there will be a house in town, or a country cottage, if that is what you prefer. And I shall pay for Robbie's schooling."

Kate heard the words, but they registered only feebly on her brain once she caught his meaning. Something inside her crumbled like a discarded piece of paper. He wanted her for his mistress. He was willing to pay her to come to his bed.

Of course it had been foolish of her to ever think she could have more from him. She had manufactured that expectation out of her own longings. But like the reckless girl who had once raced off to Gretna Green, she had clung to her hopes that somehow she could reach into his inner self and touch him as no woman ever had before. Had she not been so close to tears, she would have laughed at her folly.

"The idea does not offend you?" Knowlton asked with a tinge of apprehension.

"Offend me?" she asked, her voice sounding as numb to her ears as she felt inside. "How could I possibly take offense? You have offered to feed me, clothe me, house me, and send my son to school. And you ask so *very little* in return."

"True," he cheerfully admitted, oblivious of the sarcasm in

her voice. "But I learned long ago that when one wishes the finest quality, one must be willing to pay for it."

"Like fine horseflesh or impeccably tailored clothes?" Katherine struggled to keep herself from trembling, the anger in her voice rising with every breath. "How does it make you feel, my Lord Knowlton, to know that you cannot have a woman without paying for her first? Do you ever calculate the cost of each touch? How much do you spend for a kiss?"

She reached out and grabbed his hand, drawing it to her breast. "Is that worth a shilling? Or a new pair of stockings?"

Knowlton jerked his hand back and stared at her in surprise, his gray eyes widening in bemusement at her vehement reaction. "Stop it, Kate."

"I would be very wary of anyone I had bought," she continued in the same biting tone. "Does the price include my emotions, my lord? Or my loyalty? You would never know when a more lucrative offer might tempt me away. Or whether my pleasure was real or feigned—or do you not care about that?"

"I had only thought to ease your circumstances, not insult you," he said with a touch of irritation. "You are quite free to refuse."

"And refuse you I shall," she cried, feeling the tears beginning to well in her eyes. She struggled against them. "I would rather starve and send Robbie to school as a scholar than whore myself to you. At least I would have my pride intact." She took a few steps toward the house, then turned to him again.

"I pity you more than anything," she said, her voice cloaked in sadness. "For you are never going to know anything beyond the mere exchange of money for sex. There is so much more to life." She turned again and sped toward the house before her tears fell.

Knowlton stared after her, anger and confusion dancing through his brain. He had sadly misjudged her after all. Kate was as hopelessly respectable as he had first thought her. Foolish woman. She would rue her refusal one day, when the shadows of the poorhouse loomed darkly over her. Pride was a poor substitute for food and shelter. With a disgusted scowl, he kicked up a spray of gravel, listening to the clattering stones crack against the others on the ground. There was an abundance of other women who would jump at the chance for such an opportunity.

Katherine fled to the sanctuary of the library, knowing she could be alone there. Sinking down into one of the comfortable leather chairs, she gave full vent to her tears of anger and sadness.

Mistress. An elevated title for a woman who sold her favors as easily as a common street whore. Fine clothes, fancy houses, and flashy jewels could not hide the basic transaction. Money for sex. A simple trade. But one she could not accept.

Had she cared for him less, his offer would have provided less insult. She still would have been shocked and angry, to think that he thought he could buy her in such a way. And to dangle the dream of school for Robbie had been cruelly taunting. Yet it was the simple fact that he wanted their relationship to be on the level of a tradesman's exchange that caused the deep hurt inside her. She was, after all was said and done, nothing more than a temporary plaything for him.

It had been pure folly to delude herself with the hope that he would come to care for her. She had allowed her love to blind her to his true nature. How arrogant an assumption on her part, that *she* would be the one woman to engender tender feelings in him. He had always claimed he had no heart, and for once, she saw it was true. At this moment, she wished she did not either. For then it would not hurt so very badly.

A noise in the hall alerted her to the doctor's arrival. Katherine glanced quickly into the mirror to make certain her face no longer showed the ravages of her earlier tears. Satisfied that no one could see how deeply she bled inside, she exited the library and hastened to her son's room.

Katherine watched eagerly while the doctor removed Robbie's splint, examined the leg, and pronounced himself satisfied with its healing. He cautioned against overactivity, warned the lad to make use of a crutch or cane while he strenghtened the weak muscles, and said Robbie would be fit as ever within a month.

Even though she had expected the news, Katherine uttered a deep sigh of relief when the doctor said Robbie could go home.

She knew she could not have remained for another night under Knowlton's roof. She only wanted to get as far away from him as possible.

Katherine was also grateful that the Wentworths would be departing for their home today as well. She knew she would not be able to hide her damaged heart from Elizabeth, who was uncannily perceptive about such matters. Making her good-byes to the Wentworths, Katherine promised to consider accepting Elizabeth's invitation to their home for Christmas. She knew she would miss the countess; in their short acquaintance Katherine had found the closest thing she had ever known to a friend her own age.

Knowlton did not make an appearance as the preparations for Katherine and Robbie's return to the cottage were put into motion. There was little enough to do, she thought, but acquiesced for the last time to the assistance of the Warrenton servants. There would be plenty of time for her to take care of herself in the future.

It was only when they gathered in the entry hall, waiting for the coach to be brought round, that Knowlton made his appearance.

He tousled Robbie's red mop. "Eager to be off, eh?"

Robbie nodded.

"Now, you promise to take good care of your mama." Knowlton shot a quick glance at Kate, standing tight-lipped against the wall. "Do not make too much extra work for her, do you hear me?"

"Yes, sir," Robbie replied.

"I will keep a good eye on Atlas for you," Knowlton said, wondering if Robbie would ever be allowed to set foot at Warrenton again. "When the doctor says you are ready, we will go riding."

"You will come and play chess at the cottage?"

Robbie's plaintive query seared Knowlton. How much had changed since the lad had first asked the question this morning.

"I will be gone for a space. There are some business matters I need to take care of in London." He patted Robbie companionably on the back. "But as soon as I return, we will meet again across the board."

A footman carried Robbie to the now-waiting carriage. Knowlton turned to Kate. Her closed expression gave no indication of her feelings. Was she still angry?

"I am sorry to see both of you go, Mrs. Mayfield."

Katherine met his gaze without flinching, even though it took every ounce of strength she had not to let him see how disturbed she was. "It was most generous of you to extend your hospitality for so long, my lord."

"It was no imposition," he said. "I enjoyed it very much."

Keeping her expression calm, Katherine pasted a polite smile upon her face. "I am certain you are a gracious host to all your guests." She turned and took her bonnet from the hovering footman. "I bid you a safe journey to London, my lord." Tying the ribbons firmly under her chin, she walked down the steps, her back rigid.

With long strides, Knowlton caught up to her just as she approached the coach. Smiling blandly, he took her hand to help her into the vehicle.

"If I can offer you or your son any assistance in the future, do not hesitate to let me know," he said. Lowering his voice, he added, "I still have a care for your welfare. And I ask nothing in return."

Katherine bit her lip to keep it from trembling. Nodding briefly, she took her seat, refusing to look out the window after the door closed. She needed no last look to imprint Knowlton's features on her mind. They were etched in her heart forever.

Knowlton stood on the steps watching the carriage until it vanished from sight. There was nothing he could say or do to put matters right again, he knew. He let out a long, resigned sigh. He had held such high hopes for Kate; it was unfortunate she had turned out to be such a disappointment. It had all been an interesting diversion, but nothing more.

He rued the day he had laid eyes on that redheaded witch. His initial reservations about dallying after a lady of her ilk rushed back over him like a reproach. That was what came of dealing outside the circle of experienced ladies. He would have to remember that lesson for the future. With a careless shrug, he turned and mounted the stairs.

* * *

Robbie showed more enthusiasm at returning to the cottage than Katherine had thought he would. Even a ten-year-old appreciated the familiarity of home. The Warrenton cook sent along a cold collation so Katherine would not be faced with too many tasks on her first day home. Katherine noted in shocked puzzlement that the cottage gleamed. There was even, she noted with surprise, a new mattress on Robbie's bed. Knowlton had taken care of matters, of course. She was forced to admit a grudging gratitude for his thoughtfulness.

Robbie, worn out from excitement and the work of exercising his newly healed leg, fell asleep early. Katherine sat alongside his bed until he drifted into slumber, then made her way to the parlor.

She looked around her, really opening her eyes to what she saw. A tiny room, filled with cast-off furniture. It was the typical residence of a lady who had not the means to support a proper establishment. "Genteel poverty"—was that not the expression? Now it seemed more intolerable than ever.

Katherine had tried to count herself lucky to have a roof over her head, thinking that as long as she had Robbie with her, it was all that mattered. Material things were not important. Love and family were.

Yet she barely had either. Only Robbie. And as much as she loved her son, he would one day leave her side to make his own way in the world. And she would be so dreadfully alone.

Would it hurt so badly then, after all the years had passed? Would she look back upon this as just a foolish interlude in her life, the last gasp of her impulsive girlhood? She sincerely prayed it would be so.

But whatever the future held in store, she knew it did not include the Rose Cottage. She could tarry no longer in this neighborhood. Where, then, to go? To another cottage, in another county? To another life on the edge of poverty, scrimping and saving every penny in order to clothe Robbie? Begging and pleading to find a school somewhere that would take him without fees? Discouragement bowed her shoulders.

Katherine had caught a glimpse of what another life could be like during her stay at Warrenton. It was not the opulence of the furnishings or the expensive clothes that meant so much to her. It was the element of comfort, the security of knowing that there would be a roof over her head in the morning, that there would be ample food on the table at night, and that one could easily replace a pair of worn shoes or a torn coat without throwing the household budget into havoc. It was knowing that there was a point and purpose to the long hours Robbie spent struggling with his Latin and Greek, for there would be school and university in his future. Knowlton had offered all that, but she could not accept his terms.

The events of six years ago washed back over her. The angry words, the veiled threats, the fear and the distrust. Could she take the chance now? For there was one other place where she could find security. One other person she could turn to in order to ensure that at least Robbie had a future in which he could seek his own happiness. She had enjoyed four blissful years married to Robert. Perhaps that was all the happiness she was destined to achieve in this life. But Robbie was still young, with his whole life before him. She could still hope for more for him.

Six years ago, she had scornfully turned her back on her only other source of assistance. Now she would have to go hat in hand, pleading her case. But if Robbie benefited, it would be worth the damage to her pride.

Her pride. Katherine smiled ruefully. She had made so many decisions based on pride, and what had it earned her? A life where she and her son lived on the precarious edge of survival. A life where she was subjected to offers of the type Knowlton had made. Pride was an expensive commodity in her situation. Too expensive.

With a sigh, Katherine rose and picked up the candle. She followed the eerie shadows it threw on the wall as she mounted the stairs to her room. It was time to confront the past. She and Robbie would leave for London tomorrow.

14

'Tis time, I feel, to leave thee now,
  While yet my soul is something free;
                    —Thomas Moore, To—————

Katherine nervously clenched her hands together, staring blindly out the window as the hackney wound its way toward St. James Square. For the thousandth time, she prayed she was making the right decision. For both Robbie and herself.

As the coach pulled up in front of the modest building, a liveried footman opened the door and assisted Katherine from the carriage. He followed her up the few stone steps, where another footman held open the front door.

Adjusting her eyes to the dim light in the entry hall, Katherine looked about for her first view of the town house of the Marquess of Winslow. A silent, stern-faced butler motioned for her to follow him up the stairs. With tight self-control, she refrained from gawking at the ancient paintings and ornamental vases lining the staircase walls, but she was helpless not to come to a dead stop when she saw the painting at the head of the stairs. There was no question it was Robert—at ten or eleven, perhaps, posing with his older brother, Frederick. The painter had captured his boyish enthusiasm, the *élan* that had so swept her off her feet when she was seventeen. How she hoped Robbie could see this portrait. Despite the differing hair color, they looked so much alike.

"My lady?" The butler was correctly proper.

She started self-consciously, embarrassed at having been caught gawking like a visitor on open day. "Proceed," she directed.

While the butler held open the door to the marquess's study, Katherine halted momentarily outside the room. What fate awaited her inside? Would she be welcomed home as the prodigal daughter, or tossed out on her ear as an unwanted relative? Whatever the outcome, there was no changing her mind now. Her last hope rested inside the room. Squaring her shoulders, she stepped through the doorway.

The man behind the desk rose as she entered. Katherine struggled to suppress a small cry of shock at his appearance. In the six years since she had seen him last, he looked to have aged twenty. His hair was completely white now, and his shoulders were stooped with age. Still, he projected the aura of command that she remembered so well.

"So, my dear, you have decided to come out of hiding at last." He did not conceal the derision in his voice.

"Yes, my lord."

"Your letter mentioned that you are interested in discussing the future of my grandson. He is well, I trust."

She nodded, fighting down her nervousness. "He is still recovering from a broken leg earned in a riding accident, but otherwise enjoys excellent health."

"Trying to crowd his fences, eh?"

"Not anything so dramatic." Katherine forced a tentative smile. "He only learned to ride this past summer, and a shooting party startled his mount."

The Marquess of Winslow shook his head in a display of sympathy, and motioned for her to sit. He took his own chair and surveyed her with an assessing gaze. "Well, madam, what exactly is it that you wish to discuss?"

Katherine took a deep breath and met his piercing stare without flinching. So much depended on the outcome of this interview; if she made a mistake, antagonizing him further . . .

"Robbie needs an education, my lord. And I simply do not have the funds to send him to a school commensurate with his station—or his abilities." She unconsciously played with the folds of her skirt. "He is doing quite well at the present, taking lessons with the vicar, who has no doubt that Robbie will be able to take his place at school with no shame to his studies."

Katherine looked down briefly, steeling herself to say the words. Raising her gaze, she again met the marquess's imperious gaze. "I am asking you to pay his tuition, and perhaps use your power to find him an adequate position when he finishes his schooling."

"Hmm." The marquess sat silently for a moment.

Relief flooded Katherine at having at last made her request. It was all in his hands now; she had done what she could. She searched his lined face for a clue to the fate of her mission, but he gave no hint of his feelings.

"What career does the lad envision?" he asked at length.

"He wishes to be a cavalry officer." She gave him a small, apologetic smile. "I think he would do well at law, my lord."

The marquess toyed with his penknife, which only served to increase Katherine's agitation. Her fingers continued their nervous fumbling.

"Why now, after all these years?" His deep blue eyes stared at her coldly.

"It is school," she said simply, having practiced this answer numerous times. "Robbie deserves to have a proper education. I do not care if it is Eton or Harrow—there are other schools just as fine. Since there are so few scholarship opportunities . . . I thought I would appeal to you first."

"Have you forgotten your last words to me?" The marquess's face grew harsh.

"No, my lord, I have not." Katherine lifted her chin defiantly. "And I still believe them to be true. You had no right to accuse me of being an unfit guardian for my son, or to attempt to take him from me. If you still feel that way, I shall take my leave." She rose to her feet.

"Sit down, Katherine. You have not completely outgrown your impetuous nature, I see." The marquess leaned back in the chair, forming his fingers into a steeple. "I believe I shall make you a bargain, madam. Let me make young Robert's acquaintance. If I think that you have done an acceptable job of raising him to this point, I will do as you ask."

"And if not?"

"I will wash my hands of the both of you." His tone was abrupt.

"I think this is a bargain I shall easily win," she replied with the hint of a smile. Hope leapt within her. "He is bright, inquisitive, and eager for new experiences. Very much like his father.''

''Who was also a hotheaded young fool without an ounce of common sense when he got the bit between his teeth,'' the marquess countered.

''I am beginning to learn, with Robbie, that opposition only makes children more determined.'' Katherine spoke carefully, afraid of alienating the marquess now that she had gained a tentative victory. ''As a parent, you have to learn when to let them find their own path.''

The marquess fingered his penknife, then sighed. ''There is no question I dealt poorly with Robert on the matter of your marriage,'' he admitted. ''Perhaps it is time I make amends to you—and his son.''

''I think Robert would have been pleased to hear you say that,'' Katherine said, her voice catching.

The marquess stood up quickly.

''Where is the lad? Did you bring him with you to London, or do you still have him secreted somewhere in the countryside?''

''He is here,'' Katherine replied, allowing the first tremors of encouragement to surge through her body.

The marquess pulled out his watch and consulted it. ''Bring him around today at five,'' he ordered. ''The two of you may stay to dinner. Leave your address with Harlow and I will have the carriage sent round.''

''Thank you, my lord,'' Katherine said.

The marquess waved her out of the room, immediately turning his attention to the piles of papers on his desk as if she were no longer there.

Katherine's knees felt weak and wobbly and she was astounded they were able to carry her out into the corridor and down those intimidating stairs. She could hardly believe that the interview had gone so well. For six years she had hidden herself and her son from this man, and in the matter of a few minutes all that had been passed over as if it never happened. Has she been a prideful fool? Had those last six years of struggle and sacrifice been totally unnecessary?

Yet she still retained some nagging doubts about the marquess. He had tried to take Robbie from her once; would he do so again? She could be playing right into his hands. He could send Robbie off to school, hire the most expensive legal help in the country, and wrest him away from her—forever. The thought chilled her.

But the elderly man she had encountered today was not the same man who had threatened her after Robert's death. She was willing to concede that grief and anger had held him in their sway at that time; the years would have softened that blow. And of course, there were other grandsons now, to carry on the name. Robbie was no longer so close to the title. Perhaps the marquess spoke now in complete sincerity.

She would have to hope so. For by returning tonight, she was casting Robbie's fate, and hers, into the marquess's hands. She prayed she was not making a dreadful mistake.

"Where have you been?" Robbie's voice demanded querulously as she reentered their sleeping chamber at the posting inn.

"Visiting," Katherine replied briefly, laying her warm winter cloak carefully over the back of the chair. "Did you finish with your Latin?"

He scowled. "Almost."

She shook her head, but she was not angry. What boy of his age would be interested in Latin grammar when there was all of London to explore? Yet his leg was still weak, and not up to a rigorous traverse of the city's streets. The Latin would occupy his mind while he recovered his strength.

"We will be going out tonight," she said casually, groping for the best way to explain things to Robbie. How best to tell him all that had transpired between her and the Mayfield family? Would he understand the reasons for her actions six years ago? Or would it all be too confusing?"

"Will I have to wear my new clothes?" He grimaced.

She nodded, and sat down facing him. "Robbie, there is something important I need to discuss with you. You are ten now, and very nearly a young man, and therefore old enough to know most of the story.'' She took a deep breath as she regarded her son's quizzical eyes.

"Your father was more than a captain in the cavalry,'' she began. "He was also the son of a marquess.''

"A marquess? Papa?''

"The *son* of a marquess,'' she reiterated. "And only a younger one, which is why he was in the cavalry, for the titles and estates will go to his elder brother. When your father and I married . . .'' She paused for a moment, watching his face carefully, fearing his reaction to these revelations. "Neither his family nor mine was very happy about it. The marquess, in particular, was very angry.''

She halted in her narrative. It would be pointless to tell Robbie just how angry the marquess had been, and the words that had been exchanged between father and son when Robert had brought home his Gretna bride to the family estate. It would be best if Robbie never heard that story—or what had transpired between herself and the marquess after Robert's death.

"That is why I have not spoken of him before. But he is your grandfather, Robbie, and you have aunts and uncles and cousins here in London and in the country. I spoke with your grandfather this morning, and he is very eager to meet you.''

She would not tell him what the outcome of the meeting could mean for the both of them. School was not a primary concern of Robbie's; he was too young to know the advantages that would accrue from consorting with his peers. Or the doors that could be opened to him at the word of a marquess. Better that he looked forward only to having a family around him at last.

"Is my grandfather still angry?''

Katherine shook her head and smiled encouragingly. "He is not. That was long in the past. He has invited us to dine with him tonight, which is a great honor, for not everyone has the opportunity to dine with a marquess. That is why I wish you to wear your new clothes and demonstrate your best manners, so I can be proud of you.''

"Tell me about my cousins.''

"I know very little about them, I am afraid. Your papa had several sisters, and they all have children even older than you.

I know there are two young boys—the sons of your uncle. You can ask your grandfather about them tonight.''

She studied him closely, trying to gauge his reaction to the news. But Robbie's face only reflected his boyish curiosity.

"Does this mean," he asked at last, "that we are not going to go back to Rose Cottage?"

"Yes, Robbie. The marquess will probably find us another place to live, closer to his house.'' And far away from the Earl of Knowlton.

"What will happen to my pony?"

"When we are settled, you can write to the earl and ask him for your pony. You will not be able to ride until your leg is stronger anyway. And I would not be surprised if the marquess has some ponies of his own that he might let you ride.''

To her relief, that answer appeared to mollify his concern. She had felt a twinge of guilt at leaving Robbie's pony behind, knowing that he might never see the animal again. If the marquess did take them in, the pony could be retrieved. She knew it would reveal her location to Knowlton, but by then it would not matter. She was certain he would have little to say to her in their changed circumstances. And there was little she wished to say to him. She wished to avoid any future contact with the earl for as long as possible. Until all the dreams he had so thoroughly dashed faded from her memory.

Katherine noted with a self-conscious start that Robbie was watching her closely. This was no time for what-might-have-beens, she chided herself.

"I promised I would show you some of the sights of town today," she said, brightening. "Shall we see what we can see from the windows of a hackney?"

Robbie scowled. "My leg is fine, Mama.''

"And I intend for it to stay that way. We shall save it for more important endeavors like the Tower and the waxworks. It would be a pity to tire it out now and have to miss those sights.''

"All right," he grumbled.

Katherine sympathized. He had been inactive far too long. But he still favored the healing limb, and walked with a slight limp, particularly when he was tired. Until he was perfectly well, she did not want to take any risks.

She managed to find a hack that was not too worn or filthy inside, and once the driver got over his surprise at being ordered to drive about the streets so they could gawk like tourists, it was a pleasant journey. It was a wanton extravagance as well, Katherine noted ruefully, but if all proceeded as planned, money would no longer be of such pressing concern. With Robbie's schooling paid for, she could exist quite easily on the small competence she had. so she even had the man stop at Gunther's, where she treated Robbie to his first ice.

They dallied so long that it was a mad scramble to get themselves ready for their visit to the marquess. Katherine slicked Robbie's wayward hair to his head in hopes of his making a more presentable appearance and of disguising its brilliant red shade. She dressed herself in her serviceable gray silk, twisting her hair into a demure chignon. For once, she wished she had a decent cap she could wear. It would make her look older and more responsible. And hide that devilish red hair.

As if that would impress the marquess. Despite the favorable outcome of the morning's visit, she was still more nervous than she wished to be. As she herded Robbie into the waiting carriage, his eyes had widened at the sight of the grand town coach with its coat of arms upon the door and the liveried grooms.

"Is the marquess rich?" Robbie whispered when they were settled inside on the padded velvet seats.

She nodded. "He is."

"Will he give us money, then, so we do not have to be so poor?"

"In the first place, Robbie, we are not poor." Katherine could not keep the defensive tone from her voice. "We just do not have enough money for frivolous whims. And the marquess will do whatever he pleases with his money. It is not our concern."

What a dreadful lie, she scolded herself. Money was precisely what she was asking the marquess for. But somehow the thought of asking for tuition money did not sound so crass.

* * *

"Damn that witch!"

Knowlton stormed out the door of the Rose Cottage, his face contorted in anger. What kind of a monster did she think he was? He had accepted her refusal, had acknowledged that she considered it no compliment. There was no need for her to pack their belongings and flee from him as if he posed a danger.

Why? Why had she left, without a word to anyone, or a message to him? He knew now he had sadly misjudged her. His offer of protection had been received as a mortal insult. Knowlton felt a spasm of regret for that. But certainly she would realize her angry rejection had effectively stilled his intentions regarding her?

Had something else gone wrong while he was gone? Knowlton felt a stab of concern. He knew Kate had little money. Her furniture was gone; that would have entailed the expense of a cart for the journey to wherever she had fled. Rents could be low at this time of year, but food would grow dearer as winter neared. He knew she had supplemented what income she had with sewing, but would she have that opportunity in the new place she settled? He cringed at the thought of her and Robbie in need, hungry and cold throughout the harsh months to come.

And what was worse, he would probably never know her fate. Pain shot through him at the dismal thought. If she and Robbie arrived at some pitiful state, he would never know. It would not take many reversals to reduce them to paupers; they could find themselves on the parish rolls in short time. Why was she being such a fool? He would never have forced his intentions upon her. She was safe after she made it clear she did not want him.

But she *had* wanted him. That had been no feigned passion that night in Robbie's room. She had been as bold and wanton as any lover he had bedded, wildly exciting, achingly tender, and firing such a yearning in him as he had never known before. Even now, in the cold October wind, his body raged with desire at the remembered feel of her. He had struggled against the burning heat of his memories during his absence from Warrenton, consoling himself with knowledge that he could douse the flames in the softness of a more willing female body if he so desired. That he had not done so was his own folly.

Knowlton mounted his horse and took a long, last scowling look at the Rose Cottage. He had been driven with such plans, such ideas. Once Robbie was settled in school, he had thought to travel. Kate would have enjoyed that, he was certain. Paris, Switzerland, Italy. He wanted to share with her all the delights he had discovered there, and search for new ones they could both share. And now . . . now . . .

With a vicious tug at the reins he set his heels to his horse. He had better things to do than worry about the fate of such an ungrateful woman and her son. He had offered to help, and his offer had been refused. Very well, he would spend no more time with them. Let them seek their own fate.

15

Katherine could not shake her last-minute jitters as she and Robbie entered the marquess's town house. She was not worried about her son's impression upon the marquess—she knew that Robbie's deportment and manners were all she could wish, and he would not shame her. It was her own behavior she concerned herself with. If things began to go wrong, she did not know if she could rely on her good sense to still her tongue. The marquess still had far to go in earning her trust.

"This is even fancier than Knowlton's house," Robbie whispered to his mother as they followed the butler up the stairs. "Did my papa really live here?"

She nodded. "Not often, though. He grew up at the country estate."

"Will we go there sometime too?"

"Perhaps," she said, her lips compressing in a thin line. Her memories of her one visit to that house were bitter.

At the top of the stairs she motioned for the butler to halt, and she turned Robbie toward the picture that had so captured her imagination that morning.

"That young boy is your papa, Robbie."

"Really?" He stopped and stared. "He looks different from the miniature."

"The miniature was painted much later," Katherine explained. "Why, he must have been near your age when this painting was done. The older boy is Frederick, your uncle."

"I don't look much like him, do I?" Robbie asked with a note of regret.

"Of course you do," Katherine hastened to reassure him. "You have my hair, but otherwise you look very much like him. See how full of mischief he looks? I wager he was nearly as big a scamp as you."

The butler coughed and Katherine shot him a sharp look.

"Lord Robert could be quite a handful," he said.

"Did you know my papa?" Robbie asked eagerly. "What do you remember about him?"

"That he was always a very inquisitive lad," the butler said, and a ghost of a smile crossed his face. "Stubborn as could be when he was thwarted, and always in and out of trouble."

Katherine smiled fondly. Robbie and his father were very like—and both took after the old marquess. Her amusement faded as she remembered the confrontational scenes between Robert and his father. Would Robbie carry on the strife into the next generation? She prayed she had successfully leavened some of his willfulness. She gently nudged him forward.

"Your grandfather is waiting," she reminded him.

Robbie took one last look at the portrait and followed her down the long corridor to the drawing room. Katherine stood aside nervously to allow Robbie to enter. She had said her piece in the morning. The outcome of this evening depended upon Robbie and his grandfather.

The marquess rose from his chair as they entered, surveying his grandson with a skeptical look.

"So," he said at last. "I suppose it was too much to hope that you would have inherited your father's coloring."

"I have my mama's hair," Robbie said proudly.

Katherine knew that no matter the outcome of this interview, she would forever be proud of her son for that defiant remark.

"So you do," said the marquess, nodding his head.

"Mama says I look a lot like Papa. We saw the portrait at the top of the stairs. Was he really my age then?"

The marquess looked startled. "You may have the right of it, my boy. He could not have been more than ten or eleven when it was painted. And you are ten now?"

"Almost eleven," said Robbie. "In January."

Katherine could almost hear the marquess mentally ticking off the months. "A full ten months after the marriage," she remarked with a tinge of sarcasm.

He had the grace to look embarrassed, then turned back to Robbie. "Is this your first trip to London?"

Robbie nodded.

"And how do you find the city?"

"I have not seen that much," Robbie confessed. "Mama and I took a hackney and drove through the city this afternoon. She does not want me walking much because of my leg."

"Ah, yes, your leg. Came a cropper, did you?"

"It was my fault," Robbie said. "Mama told me not to ride near to where they were shooting, but I forgot."

"Sounds like your mama gave you some sensible advice," the marquess said. "Do you always forget what she tells you?"

"No, sir. Only once in a while."

Katherine stifled a smile.

The marquess motioned for them to sit. Katherine settled upon the low sofa, but Robbie took a chair next to the marquess.

"Mama said I was to ask you about my cousins," Robbie said. "Are there any my age?"

Katherine realized with a pang how few opportunities there had been for Robbie to develop friendships among youths his own age. It was one more thing her stubborn pride had cost him.

"Georgie's eldest is nearing eighteen," the marquess mused. "There are a gaggle of females ranging from five to fifteen, but no lads your age, I am afraid. Frederick's two boys are still in short coats; too young to be of much interest to you."

"Oh," Robbie said with a crestfallen expression.

"Wanted a playfellow, eh?"

Robbie nodded. "I miss my friend Sam."

The marquess shot Katherine a questioning look.

"One of the neighbors' boys," she explained hastily. She could only imagine what the marquess would say if he knew Robbie's playmate was a rough farmer's son.

The marquess appeared satisfied. "Your mama says you are doing well in your studies. How is your Latin?"

Robbie glanced at his mother. "Adequate," he said.

"Greek?"

"Tolerable."

"Mathematics?"

"He has outpaced his tutor in that field," Katherine said proudly, not adding that she had been that person. But she had no qualms about Robbie's ability in that area.

The marquess nodded in satisfaction. "Your mama thinks you ought to be going to school soon. We sent your papa off at eleven. What do you think of that idea?"

Robbie looked at his mother in surprise, and Katherine groaned inwardly. She had known there would be a stumbling block somewhere this evening, and they had just run straight into it. She returned Robbie a rueful smile, refusing to indicate what response she desired. Thank goodness she had never repeated Robert's stories of how he had hated life at Eton. Robbie was on his own.

"Well, I . . . I think that might be all right," he said doubtfully. "What kind of school? Would I have to leave Mama?"

"It would depend on which school you were suited for," the marquess responded. "Perhaps the best thing to do is have you examined by a qualified tutor to see how far you have progressed in your studies. If there are any deficiencies, you will need to make them up first."

"Do you really want me to go away to school?" Robbie asked his mother.

"It would give you the opportunity to be with boys your own age," she said cautiously. "You would have the chance to make many friends."

Robbie sat quietly, considering. "I will think about it," he said finally. He turned back to the marquess. "Are Mama and I going to come and live with you now?"

Katherine suppressed a grin. She was pleased to see the marquess put on the spot for once.

"It may be," he said. "Do you want to live in the city?"

"Can I have a pony in the city?"

"Still eager to ride after your accident?"

Robbie nodded. "I had to leave my pony when we came here, but Mama said you might let me bring him here. May I?"

The marquess nodded silently, and Katherine saw the ghost of a smile flit across his lips.

The butler appeared at the door. "Dinner is served, my lord."

"About time," grumbled the marquess. "You would think they wanted a body to starve around here." He eyed Robbie skeptically. "Have you creditable manners at the table, boy?"

Robbie nodded.

The marquess held out his arm to Katherine and she took it shyly.

"He'll do," the marquess whispered to her in a low undertone as they stepped into the corridor.

Katherine and Robbie moved to the town house the following day, to Robbie's great delight. He insisted on exploring every nook and cranny of the four-story building. Katherine admonished him against pestering the servants, for his first question to all of them was whether they had known his father. Surprisingly, a large number of the house workers remembered Robert and filled the eager boy with tales of his father. It did much to ease Katherine's worries about how Robbie would adjust to the change in their situation.

She had barely had the opportunity to adjust herself to their changed surroundings when Lady Durham descended upon her. Katherine had never met the wife of Robert's older brother—they had married after Robert's death—and she was curious to meet her sister-in-law for the first time. Smoothing down the skirts of her unfashionable day gown, Katherine repaired to the upper saloon to meet the woman whose children had supplanted Robbie in the inheritance. What could she expect from the countess? Acceptance, dismay, or outright resentment?

An elegantly garbed and coiffed woman, short and slender, with dark hair, was gazing with rapt attention out the window to the activity in the square below.

"Lady Durham?" Katherine questioned.

The lady turned and surveyed Katherine with an inquisitive and appraising stare. At the moment when Katherine felt her anger rising at this rude perusal, Lady Durham broke into a musical laugh.

"I can certainly see why Robert chose you over his family!"

"Can you?" Katherine's voice was icy.

"Oh, dear, I have bungled matters already, haven't I?" Lady Durham tossed her head gaily. "I always make such a mull of things. What I meant to say was that you are far more lovely than I could have imagined. It will be a delight to take you in hand."

"Take me in hand?" Katherine felt her anger rising again.

"I did not phrase that well either, did I? The marquess wishes me to advise you on the matter of your new wardrobe."

"Since he obviously does not trust me to competently choose my own. He need not fear, I will not disgrace him."

"And there is no reason to think you should," Lady Durham murmured soothingly. "I really am making a botch of this. I am certain you have excellent taste. But I do so love to shop, and Frederick is being positively *gothic* about my overrunning my allowance again this quarter and has forbidden me to make any more purchases. Helping you choose your new wardrobe will be almost as much fun. Please say you will let me accompany you."

Katherine smiled in spite of herself. She began to suspect her younger sister-in-law was a bit of a scatter-wit. "I would enjoy it if you came along, Lady Durham."

"Oh, please, call me Castalia. After all, we are sisters of a sort. Your name is Katherine, is it not? May I call you that?"

Katherine nodded, growing more and more amused by this chattering young woman.

"Do you wish to begin this morning? I know they have received some new silks at the warehouse, and I saw the most exquisite lace shawls at Plummer's last week, and—"

"I need only a few things."

Castalia paused. "The marquess said he had given you *carte blanche* for everything, top to toe. My goodness, you do not intend to turn down such a generous offer?"

"It is a munificient gesture, but I hardly see the need." Katherine shook her head doubtfully. "I own I would like to purchase a few dresses. However, my remaining needs are small."

Lady Durham laughed. "I can see why the marquess wished me to accompany you. You cannot possibly do without at least a dozen outfits.'' She ticked off the list on her fingers. "Two walking gowns, at least, and a carriage dress. Dinner gowns . . . three, I think, and three evening dresses as well. Do you ride?''

Katherine shook her head, too astounded by the woman's grandiose plans to say anything.

"Well, perhaps another carriage dress, then. And some morning gowns. With all the matching gloves, bonnets, shawls, and shoes, it will make a prodigious collection.'' Her eyes glowed with excitement. "It should entail a full week of shopping, at least.''

"But I have no need—''

"Of course you do. You do not want to disgrace the marquess or the memory of your husband when you are presented into society?''

"I hardly think I shall be much in society,'' Katherine protested. "Once the matter of Robbie's schooling is settled, I will be returning to the country.''

"You do not wish to remain in London?'' Incredulity lit Lady Durham's face. "Why ever not?''

"I have no reason to be in the city. I have no connections with whom to renew acquaintances.''

"Then you will have ample opportunity to make new ones,'' Lady Durham declared emphatically. "Goodness, Katherine, the Little Season is in full swing already. If we do not get you about soon, everyone will have deserted the city for country estates and you will have to wait until spring.''

Katherine suspected that she was going to be swept along into whatever plans the marquess and Castalia had for her, whether she wished to be or not. This woman might be frivolous, but Katherine suspected she had a will of steel beneath her flighty exterior.

"I will acquiesce to perhaps half that number of outfits'' she said firmly. She did not wish to be more indebted to the marquess than she had to.

Castilia airily waved a hand. "Six, eight, twelve. It is much the same. Shall we leave now?''

Katherine suppressed the urge to laugh at her sister-in-law's determination. "I will get my cloak.''

Katherine was much less in favor of Castalia's enthusiasm when they finally returned to St. James Square. It was not the countess who had been required to stand stiff as a statue while she was being measured, poked, prodded, and pinned for what seemed an eternity. Despite Katherine's protests, Castalia proceeded to order all the gowns on her required list, plus a few extra. When measurements had been taken, the fabrics chosen, and delivery dates promised, Castalia then dragged her to the vast warehouses where she forced stockings, handkerchiefs, chemises, gloves, and every manner of item on the protesting Katherine. She had wondered at the two footmen who had accompanied the carriage, but saw the wisdom in their presence when they followed the two ladies from the shop with an enormous burden of packages in their arms.

Katherine sank back against the carriage cushions in exhaustion.

"Now, of course, we will have to plan your entrance into society." Castalia bubbled with enthusiasm. "I know Lady Trumball is having a rout next week; that might make a nice beginning. We can have our own ball the following week, and—"

"Castalia, it really is not necessary to go to such trouble. I assure you, I have no desire to cut a dash in society. I am merely a simple country widow."

"But Frederick has been so reluctant to give his permission for a ball. If it was in your honor, he could hardly refuse, could he?"

The pleading look Castalia directed at her did little to alleviate Katherine's misgivings. Her only desire had been for Robbie's future when she repaired the breach with his grandfather. She had never intended for the marquess to provide for her; now she had acquired this overwhelming wardrobe and her in-laws were determined to introduce her to society. Katherine feared she would be woefully out of place among the elevated reaches of the *ton*.

Katherine's protestations were ignored and Castalia merrily planned a ball more suitable to the debut of an Incomparable than the mere introduction of the inconsequential widow of a long-dead younger son. And Katherine began to have grave suspicions as to the reasoning behind this. No one had actually said anything outright to her, but it did not take long for Katherine to notice that Castalia, and the marquess himself, took great pains to introduce her to every bachelor they met.

Katherine shook her head at their faulty reasoning. She had given them no indication that she wished to remarry. And she grew suspicious of their motives. Marriage would cut her legal ties to the Mayfields—would they use that as an excuse to attempt to take Robbie from her again?

And even if she did not have that worry, she saw no reason to take another man to husband. Short as it had been, her marriage to Robert had been all that she could have wanted. It would be an impossible task to attempt to recreate that magic with another man. And if the image of a pair of cynical gray eyes belied her protestations, she had the cold comfort of knowing that he held out no offer of marriage.

She felt as if she were being swept along by a swift river current. With no hope of struggling against it, she was forced to acquiesce and follow where it led her. And if it involved routs and balls and theater parties, well, there was a growing part of her that admitted that the enjoyments of even the Little Season were more than she had ever hoped to experience. As long as she accepted that they were to be a temporary happenstance, she could relax her qualms and attempt to enjoy herself. It might be her only opportunity.

Despite his growing dissatisfaction, Knowlton felt himself strangely reluctant to leave Warrenton, even though he felt restless and bored within its walls. In the past few weeks the servants had learned to tread lightly when in the presence of the earl. The merest slip, an awkward appearance, or a perfectly respectable performance of their duties was likely to earn them a blistering tirade from Knowlton.

He sought comfort in exhaustion. From morning to afternoon he was in the saddle, riding about the county in a reckless manner that left him physically tired but mentally alert. When not ahorse, he stalked the estate with his shotgun, bagging enough birds to feed the entire county. By dinnertime he could barely keep his eyes open, and it took only small quantities of brandy or port to tumble him into sleep, usually in his chair in the study.

He studiously avoided Katherine's old cottage on his wild rambles, riding miles in the other direction to avoid any place associated with her. Yet every sight of his own stable brought Robbie's abandoned pony to mind. How could she have been so cruel as to leave the poor beast behind? Robbie would be grieved at the loss. She was intolerably selfish, thinking only of herself. If he ever got his hands on her again, he would be sorely tempted to throttle her.

Knowlton grew more discontented with every passing day. Warrenton held too many reminders of the pleasant hours he had spent in Kate's company. Every night, as he took to his bed, he was assailed with vivid reminders of that impassioned kiss in Robbie's room. Knowlton's body ached for her. He struggled against his desire, willed his body to obey his mind, but more often than not his efforts resulted in dismal failure.

The peace of mind he had thought to find at Warrenton when he arrived from London all those months ago completely eluded him with Kate's abrupt departure. And short of filling his house with an assortment of unwanted guests, there was little he could do to restore his sympathy with life here. Perhaps it was time to return to London. There would still be a flurry of activity before the *ton* left town for the winter holiday. Time enough to sample the pleasures of the city. After a four-month absence, they might not look so discouraging.

Yes, he decided, he would go to town. It was only the solitude of Warrenton that made the memories of Kate Mayfield so difficult to abandon. He would wager that within a week of his arrival in the city, her memory would cease to taunt him. In London, there was no shortage of ladies who would be quite willing to accept his patronage. With a sudden spurt of enthusiasm, he rang for Rigsby and ordered him to prepare to depart the following day.

16

Woman, that fair and fond deceiver
How fond are striplings to believe her!

—Byron, *To Woman*

Katherine's arrival on the scene was greeted by the *ton* with
curiosity and questions, which the family explained away as a
lengthy period of mourning for the long-dead Robert. This
explanation was met with complete acceptance. Katherine
continued to make mild protests against the family's attempts
to turn her into a social matron, which Castalia dismissed as
the typical nervousness due any young lady making her bow
in London. Katherine *was* nervous about it. Raised in a simple
home, the grandest entertainments she had ever attended were
the local assemblies, where she had met Robert. Her subsequent
life as an underfunded officer's wife had not been overly
exciting. And certainly since his death she had lived as retired
a life as one could imagine. Those weeks at Warrenton had been
her only contact with members of the *ton*. Now her in-laws
expected her to take that association as a matter of course.

It was not that Katherine did not wish to enter society. She
confessed she enjoyed the small dinners and musical entertainments she attended, and the theater was as entrancing as
she remembered from her lone visit with Robert. It was only
the lack of purpose for her participation that caused her to pause.
All she wanted from Robert's family was a gentleman's
education for her son; she never planned to ask for anything
for herself. But they acted as if it were all a matter of course,
and Katherine suspected that only downright defiance would
cause them to lay down their plans. And there was just enough
of a luxury-loving woman in her not to go that far. She would
never take her new position for granted, but while it was offered,
she would be foolish to refuse. When Robbie went off to school

next year, she could take up the threads of her own life again.

Katherine felt the tiniest twinges of doubt about the ball that Castalia organized in her honor. It seemed to be far too grand an affair for introducing a widowed sister-in-law. Indeed, it looked more appropriate for the come-out of the daughter of an exalted family. But Castalia just laughed off her protests and blithely went her own way. Katherine submerged her doubts and followed along. And she had to admit that the gorgeous green silk Castalia forced upon her made up into an admirable dress.

Katherine fought against her nerves as she followed Castalia into the main drawing room. No other young lady making her first bow into society could feel more apprehensive. The falseness of her position plagued her. She was *not* an innocent miss in search of a husband. Why, then, had she allowed them to subject her to this public perusal?

Because it pleased them, and that pleasure reflected on what the marquess was willing to do for Robbie. And that was why she found herself at the Earl of Durham's house, dressed in all her new finery, waiting for the ball in her honor to begin. At least this sacrifice was more pleasant than the one she had made six years ago. The results of her current capitulation were worth it, of course, for the marquess was completely reconciled to her guardianship of Robbie. She had achieved all she could have asked for.

Still, she felt the stirrings of regret for Knowlton and what might have been. If only she had been able to reach his heart . . . even a few months in his arms would have been worth the lifetime of loneliness that followed. But he had made it abundantly clear that he felt no emotion for her beyond lust. Once again she wished she had listened to her head instead of her heart in her dealings with him.

Castalia's voice intruded into her thoughts.

"Now, Katherine, I will take it upon myself to introduce you to a number of suitable dancing partners. Rumors of your presence have already been circulating among the *ton*, so you can be assured of a great deal of interest."

"How wonderful," Katherine responded dryly. Just the thing to set her at ease.

Castalia laughed. "I assure you, it is much more pleasant to be making your debut at twenty-eight than at seventeen."

"I still find the whole idea foolish," Katherine said. "I would much rather cultivate the role of secluded widow."

"Nonsense," Castalia replied, tapping her lightly on the arm with her fan. "You deserve to have what Winslow's stubbornness and Robert's untimely death deprived you of. You are the daughter-in-law of a marquess, remember, and that gives you enormous social consequence. And with my backing, you will go far."

"You will be a wicked marchioness," Katherine said, a smile lighting her face.

"I know," Castalia responded with a self-satisfied smile.

By midnight Katherine was laughing at all her earlier nervousness, swept up by the excitement of the evening, the attentions of her numerous partners, and the glittering company she found herself in. She had often wondered what her life would have been like if not for the estrangement between Robert and his father, if they had taken their rightful place in society. She was rapidly discovering that it might not be such a bad life after all.

Fanning herself against the heat generated by too many people crowded into too small a space, Katherine scanned the crowd for a familiar face. She would be forced to navigate the crush herself to find the punch if she could not find a willing assistant. Resigned to the trek, she turned toward the door, then stopped, frozen in place.

He was the last person she had ever dreamed of seeing this evening, and she instantly acknowledged her foolishness. She had assumed they would meet again, someday, but not so soon. He'd said he planned to winter peacefully on his estate—so why was he here now in London, in November? And why, oh why, was he at this house?

Katherine edged her way back into the center of the room, her gaze darting about in frantic search of Castalia. But fatally, she looked in his direction one more time, and their gazes locked.

She did not mistake the brief shock that registered in his eyes before his usual cool, mocking expression returned. Ignoring the image she presented, she turned and pushed her way through the crowd. Flight was the foremost thing on her mind.

She found Castalia in the next room and grasped her arm in relief.

"I am feeling unwell," she gulped.

"It is this heat," the countess murmured sympathetically. "Let me find someone to get you a glass of punch."

"No, really, I think I would feel better if I—"

"Ah, Lady Durham." Knowlton crossed the room with impatient strides and took Castalia's hand and raised it to his lips. "A dreadful crush, as usual. Your reputation as London's premier hostess is in no danger tonight."

"Nor is yours as a flirt," she responded, rapping his knuckles with her fan until he released her hand.

He turned expectantly toward Katherine.

"I do not think I have had the pleasure of meeting your exquisite companion," Knowlton said with a mocking smile. "Please, do the honors."

"Certainly. But I warn you, Knowlton, do not try to set up one of your flirtations with her. She is a highly respectable lady, not your type at all. Do you remember Frederick's younger brother, Robert? This is his widow. Lord Knowlton, may I present Lady Robert Mayfield."

"Enchanting," he said, drawing her hand to his lips. "How could such a fair light have denied us her presence for so long?"

"Now, Katherine," Castalia warned, "do not take a word he says seriously. Knowlton is an incorrigible flirt, and terribly spoiled by the adulation of countless women who are less than ladies. In short, he is a rogue."

He brought his hand to his chest as if reeling from a blow. "You wound me, Lady Durham."

Katherine felt like a tongue-tied idiot, but she could not have uttered a word if her life depended on it. She prayed he would go away.

"It is quite warm in here," he said, taking in her pale face. "Let me escort you to the refreshments, Lady Robert."

"Thank you, but I shall be fine," she whispered, preparing to flee.

"No, I insist," he said, grabbing her elbow in a firm grip and leading her none too gently across the room.

In the relative emptiness of the corridor, Katherine tried to shrug his hand loose, but he only clasped her arm tighter.

"Unless you want an embarrassing scene, you shall come with me," he said between gritted teeth, dragging her down the hall. Pushing open the first door he came to, he gave a satisfied sigh as he shoved her inside the room and firmly shut the door.

Katherine rubbed her arm. She would have bruises tomorrow.

Knowlton turned his steady gaze upon her. God, she looked beautiful. That flowing emerald gown accentuated every luscious curve; the fashionably low décolletage did more than hint of the full breasts that lay below. It took no imagination at all to envision her naked form. Anger, hurt, longing, and lust warred within him as he confronted the woman who had so disturbed his life these last weeks.

"I suppose you want an explanation," she said lamely.

"I? What right do I have to demand anything from you?" He glared at her fiercely. "I have no claim on you, *Lady Robert*."

She fumbled with the clasp of her fan. This was going to be as dreadfully awkward as she had feared.

"I assume you really *are* Lady Robert? Or is it only another of your false identities?"

"I never lied about who I was," she retorted. "I am Robert's widow."

"Of course, *Mrs.* Mayfield," he said sarcastically. "The fact you are the daughter-in-law of a marquess is irrelevant."

"It was and is," she said angrily, trying to brush past him.

"You fool." He grabbed her arm roughly. "What game were you playing, masquerading as an impoverished widow?"

"It was no game," she said. "The marquess did not approve of my marriage to Robert, and dealt with me accordingly."

"And left you totally without funds at your husband's demise? Difficult to believe."

"It is true!" Damn his arrogant assumptions. "When Robert died, the marquess tried to take Robbie from me. I had to live in hiding, else he would have found me."

"Now suddenly you are cozy as an inkle-weaver with the whole family? It does not wash, Kate."

Her name on his lips sliced through her like a knife.

"I did it for Robbie," she said quietly, turning away to get hold of her emotions. "He has a right to know his family and his heritage."

"Of course, there is the added advantage to you of the sponsorship of the marquess's family." He coolly appraised her elegantly clad form. "I must say, Katherine, you have done well for yourself."

Anger boiled up inside her. "I did not do this for myself," she said icily.

He stepped back a pace and subjected her to a long, lingering perusal. "I suppose they forced that gown upon you."

Katherine's cheeks flamed. How dare he accuse her of mercenary motives! "Had I wanted only elegant gowns, I recall you were only too eager to provide them."

She turned away again, running her fingertips along the edge of the rosewood table. Katherine did not want him to see how, even now, his presence disturbed her composure.

Knowlton realized with a sudden stab of pain that his improper proposal had driven her back into the family circle. His offer to pay for Robbie's schooling no doubt reminded her of the advantages that would accrue to him as the grandson of a marquess. What had he forced her to do?

"Kate," he said with a new degree of warmth in his voice, "are they treating you well?"

A twinge of irony touched her laugh. "In point of fact, they are. The marquess has virtually apologized for his actions six years ago and made me feel like the veriest fool for not getting in touch with him sooner."

Relief crossed his face. This forced reunion with her husband's family was not hateful to her. She would be well-taken-care-of, and protected. Yet he felt a trace of sadness, knowing she had no need of his help now. The one thing he could offer her—an easy life—had been taken care of.

"So now you can return to the life you left," he said lightly. "There will be more fine dresses of silk and lace, parties and—"

"I had never set foot in this house before last month," she said, sighing with remembrance and regret. "Neither the marquess nor my own parents countenanced my marriage to Robert. We eloped, a true Gretna Green marriage. The scandal alone would have put us beyond the pale, but the marquess exacerbated the situation by publicly disowning Robert for 'lowering' the family's standards by marrying a mere country vicar's daughter."

"You are a vicar's daughter?" Disbelief washed over his face.

"A rather rebellious and willful one, I fear," she acknowledged with a sad smile.

Knowlton's guilt over what he had proposed to her deepened. How could he have asked the daughter of a *vicar* to become his mistress? "What did your parents do? Certainly they must have been pleased to see you married so well."

"They sided with the marquess, about both the marriage and Robbie. They thought it a folly for me to try to raise him alone on the mere pittance Robert left me." She shrugged. "I managed to reach a tolerable accommodation with my father before he died."

Pity and guilt washed over Knowlton. He had not known how deep an insult his offer had been. It had endangered not only her own respectability but also her son's entire future. No wonder she had rejected him so vehemently.

"Under the circumstances," he began, "I find that my previous offer to you was highly inappropriate. I apologize if I offended you, Lady Robert. I had meant it as a compliment."

"I hardly took it as such." Her gaze met his without flinching. Only she knew how much her studied dispassion caused her. He looked as calm and unperturbed as always. Her defection had not troubled his dreams, she was certain. She was the only one filled with regret and longing.

"I regret we parted on such violent terms. You never did allow me to say good-bye properly, you know," he chided in a voice suddenly grown husky. He had been living on dreams of her for weeks now; certainly, once he experienced the reality again, it would banish those foolish flights of fancy. The real Kate Mayfield could not come near to his maudlin imaginings. He could free himself from her spell once and for all.

Katherine was unable to turn her gaze away from the grip of those piercing gray eyes, and when he took a step toward her, she did not fall back. He would never know of the storm that raged within her as she fought against her longing.

"It is not necessary," she said hastily. His nearness wreaked havoc with her senses. She must get away from him. But her feet would not move; she watched him, entranced, as he took another step toward her.

"Oh, but I insist." He laid his hands lightly on her shoulders, drawing her toward him while he lowered his head to kiss her.

He nearly groaned at the moment of contact, knowing instantly that this had been an act of pure folly. He was still ensorcelled by this redheaded witch. Just the touch of those soft lips to his brought back a flood of memories of her passion. Heat diffused through his body; his hold on her shoulders tightened as he pressed her against him. Kate, Kate . . .

He released her so suddenly she nearly lost her balance.

"Our paths will undoubtedly cross here in town," he said, covering his unsteady voice with a mocking smile. "But you need not fear I will touch you again. This is good-bye, Kate." He turned on his heel and left the room.

Katherine stood for she did not know how long, staring at the closed door through the mist of tears in her eyes. She had been fooling herself in thinking she could maintain her composure when she saw Knowlton again. No amount of time would ever make it easy. It had been pure, hellish agony. Every portion of her body screamed for his touch, his caress. She touched her shoulder, where the mark of his fingers still remained. She longed to be in his arms again.

It had been sheer madness for her to think she could enter the elevated reaches of the *ton*. She did not belong here, for she did not have the skill to play the game. Like a foolish young chit, she had lost her heart to Knowlton, and neither shimmering dresses nor glittering jewels could ease the aching pain of knowing he would never be hers. A wiser woman would have been able to match Knowlton's indifference with her own, conducted a discreet affair, and not have lost a night's sleep when it was over. But she could not overcome the rigid upbringing of her childhood that easily. She had veered so very close, but she had wavered out of love—an emotion most of the *ton* held in disdain. No, she was not meant to live in this world. And knowing she would eventually encounter Knowlton again in town, she only wanted to flee to the furthest reaches of the island.

Knowlton went directly from his talk with Kate to the door, ordering his carriage brought round immediately. He stood on the steps, the cool night air working like a bucket of cold water on his overheated soul.

How could one simple kiss disconcert him so? He half-believed she was a witch. He had kissed her not above a dozen times, and the memories of those encounters were burned into his brain as if they had been lovers for years. What strange hold did Kate Mayfield have over him that no other woman had ever had?

Scowling, he stepped into his carriage. He needed a woman. Badly. It was the only cure to this madness that held him in its grip. One night in the arms of a skilled practitioner of the art of love would wipe out all memories of his modest little widow. He leaned out and gave his coachman the address of a house in the north end of Mayfair. He would find what he needed there. By morning his desire for Kate Mayfield would be only a dim memory.

17

One struggle more, and I am free
 From pangs that rend my heart in twain;
One last long sigh to love and thee,
Then back to busy life again.
                    —Byron, *One Struggle More, and I Am Free*

"Mama, Mama!" Robbie bounced exuberantly into the front drawing room. "Atlas is here. In the mews."

A sharp shaft of pain shot through Katherine and she closed the book in her lap. One more reminder of Knowlton to add to her torment. And a reprimand to her as well. She should have sent for Atlas as soon as she and Robbie were ensconced at the Winslow house. But she had hesitated to make Knowlton aware of her present location. He must have sent word to Warrenton the morning after the ball. "How nice of Lord Knowlton to have arranged such a thing."

"May I ride in the park today?"

"I do not think you are quite ready for riding yet, Robbie." She ignored the pleading look in his face. There would be time and enough for riding after his leg had healed further.

"Of course he is," the marquess said, peering over the top of his newspaper. "You are coddling the lad."

Katherine's lips compressed into a thin line. "Perhaps you are right."

"Of course I am right," the marquess chortled. "Get Hodges to saddle up your pony and take you to the park, lad."

Robbie glanced nervously at his mother. "May I?"

She nodded reluctantly. Robbie gave her a swift hug and raced out of the room as quickly as he had arrived.

"Must you contradict me at every turn?" she demanded icily of the marquess when Robbbie was gone.

"Only when I think you are doing the lad no favors," the

marquess retorted. "He's been clinging behind your skirts long enough. If he's to be off to school next year, he will need some toughening up."

"And you think that teaching him disrespect for his mother is going to help?" Katherine cringed at the shrill tone of her voice.

"You saw how he looked to you for the final word," the marquess said. "He still knows who is in command."

Katherine sighed. It did seem petty, arguing over these minor points. But every day they remained in this house, she felt her control over Robbie undermined at every turn. The longer they remained, the more she would be pushed into the background. She yearned for the freedom of her own establishment. Tomorrow, maybe, she would broach the subject with the marquess. They had availed themselves of his hospitality for far too long. She was eager to be out of the city—particularly now that she knew Knowlton was here.

"You are sorely blue-deviled of late," the marquess said, scowling. "Order the carriage and go shopping. Always used to put the marchioness in a better frame of mind."

"There is nothing I have a need for. You have provided me with so much already." There was a hint of reproach in her voice. She could not help but feel she was living on the marquess's charity.

"Go visiting, then. Castalia will welcome you. You are giving me the fidgets."

Katherine considered the idea. "Perhaps I will," she said slowly, setting her book on the table. There was little else to occupy her time. She was rapidly discovering just how dull life as a "lady of leisure" could be. It was difficult to remain glum in the young countess's presence. Castalia could charm anyone out of the crotchets.

Katherine was forced to admit she did feel better after talking with Castalia. Infectious gaiety and amusing gossip were exactly what Katherine's bruised spirits needed. And despite her earlier protestations, she was quite willing to join her sister-in-law for a morning of shopping. Anything to keep her mind off that disastrous meeting with Knowlton. She began to understand why so many matrons overspent their allowances. A new parasol overcame a multitude of hurts.

Upon exiting the shop where Castalia had ordered another two winter bonnets, Katherine recognized Lady Wentworth alighting from a carriage.

"Elizabeth!" she cried joyfully.

Lady Wentworth looked bemused for a moment and then recognition creased her face. "Katherine! Whatever are you doing in London?"

"It is a complicated tale," Katherine replied, turning to Castalia. "Are you acquainted with my sister-in-law, Lady Durham? This is the Countess Wentworth."

"It is a pleasure to meet you," replied Elizabeth. "But how is she your sister-in-law?"

"My deceased husband was a son of the marquess of Winslow," Katherine confessed.

"Oh," said Elizabeth, her eyes widening. "And you never told me. Shame on you, Katherine."

"The marquess and I had not been on friendly terms for years," Katherine explained defensively. She did not miss the slight hurt in Elizabeth's eyes, and felt a pang of regret for having deceived her friend.

"And now you are?"

Katherine nodded.

Elizabeth raised a questioning brow. "Does Knowlton know?"

Katherine did not miss Castalia's unveiled look of interest at the mention of the earl's name. "He does," she replied softly, hoping Elizabeth would say no more.

"What a delightful surprise this all is," Elizabeth said. "I insist you visit tomorrow and tell me the whole story."

"Are you to be in town long?"

"Somers insisted that we come up, since I have been too wrapped up with Caro to even care much for society this last year." Elizabeth laughed. "Spending the Little Season in town is my penance."

"Did you bring Caro with you?" Katherine had grown fond of the little girl during her stay at Warrenton.

"Of course. And you will have to visit her as well tomorrow. The town nursery is a great big barn of a room, but she has settled in rather well. I shall see you then. Lady Durham." Elizabeth nodded her farewell and continued on her way.

Castalia said nothing until she and Katherine were seated in the carriage.

"You did not tell me you were acquainted with Lord Knowlton." The reproof in her voice was strong.

Katherine ducked her head deferentially. "We were merely neighbors."

"Katherine!"

"Robbie and I rented a cottage on his estate," Katherine said quickly. Elizabeth would keep her counsel. Castalia would not. She had no need to know about what was now firmly in the past. "He was very kind to Robbie."

"Knowlton never struck me as the type who would put himself out for a small boy." Castalia surveyed Katherine with open suspicion.

"I own his reputation with women is dreadful, but he is well-thought-of at his home." Katherine felt odd defending the man who once wished to make her his mistress. But it was the truth. Just as she had come to know the Knowlton who lay beneath the cynical exterior, she wanted Castalia to know that there was more to him than his reputation allowed. "He is a conscientious landlord, liked by both tenants and neighbors."

"What stories I will have to tell the *ton*." Castalia's eyes twinkled. "The dreadful Lord Knowlton befriends young boys, widows in distress, and farmers."

"Do not say anything," Katherine pleaded quickly. She did not want her name linked to Knowlton's in any manner. He would detest such gossip as much as she.

Castalia eyed her curiously but said no more.

Katherine was pleased to find Caro with Elizabeth when she arrived at their elegant Grosvenor Square house the following morning. She played games with the girl for half an hour before Caro was returned to the nursery.

"Now, tell me about your estrangement from the marquess,"

Elizabeth eagerly leaned forward in her chair. "It all sounds so deliciously mysterious!"

"It is all rather silly, in retrospect," Katherine said, shaking her head in self-deprecation. "Winslow was less than delighted when Robert and I eloped, and when Robert was killed, the marquess tried to take Robbie from my care."

"How dreadful!"

"Frederick had not married then, and Robbie was next in line to the title," Katherine explained, although even after six years she still did not completely absolve the marquess for his actions. "Now that Castalia has the boys, Robbie is not so important."

"So the old marquess accepts you now?"

"More for Robbie's sake than mine, I fear." Katherine smiled wryly. "But we are able to tolerate each other. And I cannot complain about his generosity. He is allowing us to make our home with him until Robbie goes to school next year."

"How interesting, to discover such a similarity in our lives. For I was estranged from my family for the longest time, until Somers drew us back together." Elizabeth smiled fondly. "Perhaps that is why we developed such a quick friendship."

Katherine nodded. She had felt it also, that sense of having found a kindred spirit in Elizabeth.

"What are your plans after Robbie goes away to school?"

Katherine contemplated her fingers. "I am not certain. There is a dower house on Winslow's country estate—"

"Do not say you intend to lose yourself in the country again?" Elizabeth's eyes flashed in protest. "You are much too young and pretty to settle for such a thing. You should be on the lookout for another husband."

"The idea does not appeal to me," Katherine replied stiffly. Was she to be badgered on this topic by Elizabeth as well?

"Nonsense. Surely Winslow would set you up with a reasonable dowry. I know any number of men who would be interested, no matter what size settlement you brought." She gave Katherine a sidelong glance. "Although I rather thought that you and Knowlton—"

"There was never anything between the earl and me," Katherine interjected hastily.

"And pigs fly," Elizabeth retorted. "I am not blind, Katherine. I noticed the way he looked at you. And the way you viewed him in return."

"Knowlton has no inclination to marry," Katherine said, more vehemently than she intended.

"And you wish it otherwise, don't you?" Elizabeth squeezed Katherine's hand in sympathy. "Are you dreadfully fond of him?"

Katherine nodded, swallowing against the lump in her throat. "I know it is pure folly, but I could not help myself. He has such a dreadful reputation, but he is one of the warmest, most caring men I have ever known."

"I shall have to speak to him and knock some sense into that brain of his."

Katherine grabbed Elizabeth's hand. "Do not! He never misrepresented his intentions. I have only myself to blame for my foolishness."

"Do not worry, Katherine. I will say nothing to Knowlton if you do not wish it. But I still insist the man is a fool to allow you to slip from his fingers."

"He is doing it of his own volition."

"Have you seen him in town? Does he know of your connection with Winslow?"

Katherine nodded. "Knowlton is determined to remain free from the chains of wedlock," she said, a thread of sadness in her voice. "There is nothing I can do to change the situation. So I have resolved to think of him no more."

"Then we shall have to find you a husband elsewhere," Elizabeth announced emphatically. "I am certain there will be several suitable candidates in town this fall. This makes me look forward to the Season even more."

"I do not wish to marry again," Katherine protested, knowing that it would be as futile to argue with Elizabeth as it had been with Castalia. Trust her luck to have fallen in with such confirmed matchmakers.

"We shall see," Elizabeth said dryly. "Now that you have family around you, I assume it is too much to expect that you will visit with us over Christmas."

"I own I had not thought that far ahead," Katherine said.

"I do not know what sort of celebration the family plans. I would like to visit you.''

"It will be quite sedate, I fear.'' Elizabeth leaned closer and patted her abdomen. ''It seems we are to be blessed with a permanent reminder of our stay at Warrenton.''

Katherine winced inwardly at Elizabeth's happy news. Another joy she would never experience again. ''How wonderful,'' she said with unfeigned enthusiasm to Elizabeth, and the conversation turned toward domestic matters.

Knowlton expertly guided his prancing stallion through the empty park lanes. The early-morning gallop went far to restore his equanimity and clear his head, as did the cool morning air. His thinking had been woefully fuzzy these last few days, since seeing Katherine again.

It had been more than a shock to discover that his prim little widow was connected with one of the premier families in the realm. He felt a measure of satisfaction in knowing that his dishonorable pursuit had driven her back into the secure hold of her husband's relatives. They would take good care of her. It was the one thing he had worried about when he discovered Kate's precipitate flight—that she would be in want. Knowing now that she was well-taken-care-of, he could rid his mind of her once and for all.

He chose to ignore the fact that he had thought the same thing at Lady Durham's, when he had hastened from the ball into the arms of one of London's leading Cyprians. If that liaison had proved less than satisfactory, it could only be because of his disordered mood. The lovely lady had performed with admirable skill and talent, and he had merely not been in the proper frame of mind to appreciate it. He suspected he would be more entranced with the lovely opera dancer he planned to see tonight. He had deliberately waited a few days to make his conquest of her, knowing how well anticipation whetted his appetite. He had no doubts that tonight's adventure would be very pleasurable.

''Knowlton! Knowlton!''

The earl's head twisted around to identify his importuning caller.

"Robbie!" A genuine smile crossed Knowlton's face at the sight of the tousled red head. Knowlton reined in his mount and watched with amusement as Robbie bounced along on his pony, a groom dutifully trailing behind him.

"Thank you for sending Atlas! It is ever so wonderful to be back on him again."

"He was eating me out of hay and oats." Knowlton laughed. "How is your leg?" Healing properly?"

Robbie nodded. "Mama did not want me to start riding so soon, but my grandfather said I could. Do you know I have a grandfather who is a marquess?"

"Yes, I do," Knowlton said. "It must be pleasant to discover you have a family."

Robbie considered. "Well, Grandpapa is nice, and I like Aunt Castalia and Uncle Frederick. But most of the cousins, well, they are either girls or babies."

Knowlton laughed inwardly at the note of disgust in Robbie's voice. It would not be many years before he changed his view.

"I did not know you were in London," Robbie said with a faint hint of accusation in his voice.

"It was an unexpected trip," Knowlton lied. He keenly felt the boy's disappointment. He had not stopped to consider how the break with Katherine also affected his relationship with Robbie. "Are you practicing your chess and whist?"

Robbie scowled. "Grandpapa will not play with me. Uncle Frederick played a game of chess with me last week, but he is not at our house very often." His face brightened hopefully. "Could you come to the house and play with me?"

Knowlton winced at that plea. "I am afraid not, Robbie." The lad's crestfallen face smote him. He must do something for the boy. "Perhaps there is something else you and I could do together. Have you been to Astley's yet?"

Robbie shook his head, his eyes widening with hope. "Will you take me?"

"You shall have to ask your mother," Knowlton said. "If she approves, we shall go. Ask her if Tuesday will be acceptable."

"Oh, I am certain it will be." Robbie's face beamed with pleasure at the anticipated treat.

Knowlton felt a twinge of regret for the relationship that must, by necessity, die away. Robbie was a good lad. In other circumstances, Knowlton would not mind keeping up the friendship. But it took only one glimpse of Robbie's unruly red hair to bring the image of his mother to mind. He would take him to Astley's to soothe his conscience. Robbie would gradually acquire his own circle of friends and not need him anymore.

"Send a note round to Upper Brook Street when you find out," Knowlton said. "And you be careful with that leg. We don't want you laid up again."

"Yes, sir," said Robbie. "Thank you again for sending Atlas."

"My pleasure." Knowlton touched his hat and urged his horse forward. He could feel Robbie's hero-worshipping gaze boring into his back as he trotted down the path. Damn!

It had not seemed to be such a bad idea back at Warrenton, befriending the boy as he had. Even if he and Katherine had not made an arrangement, Robbie could have come and gone as he pleased at the house. But here in London, with eyes and ears everywhere . . . Any attention he directed at Robbie would be instantly scrutinized and analyzed with an eye to his mother. From Lady Durham's introductions at that disastrous ball, it was quite apparent that Kate had said nothing of him to her new family. He hoped that the revelation of this chance meeting with Robbie would not cause her distress.

He knew that Kate would not like the proposed trip to Astley's, but hoped that she, like him, would see the necessity of a gradual sundering of his ties with Robbie. As he and his mother were drawn deeper into the Winslow circle, there would be little need for Knowlton to entertain the boy. And Knowlton was certain that Robbie would be headed off to school soon, which would effectively solve the whole problem. There was no deep cause for concern.

Then why was he filled with such regret?

18

Is it thy will thy image should keep open
My heavy eyelids to the weary night?
—Shakespeare, *Sonnet 61*

The death of the old queen brought an abrupt halt to Katherine's debut into society. Not that the *ton* called a complete stop to their entertainments. The theaters closed for a respectable length of time, and dancing parties were curtailed, but little else changed—except the necessity of acquiring an entire new mourning wardrobe.

However, the Winslow circle considered the event a chance to retreat to the country earlier than planned, so before December arrived, Katherine found herself back where she had longed to be—in the English countryside. To her dismay, the removal from London did not bring her the peace of mind she desired. She had thought that in the country, with no chance of another awkward encounter with Knowlton, she would be free from her memories. But it proved otherwise. Perhaps it was because her only other visit to the country home of the Winslows had been in Robert's company, and had ended with the permanent breach between father and son. There were no fond remembrances here to lull her into serenity.

And the country brought with it too many memories of the summer and fall in Lincolnshire. London was not fraught with experiences shared with Knowlton. But the country abounded with reminders. Neatly tilled fields evoked the heated days of harvest. The well-tended flowerbeds suggested the garden at Warrenton, where she and Knowlton had walked and talked, and where he had kissed her for the first time. And every sight of Robbie and his precious pony brought Knowlton's face to mind.

Even the gaiety of the Christmas and Twelfth Night celebrations did not soothe her spirits. Katherine treasured no fond memories of such opulent markers of the season; Christmas in the rectory had been a time for quiet reflection, and there had been only one Christmas with Robert. Like everything else, the Winslows celebrated the season with uncommon enthusiasm. Katherine allowed herself to be drawn into the merriment, accepting chaste kisses from her relatives under the kissing ball, playing charades long into the night. But her enthusiasm was forced. The country did not bring the enjoyment she had hoped for.

Yet she loathed the idea of returning to the city even more. Indeed, she managed to find any number of excuses to remain in the country while the rest of the family drifted back to the city. Castalia's younger son developed the sniffles and Katherine volunteered to stay with him when the marquess returned to town for the opening of Parliament. Unfortunately, Castalia decided to remain as well, so Katherine was not freed from her sister-in-law's determined plans for her future. At least there was little opportunity for them to be put into action while Katherine remained out of town.

The long months of separation did little to dim her memories of Knowlton. Katherine did not think there were enough years left in her life for that to occur. But she reached an accommodation of sorts with her wayward heart. The sharp pain of the early parting receded into a dull ache, and she realized one day that she no longer thought of him every hour. Yet memories flooded back over her at the oddest times. The first spring flowers peeking their heads aboveground reminded her of the Harvest Home, when they had walked in his garden and he had promised to send her bulbs. The aroma of brandy brought back their lengthy cozy chats in the library at Warrenton. And every fond glance exchanged between Castalia and Frederick reminded Katherine with a pang that she was quite alone.

When at last the countess announced that Katherine simply must accompany her to London, she could not bring herself to refuse. Particularly since Robbie had been begging her with every breath to return to the fascination of the city. With children and tutor in tow, they made the journey.

* * *

Knowlton grimaced with relief as his carriage clattered down the driveway. He had endured enough country parties to last him for the remainder of his life. The forced conviviality of the drawing room before dinner drove him mad, the mad scramble for partners in the long hours between dinner and bed grew tedious. Even cold, dirty, midwinter London held a greater appeal. In the house at Upper Brook Street, he could lock himself away for days at a time without fear of interruption. If he went a week without seeing another face, he would not complain.

His face twisted into a grimace. Holidays were an intolerable invention. The insistence on trying to outdo all others in Christmas cheerfulness escaped his understanding. There was not much to be gay about during this dark time of the year, when one was tucked away in some damp, cold house in some wretched corner of the country, where the chimneys smoked, the ladies giggled inanely, and the food was bland. He should have stayed at Warrenton.

But it was precisely Warrenton he wanted to avoid when he had ill-advisedly accepted all those invitations in December. He did not want to spend any more time in the empty corridors, with the ghost of Kate still haunting them the way she haunted his mind. In the company of other revelers, surely he would easily forget her.

Yet even in the midst of the largest groups, his thoughts often strayed to her, quite against his will. At the oddest moments something would trigger his memory, and images of Kate would torture his mind. Her embarrassment when he had bared his chest in front of her at harvest. Her gentle chiding over his past excesses when they talked long into the night at Warrenton. That first, lingering kiss in the garden.

Never had a woman so filled his mind for such a length of time. Usually women were nothing more than amusing creatures who provided entertainment and pleasure and then were forgotten as quickly as they had come. But Kate . . .

It was her abrupt departure from Warrenton, the long weeks of worry and anger, and the final discovery of her subterfuge that so embellished her memory. She was the first woman in years to have refused him, and he theorized it was that which made her so unforgettable. Had matters run their normal course, he would have grown tired of her and brought their liaison to an end. The fact that *she* had ended it, before it had barely begun, rankled.

He shrugged. Ah, well. London lay at the end of the road, a city full of the most beautiful and willing women in the world. He was bound to find another to capture his fancy before more than a few days passed. His attempts last year had been too halfhearted. This time he would find a lady who could drive even the memory of his own name from his brain.

The difference between the Little Season last fall and the full Season of the spring quickly became evident to Katherine. Invitations arrived at St. James Square in a never-ending stream. She thought that by staying with the marquess she would draw little attention, but those she had met in the fall were eager to see her again and those who had not were curious about the widow. Katherine limited her attendance to those events that either the marquess or the Durhams graced with their presence. She was determined to preserve the mantle of respectability she had paid for so dearly.

Katherine inwardly groaned when she saw Castalia bearing down on her at Lady Winthrop's musicale. She had hoped to spend at least one night free from her sister-in-law's matchmaking. Be it musicale or rout, Castalia never abandoned any opportunity to present Katherine with promising suitors.

"Katherine, dear, I would like you to meet Lord Belton." Castalia grabbed Katherine's hand and virtually dragged her across the carpeted music room. "He is a viscount, dreadfully plump in the pockets, and most polite."

"He sounds irresistible," Katherine said through gritted teeth.

"Belton! How nice to see you this evening. A sad crush, is it not?" Castalia beamed in anticipation. "I must make you known to my sister-in-law, Lady Robert Mayfield. Poor Robert was killed in the Peninsula, you know, leaving Katherine alone with a small child." Castalia attempted to stiffle a sigh. "Katherine has done such a marvelous job raising the lad on her own, but we are well pleased she has joined us in London at last."

Katherine turned three shades of red at Castalia's ridiculous babbling. It made her sound like some bedraggled heroine in a poorly written tragedy. She simply must have a long talk with her sister-in-law.

"Lady Robert." Belton bowed low in greeting.

"My lord." Katherine fitted a polite social smile on her face. He looked exactly as one of Castalia's candidates would—conservative dress, a pleasing but not overly handsome countenance, and an aura of placid respectability.

"Oh, there is Lady Wallace. I must speak with her." With a wave of her fan, Castalia flitted across the room.

Katherine dared to raise her eyes to Lord Belton's and was struck by the look of amusement in the blue depths.

"I am afraid Lady Durham is—"

"As transparent as a sheet of glass?" Lord Belton offered. They broke into shared laughter.

"She almost had me wishing to make a donation to the poor widows' fund," Katherine confessed, taking a closer look at the viscount. His light-brown hair was nearly the shade Robert's had been. "I pray that you will not hold her dramatics against me, my lord."

"Not at all. I have known Lady Durham long enough to know to discount three-quarters of what she says. However, one must pay attention to the other quarter. You have a son, then? How old is he?"

"Eleven," Katherine replied.

"And probably a bundle of mischief, if I remember life at that age," Lord Belton said kindly.

Katherine smiled. "That he is. But I am certain you do not wish to hear of my son, my lord. Are you in town for business or pleasure?"

"I am not certain," he said. "I came up last week for an auction, intending to stay for only a short while, but I might have reason to reconsider that plan."

Katherine vainly fought against her blush at the appreciative look she saw in his eyes. "What type of auction did you attend?"

"A book sale. An unfortunate gentleman outspent his income and was selling off his library."

"You must be a collector of books, then." Katherine relaxed

slightly. There was something comforting in such an innocuous endeavor.

He smiled. " 'Collector' may be too formal a term. 'Accumulator' is more apt. I do not have many rare or fine works, but I like them all the same.''

"Do you collect books on special topics?''

Belton shook his head. "Whatever strikes my fancy, I am afraid. Or whatever is offered for sale. But certainly, Lady Robert, you did not plan to discuss books when you attended a musicale. Did you enjoy the soloist?''

"I own I am rather indifferent to operatic airs,'' she admitted with a rueful smile.

"I also!'' Belton looked around in mock dismay. "But it would not do either of our reputations good to have that overheard.''

Katherine laughed again.

"Did you plan to eat with the Durhams, or may I take you in to supper?''

His suggestion delighted Katherine. It was wonderful to find someone she enjoyed conversing with. "I should like that very much,'' she said, extending him her hand.

As they entered the supper room, Katherine felt a moment's hesitation, remembering Castalia's deliberate maneuverings to bring her together with Lord Belton. Then she willed herself to relax. Lord Belton *was* nice and it was foolish for her to deny herself pleasant company out of some vague apprehension. He was certainly the least intimidating man Castalia had introduced to her.

Katherine was not certain how it happened, but over the next few weeks it seemed she saw more and more of Lord Belton. It was rarely by prearrangement. Oh, he took her for an occasional drive in the park and even consented to accompany her and Robbie on a visit to the British Museum. Katherine still retained the Durhams' escort to the parties she attended, and they always saw her home, but she found she spent more and more time in Lord Belton's company during the intervening hours. If she entertained suspicions about Castalia's connivance in alerting Belton to their plans, she did not complain.

She did enjoy his company. He was amusing, modest, and eminently likable. What was more, Katherine felt totally safe in his company. He treated her with polite circumspection, and any fears she may have entertained about his interest in her soon faded after hours of his unexceptionable company. He made no untoward moves, treating her in the same refined manner he did Castalia. Katherine even dared to look forward to seeing him whenever she went out.

Katherine genuinely began to enjoy herself in the hectic social world of London. She dampened the pretensions of any importuning men she met, and could always rely on Castalia, Lord Durham, or the marquess to provide her with protection if she needed it.

Tonight's fete was a severe crush, which of course made it a great success. Katherine fanned herself unsuccessfully, too hot and uncomfortable to concentrate on Castalia's bright chatter. It had been a long week and she looked forward to spending tomorrow night at home. Robbie had complained more than once that he saw little of his mother. She felt a nagging guilt at her unintended neglect and resolved to spend more time with him. In the fall he would be away at school and she would seldom see him.

Katherine's languidly waving fan hesitated fractionally as she caught a glimpse of Knowlton across the room. The mere sight of him caused a tingling awareness to sweep over her body. Forcefully, she willed herself to calm. It was inevitable that they would encounter each other in society; they could certainly behave in an amiable manner when it happened. That thought did little to still the pounding of her heart. Dismayed at her reaction, she turned and addressed an innocuous remark to Castalia.

Normally Katherine enjoyed listening to Castalia's artful prattle, but she was no longer in the mood for any polite chatter. Her glimpse of Knowlton had ruined the evening for her. She was torn between expectation and dread that she would suddenly find him at her shoulder. How could she decently extricate herself and return home?

She almost collapsed in relief when she saw Lord Belton standing at the door, looking about with an air of expectant anticipation. But when she saw the smile of recognition that lit his face when he spotted her, she felt the tiniest qualm in her stomach. It seemed . . . No, she was reading too much into an innocent smile. She would have greeted him in the same way if she had picked him out in a crowded room. She valued his friendship, as he did hers. There was nothing more to their relationship than that.

"Lady Durham, Lady Robert." Belton greeted them with an affable smile. "A sad crush, is it not?"

Castalia nodded. "I am certain Lady Steventon had no intention of hosting half of London here tonight."

"If I may offer my assistance in trying to clear a path to the refreshments . . . ?"

Castalia shot a knowing glance at Katherine. "We would be most delighted, my lord."

Katherine dutifully followed them into the crowded supper room, where Belton appropriated three chairs. She fidgeted with her gloves while she waited for his return. Why, of all nights, had Knowlton chosen this one to appear? Her initial relief at seeing Belton soon changed to dismay. She felt uncomfortable at the idea of Knowlton seeing them together, which was in itself ridiculous. One could not read into the situation that which was not there.

Katherine stifled the thought with a surge of anger. It did not matter *what* Knowlton thought. If he even thought of her at all. A man who only wanted her for his mistress would have little reaction if he saw her receiving the attentions of another. Katherine smiled weakly. It might even please him to discover he need not fear any chastisement for his dishonorable proposal. She knew that fear had been uppermost in his mind when he first discovered her identity. Let him see he no longer concerned her either.

Katherine talked herself into a state of composure until she saw Knowlton enter the supper room—this time in the company of an exquisitely beautiful lady. She nudged Castalia.

"Who is that with Knowlton?"

Castalia turned and stared boldly, to Katherine's chagrin. "Do not be so obvious," she commanded.

A mischievous smile flitted across Castalia's face. "That is

Lady Taunton. A lovely lady, married at a young age to an aging lord who then conveniently died, leaving her a *very* rich widow.''

"Do you know her well?"

Castalia wrinkled her nose. "She is not, shall we say, of the highest *ton*. She is much more popular among the gentleman than their ladies."

"Is she Knowlton's mistress?" Katherine asked bluntly, inwardly berating herself for wanting to know.

Castalia shrugged. "Who knows? It is said Lady Taunton prefers to have several men at her beck and call at any one time. Goodness, you know Knowlton better than I. Why do you not ask him?"

Belton's arrival with their food saved Katherine the necessity of a reply. She looked up and thanked him with a radiant smile.

Knowlton sensed Katherine's presence in the crowded saloon even before he saw her in the far corner of the room. God, she looked beautiful tonight. Every time he saw her she looked even more ravishing, her creamy white skin begging to be touched, her golden-red hair a living, glowing flame. Involuntarily, his body responded.

He struggled against his impulse to glower across the room at Belton, who bent over Katherine in a very proprietary way. Damn, he had no right to feel this way. He knew perfectly well why she had rejected him. No respectable lady would entertain an offer such as he had made. It had been a grievous insult.

And if respectability was what Kate truly wanted, she could not do better than Belton. Knowlton doubted the viscount would even dare to kiss a woman without having first offered a declaration of marriage. And marriage, the one thing he himself was unprepared to give her, was what Katherine wanted most of all. So let her look for it elsewhere—in Belton she had a likely candidate.

"I am feeling sadly neglected, Knowlton." Lady Taunton's voice was soft in his ear.

"You were the one who insisted on coming here tonight," he growled. "I told you I would be a poor substitute for Seb."

"You also promised Seb to keep me entertained while he was

gone," she warned. "He will not be pleased if I expire from boredom before he returns."

"I am sure Seb will be reasonable about the matter," Knowlton drawled in bored tones.

She rapped him on the arm with her fan. "You are incorrigible." Lady Taunton glanced quickly across the room. "Who is the fair lady who inspires such a look of gloom upon your face? Surely not Lady Durham—apart from being a widgeon, she is boringly happy in her marriage. Perhaps the lovely redhead at her side?" She smiled as Knowlton's scowl deepened.

"And Belton is so attentive. Do not tell me you two are engaged in a rivalry for the favors of such a striking lady?"

"Not at all," Knowlton said smoothly, taking her arm and steering her out of the room. "No lady who could be content with Belton's placid nature would ever interest me."

19

Fill for me a brimming bowl
And let me in it drown my soul:
But put therein some drug, designed
To banish woman from my mind.
                    —Keats, *Fill for Me a Brimming Bowl*

"Look, Mama, there is Knowlton!"

Katherine looked across the park to where Robbie pointed, then quickly averted her eyes from the two mounted riders.

Damn him. Why today, of all days, did she have to encounter him in the park, when she was in the presence of both Robbie and Lord Belton? Robbie would demand to stop, Belton would notice her discomfort. He would be too polite to ask why, but he would wonder just the same. She looked up, startled, when she felt the carriage speed up.

"Why did we not stop?" Robbie asked plaintively.

Belton exchanged a quick embarrassed look with Katherine. "I do not think your mama wished to," he said quietly.

Katherine clenched her fists to resist the urge to swivel her head around and catch a better glimpse of the woman who rode at Knowlton's side. She wished she had taken a longer look when she had the opportunity. Belton's reaction left her with no doubt of the woman's status.

So. Knowlton was openly displaying his latest mistress in the park. At least Katherine now knew he entertained no regrets for her refusal. He had obviously found a suitable replacement.

Katherine remained quiet as they returned to the house in St. James. Robbie bounded from the carriage while Katherine waited for Belton to assist her.

"Thank you," she said, giving him a grateful smile.

"I did not want to place you in an awkward situation," he said. "I did not know how best to explain things to your son."

She sighed. "I imagine that it is time he learned of such matters."

Belton cleared his throat. "If you like, I could . . . I could explain the situation to him."

Katherine was touched by his offer, yet felt a twinge of apprehension at the same time. It was not the action of a casual friend—and she hesitated to think of him as more than that. "Thank you, my lord, but I believe that is something I will have to undertake on my own—unless Robbie grows uncomfortable. I will certainly not hesitate to send him to you with questions in that event, if you do not object."

"I would be most willing to assist you," Belton said, pressing her fingers slightly.

Katherine gathered her wits and edged away toward the house. "Thank you for the drive. I look forward to the theater tonight."

"So do I," said Belton as he climbed back into the carriage and drove away.

Why had she felt the need to feign enthusiasm for their outing tonight? At times, she found Belton's solicitous kindness overwhelming. She was grateful and appreciative, but also felt guilty that those were her only reactions to his attentions. His tentative squeeze of her fingers had not sent a thrill of delight up her spine. His offer to explain the role of impure ladies to Robbie had been generous, but bordered on an intimacy with her family that she was not certain she wished to acknowledge.

Why was it that whenever she began to imagine she could find some form of happiness with Belton, or someone like him, Knowlton always appeared on the scene and exposed her wishes for the lies they were? He loomed as a nemesis in her life, unwilling to free her from his unnatural hold. She had never been one to pursue lost causes, but for some reason her heart had been frozen forever with the image of Knowlton engraved upon it. She fought, railed, and kicked against his hold, but she could not free herself from his grasp.

And now he flaunted his present mistress in front of all the town, a constant reminder to Katherine that he had once intended her for that role. It only marked her failure as complete. She had been nothing more than a passing fancy to him. How she wished she could say the same of Knowlton. Memories of that torrid embrace at Warrenton were ground into every fiber of her body. She could no more cut them away than she could cut off a finger or toe. Would she have to live with them for the remainder of her life?

By the time she had reached her room, Katherine felt the beginning of an enormous headache. Her temples throbbed and it was all she could do to grit her teeth and endure while the maid helped her from her dress. Katherine gratefully curled up in a ball and pulled the covers over her head to shut out the world.

The last person Knowlton had expected to encounter in the park that morning was Katherine—and Robbie. What fool impulse had guided him into taking that Cyprian riding? He had been less than enchanted at their first dealings, but since that seemed to be his reaction to every woman he took to bed these days, he had decided to give her another chance. By the time they returned to her set of rooms, any flickerings of desire had fled. He gave her a vague promise of a future engagement, and returned the horses to the mews.

What was wrong with him? This was a thousand times worse than his *ennui* of the previous spring. Then, it had been a general but vague dissatisfaction. Now it was a yawning chasm of disinterest. He had spent the better part of a month working his way through the muslin company, and not one single woman had inspired him to a repeat visit. In fact, he had more than once been inclined to depart before the activities commenced. But he soldiered on, needing to prove to himself that this was only a temporary aberration.

And what was worse, these numerous liaisons did little to slake his burning need. His expression darkened. Even at the moment of release, he felt the dissatisfaction welling up within him again, his desires unsatisfied. Not since Kate . . .

As he entered his bedchamber he ripped off his cravat and flung it across the dressing table in a fit of anger. There was nothing special about her. It had only been that long, seductive courtship that had heightened his interest so. He laughed derisively. How could he possibly compare a few fumbling kisses with a prim-and-proper widow to the pleasures of the most skilled courtesans of the city? It was obvious that his mind merely exaggerated the effect of Kate's kisses.

He only needed to look to her escort to convince himself of that. Belton was as dull a fellow as he could imagine—and it seemed every time he saw Kate she was in the prosy bore's company. He laughed harshly. They suited each other. She might be breathtakingly beautiful, but her manner was quite ordinary. She only wanted a respectable husband, a house full of screaming brats, and the usual round of ladies' teas and gossip. He was lucky she had refused him—else he would have been forced to cast her off quite soon, he was certain.

No, he had made a great error in judgment regarding Kate Mayfield. He had allowed lust to blind him to her true nature. It angered him that he had wasted so much time and thought on her.

To her regret, Katherine's headache departed during the long afternoon, and she could devise no valid reason to excuse herself from the theater that evening. A night of Castalia's lighthearted prattle and Belton's increasingly overwhelming attentions would do little to improve her spirits. Despite her misgivings, she found herself that evening seated next to Belton in the marquess's box at Drury Lane.

Katherine sat deep in her own musings throughout the production, oblivious of the words spoken onstage. It was a surprise when the final lights rose and the theatergoers began to stream from their seats.

"You were very quiet tonight," Belton remarked as he escorted her through the corridor.

"I found the play very diverting," she lied smoothly. "Did you not find it so?"

She turned to look at Belton, and was startled to see the man who stood by his side. Katherine's step faltered at the sight of Knowlton and the overdressed woman with him, and she gripped Belton's arm tightly to keep from stumbling.

"Belton, Lady Robert." Knowlton inclined his head in greeting.

In the crowded corridor she was trapped, and short of ignoring him completely, there was little Katherine could do to make her dismay known. Giving Knowlton the cut direct would cause worse gossip than to be spotted here chatting with him as if . . . as if he did not have *that* kind of woman on his arm. She nodded in a fractional acknowledgment.

Appraising the woman at his side, Katherine realized with a shock that it was not the same one he had been with that morning. The brunette was brazenly beautiful, expensively dressed, and clinging to Knowlton's arm as if her life depended upon it. Which it might, Katherine thought wryly, remembering how generous his offer to her had been.

She was grateful for Belton's gentle tug on her arm. Katherine could not have consciously moved.

Knowlton smiled his mocking grin. "So nice to see you again, Lady Robert." He stepped aside to let them pass.

"The nerve of that man." Belton was furious. "The insult to you . . ."

"I did not perceive it as such," Katherine replied, trying to compose her own shattered nerves. Had Knowlton sought her out deliberately to flaunt his lightskirt before her? Did he taunt her on purpose, showing her that he had no problem finding other women to fill his bed?

"It was not at all the thing."

"The less said, the better," Katherine replied curtly, which only had the effect of eliciting an odd glance from Belton. She firmly directed her gaze straight ahead. This day had been an unmitigated disaster and she only wished to go home.

But the mansion in St. James Square provided no refuge, and Katherine lay awake long into the night. Today had been full of revelations. Knowlton was certainly doing nothing to demonstrate the qualities that had so endeared him to her. In fact, it looked as if he was embarking on a course of dissipation that surpassed even his own reputation—two ladies in one day! It was outside of enough to have been in Belton's presence at both encounters.

Belton's reaction to each situation gave her pause. He cared for her, she knew. There was every likelihood he would make her an offer. Katherine only wished to stay his hand for a while longer, until she could bring some semblance of order to her confused mind. She was in no position to make any critical decisions right now.

Especially since she had discovered just how strong her feelings for Knowlton still were. It would take only the slightest encouragement from him to bring them to the fore again. She had thought she had resigned herself to the situation. After all, he had brutally dashed all her hopes with his cold-blooded offer of protection. She wondered if there was any way to accomplish that task. She would pay gladly for the solution.

Over the next weeks it seemed she encountered Knowlton everywhere. He was often in the park, driving a carriage or riding alongside a changing panoply of women, each lovelier than the last. At the parties where their kind would not be welcome, he was seen at the side of various ladies about whom rumors circulated, but who still were held to be of the highest *ton*. The only mote of comfort Katherine could derive from all this was that she rarely saw him with the same woman twice. Was that significant? Or was he just embarking on a new streak of licentiousness that would put his old reputation to shame?

The unexpected arrival in town of Elizabeth and her husband was one of the few bright spots in Katherine's existence. She eagerly accepted their invitation to dine, hoping there would be time for a long chat with Elizabeth.

"I am so pleased you could come on such short notice," Elizabeth greeted Katherine warmly. "I had no intention of being in London this spring, but when Somers needed to come to town, I decided to accompany him. It may be my last chance to get out in a while!"

Katherine smiled warmly as Elizabeth patted the notable bulge in her abdomen. She had missed Elizabeth's company, particularly over the last month, as her misery over Knowlton grew.

"I understand you have acquired a very attentive suitor." Elizabeth's voice was teasing.

Katherine ducked her head modestly. "It is an unexceptionable relationship."

"Unexceptionable?" Elizabeth laughed heartily. "Katherine,

the entire town is talking about you and Belton. I would not be surprised to find it in the betting book at White's.''

Anger crossed Katherine's face. ''Do not those silly men have better things to do with their time?''

Elizabeth patted her hand. ''Now, now. You must admit that your mysterious appearance last fall had all the tongues wagging. People were bound to notice, whatever you did.''

''How many are coming for dinner tonight?'' Katherine firmly changed the subject.

''Oh, a few close friends.'' Elizabeth airily waved her hand.

Elizabeth's idea of a ''few'' was slightly different from her own, Katherine shortly discovered, for it numbered closer to twenty. Most were familiar faces, and Katherine soon found herself drawn into conversation.

She had just accepted a glass of wine from her host when a familiar voice caused her to freeze. Knowlton! She was instantly filled with anger. Elizabeth had deliberately not told her he would be here. She scanned the crowded drawing room, trying to catch her friend's eye. Their gazes met momentarily, then Elizabeth looked away in embarrassment. Katherine vowed to give Elizabeth a piece of her mind when they were next alone.

Katherine's discomfort reached new heights when she saw the seating arrangements had placed her on Knowlton's left! She halted beside the table, looking for any other place to sit, but it would have caused a dramatic commotion to displace another. Biting back her anger, she allowed the footman to seat her.

''I believe Elizabeth is playing games this evening.'' Knowlton leaned imperceptibly toward Katherine, speaking in a low undertone.

''Quite,'' she replied stiffly.

''I do not find it a totally intolerable situation. Do you not concur, *Lady* Robert?''

Katherine winced at his inflection. ''You know perfectly well how awkward this is—for both of us.''

''How so?'' His eyes lit mischievously. ''I am never averse to sitting beside a beautiful lady.'' His voice dropped lower. ''And you are exceptionally lovely tonight, Kate.''

"Do not call me that," she hissed, keeping her gaze firmly on her plate.

"My apologies, Lady Robert. I forget you hold a more exalted position these days."

Katherine fought down the overwhelming urge to empty her wineglass over his head. He knew exactly how uncomfortable she was, and he was doing everything he could to make her discomfort worse. She would throttle Elizabeth when this was over.

As if to confound her, Knowlton conversed with her no more for the remainder of the meal. But he made his presence constantly known. With only a hairbreadth of distance between their chairs, it was no challenge for his muscular thigh to press against hers. The first time he made contact, Katherine nearly jumped at the shock to her senses. He turned slightly, surveying her with a mocking grin before returning his attention to the lady on his right. Then all too soon she felt his foot rubbing against her ankle.

"Stop that!" she whispered. He did not indicate he heard, but she no longer felt his touch.

Whatever appetite she had once possessed vanished completely. Katherine toyed with the idea of feigning illness, but such an announcement would only draw unwanted attention. Perhaps if she ignored him . . .

She nearly jumped up from her chair when she felt his fingers stroke sensuously along her leg while he pretended to fumble for his napkin. She quickly slipped her own hand down to her lap, but he caught her fingers in his, squeezing them so tightly she nearly winced.

As the dinner dragged on for an interminable time, Katherine grew close to tears. Why did he seek to humiliate her so? He knew she had put their relationship behind her; knew that when she had refused his offer she had determined on a life that did not include him. She had made her choice; why would he not accept it?

Knowlton kept Katherine under close study. She was thoroughly uncomfortable, he noted with malicious pleasure. He had felt her startled movement when he furtively rubbed her thigh. His touch still had the power to thrill her. Despite the modest front she maintained before the *ton*, it was obvious that there was still a trace of passion left within his wanton little widow. He fought down the heat rising in his own body. He was *firmly* in control of this situation. He only wanted to see how far he could push her. Knowlton blessed Elizabeth's seating arrangement. This was the most entertaining evening he had enjoyed in weeks.

"Pardon me," he said, reaching past Kate for the salt cellar. He made certain his arm brushed against hers. He smiled at the faint flush that rose in her cheeks, and pressed his thigh against her again, watching her heightened color. Lord, she blushed like an angel.

Pretending to pay attention to his food, he surreptitiously watched the gentle rise and fall of her chest. Whoever was making her dresses certainly knew how to set off those snowy breasts to perfection, he thought. Kate was obviously not covering her assets with a demure neckline. Of course, he thought scornfully, she was more likely to snare a husband with such a prominent display of her charms. He rubbed his leg against hers and saw how quickly her breathing increased.

He knew he could get her alone if he wished. Her reaction to him tonight told him she was less indifferent to his presence than she pretended. It might be just the thing to stifle this maddening obsession he had for her. He had the opportunity now to make a very deliberate comparison of her talents. He felt certain she would not live up to his inflated memory.

The more he thought on it, the more he embraced the idea. He could contrive some excuse for drawing her away from the other guests. It would take only a few moments to whisk her away to some unoccupied room, where he could avail himself of another sample. He needed to set his mind at rest about her once and for all. Knowlton grinned in anticipation.

When the ladies at last rose to retire to the drawing room, Katherine immediately sought out Elizabeth.

"What could you have been thinking of to seat me next to Knowlton?" she demanded.

"Oh, dear. Did I create a problem?" Elizabeth was all wide-eyed innocence."

"The man is a total boor," Katherine said bitterly.

"How dreadful." Elizabeth sounded truly sympathetic. "I had thought you were friends, at least."

"We are not," Katherine said stonily. "I feel perfectly dreadful, I have a throbbing headache, and I only wish to go home. Can you order the carriage round?"

Elizabeth nodded. "Wait in the library. I will explain to the other guests that you are unwell." She pressed Katherine's hand. "I am truly sorry. I had no idea I would create such a disaster."

Katherine offered her a woebegone smile. "I know you meant no harm. But he has changed, somehow, from the man I knew last fall, and I do not like the new Knowlton."

After making her way to the library, Katherine gratefully sank into one of the deep upholstered chairs. It would be some minutes before the Wentworths' carriage would be ready to take her home. At least here, in the darkened shadows, she could relax and try to will her headache away.

In the cozy heat of the room, the tension drained from her body and the pounding in her head was reduced to a mild tapping. Katherine lay back in the chair, eyes closed. Shortly she would be home in her own bed; by tomorrow she would feel quite the thing again.

Knowlton slipped silently into the room, grinning at his discovery of Katherine's hiding place. "So this is where you have hidden yourself." He stood before her, hands on hips. "You need not have gone to such great lengths, Kate. You could hardly expect me to ravish you in full view of all the company."

Her eyes snapped open at his mocking tones. "With your behavior at dinner as an example, I would not put such a thing past you," she said, her voice filled with scorn.

"My, we are upset. What you need is a good glass of brandy to relax you." Knowlton turned to the side table and filled two glasses.

Katherine looked down as he forced a tumbler into her hand, and she did not see him circle behind her. She jumped when she felt the touch of his hands on her shoulders.

"Do not touch me." She shrugged out of his grasp.

"Oh, but, Kate, you are so tense. Let me ease the knots from those muscles." He began kneading the base of her neck.

Even with his gloves on, the touch of his fingers sent a delicious thrill dancing through her body. Perhaps if she ignored him he would tire of this new game and go away.

"Drink," he commanded, and she obediently took a swallow from the glass in her hand.

Despite her intentions, Katherine found herself relaxing beneath the ministrations of his hands. A slow languor crept over her as he stroked away the stiffness in her neck. Her eyes drifted shut and her shoulders drooped in a relaxed attitude. She did not move when he removed his hands, feeling almost as if she were floating along on an airy cloud. Then she jumped in surprise and pleasure as his warm fingers stroked along her neck.

"Much nicer," he murmured into her ear. "Gloves are *such* a nuisance."

His heated breath against her neck left gooseflesh in its wake. "My lord . . ." she began in protest. She simply must send him away.

"Hush," he commanded. "Relax."

She complied, her body drained of will. His stroking fingers had a hypnotic effect. It did feel so wonderful . . .

Katherine sat bolt upright when Knowlton's lips brushed her neck. Swiveling around, she glared at him in anger. "I did not give you leave to do that."

His lips formed an apologetic, almost boyish smile. "My pardon, Lady Robert. I sometimes forget myself when I am so close to such loveliness."

Katherine stood up, setting her half-finished brandy on the table. She let out a deep sigh. "I suppose it was too much to expect that you would behave yourself." She leaned over to pick up her shawl, but Knowlton laid a staying hand on her arm.

"Are you so certain my behavior offends you?" he asked, his gray eyes dark in the shadowed room. "Methinks the lady doth protest too much."

She reached again for her shawl, but he quickly drew it out of reach.

"You should have watched yourself more closely in the mirror at dinner," he said, his voice low and seductive. "You would have seen how that lovely flush crept over your cheeks every time our bodies touched. Or how your breathing quickened when I ran my hand down your thigh.''

''The only feeling I entertained was disgust at your boorish behavior,'' she retorted.

''I think not, Kate.'' He stepped out from behind the chair and lifted her chin with his finger. ''I think you were recalling how very pleasurable the touch of my hands could be on your creamy skin.'' His voice dropped lower. ''I think you remember exactly how much you enjoyed our little interlude at Warrenton.''

''Never.''

''Prove it.'' He pinned her with a challenging stare.

''You are being foolish,'' she said with a nervous laugh.

''I think not. I think behind the elegant and reserved Lady Robert is the redheaded Kate who came so eagerly into my arms. Do not pretend you would not like my lips and hands caressing you again.''

She struck him a ringing blow across the cheek.

''Damn you,'' he cried, grabbing her arms and jerking her against his body. He forced his lips on hers, brutally grinding them against her tightly closed mouth. As his grip on her arms tightened, she moaned in pain and he forced his tongue between her lips. Burning lust quickly replaced his anger as he held the woman who had driven him to near-madness. He pressed his body against her, letting her feel the hardness in his groin. His tongue thrust rhythmically; the taste and smell of her built the heat inside him to the boiling point. He felt her resistance crumbling against his physical onslaught and felt a thrill of triumph.

He would succeed now. He berated himself for not having locked the door behind him when he entered. She would be close to capitulation in no time, yet they risked discovery in this room. With a muffled groan he tore his mouth away and planted hot, wet kisses across her neck and face. He enfolded her in his arms.

''Come away with me tonight,'' he whispered, nipping at her ear. Without waiting for her reply, he again sought her mouth, seeking, teasing her own tongue into a flurried response.

''Katherine, the carriage is . . .''

Knowlton looked up in surprise at Somers, standing in the

doorway with a look of mingled shock and amusement on his face. Katherine immediately pulled free from Knowlton's arms and fled past Somers into the corridor.

"Not quite the thing to be seducing the guests." Somers grinned.

Knowlton turned away, struggling to control his impassioned breathing. "Take a damper, Somers. It is none of your concern."

Damn. Knowlton expelled his breath in a loud whoosh. He had been within minutes of having Kate fall into his hands like a ripe plum. He could have spent an enjoyable evening sampling the delights of his redheaded witch before he sent her on her way like all the other women whose charms faded in the cool light of morning. Now he would be forced to the trouble of seeking out another female to sate his lust this night. Such a bother.

As he turned to exit the room, he spied Kate's shawl, crumpled in a heap on the floor. Bending down, he picked it up and held it to his nose, reveling in the faint scent. Lavender. Kate.

20

O, Beware, my lord, of jealousy!
It is the green-ey'd monster which doth mock
The meat it feeds on

—Shakespeare, *Othello*

The spring sky was lightening in the east when Knowlton dragged his body from the carriage. He staggered slightly as he climbed the stairs, fumbling in his inner pocket for his key, which seemed to have vanished. With an angry snarl he jerked the bell rope and in moments a sleepy-eyed footman opened the door. Knowlton quelled him with a fierce look and stumbled up the next set of stairs to his room. He flung himself backward onto the bed, his legs dangling down over the sides.

He was doomed. There was no other word for it. He was totally, utterly, miserably doomed. For the rest of his life. Because only death could release him from Kate Mayfield's hold.

He had been a fool to think that a successful seduction last night would drive her from his thoughts. My God, it would only have wrapped the chains tighter. Although he wondered if that was possible.

He had tried, oh, how he had tried to free himself of her memory. He had picked the loveliest lady from the milling crowd in the Green Room, one who was new and fresh and eager to please a noble client. But when the moment came, he had only wanted to bolt from her room in dismay. Only by imagining that it was Kate's lips he kissed, Kate's breast he suckled, Kate's body he sheathed himself in, could he find a trace of pleasure in the transaction. And even then the pleasure was so transitory as to be almost nonexistent. One chaste kiss from Kate was more enjoyable than three bouts of sexual gymnastics with any dancer.

He laughed harshly. After his cruel treatment of Kate, there was little chance she would ever look upon him with favor again. He had tormented her at dinner, then rudely insulted her with his forced attentions in the library. He could still feel the stinging slap of her palm against his cheek. He had deserved far more than that. It would take a man of more diplomacy and tact than he to erase the humiliations of that evening from her mind. He might spend a lifetime at it and never succeed in regaining her respect. What had he done?

Katherine awoke with a deep, unnamed yearning in her breast that was painful in its intensity. Memory of Knowlton's erratic behavior washed over her. He had been cruel in his taunting, brutal in his attentions. And she had still responded, still clung to him as if her life depended upon it. Had Somers not intruded when he did . . . There was no doubt she would have done whatever Knowlton had asked of her.

Her cheeks flushed with shame. How could her body behave so traitorously, rebelling against all her sense? No matter how much temporary happiness she would find with him, Knowlton would eventually cause her deep, searing pain. He would never give her the only thing she wanted—his heart. If he had ever possessed such an organ, it was buried so deep within him that she doubted it could ever be found again.

She turned her face into her pillow, tears stinging at her eyes. How could she continue to be so foolishly in love with him? It was maddeningly pointless, yet no matter how hard she fought against it, it was impossible to free herself.

Katherine resolved, when going down to breakfast, that she would be most careful with her social calendar in the future. She would avoid any entertainment that might draw Knowlton's presence. That this would bar her from most events did not cause her dismay. In truth, the excitement of life in the fashionable world had paled. It was frivolous and fun, but now that she was in the middle of it, she realized that it was no more satisfying than her old life had been. It would be all too easy to let herself drift along, following in Castalia's pattern. But she did not want that for herself. A nice quiet cottage in the country sounded like heaven.

The sight of the enormous container of creamy white hot-house roses caused Katherine to pause upon entry into the breakfast parlor. The marquess eyed her with an eager expression.

"You have made an impression on someone, my girl."

"For me?" she asked with a sinking feeling. Her trembling hand reached for the card.

> Words cannot express my regret over my insufferable behavior last evening. Know that I never wished to hurt you, Kate. My only excuse is that your bewitching presence does strange things to my judgment. You have my promise that there will never be a repetition.
>
> Knowlton

Clutching the note to her bosom, Kate fled from the room, tears streaming from her eyes. Her initial relief at Knowlton's promise was overlaid with sorrow that she would never again be encircled by his arms. Yet that was what she wanted—was it not?

Katherine kept to her resolve to curtail her social engagements. She fobbed Castalia off with excuses of minor ailments, and when that no longer sufficed, pleaded exhaustion and the need to spend more time with Robbie. Although she felt a lingering sense of guilt at treating Lord Belton so shabbily, she ordered the butler to turn all visitors away. Only when both the marquess and Castalia descended upon her in force did Katherine allow herself to be persuaded to go out for one evening.

She winced at the eager look in Lord Belton's eyes when he saw her enter the music room. He hastened to her side, urging her toward a seat.

Belton leaned toward Katherine while the harpist arranged her music. "You have been far too seldom in company this last week," he gently chastised.

"I have been tired," she explained, grateful that he did not press her too closely. "I find I am unused to the hectic pace of the Season."

"I appreciate your sentiments," he murmured. "I, too, find

London can grow wearisome.'' He gave her a meaningful glance. ''I think we would both enjoy a restorative visit to the country.''

She nodded briefly, sitting back with relief when the musical program began and he was unable to continue. At this moment, the last thing she wanted was a further opportunity for Belton to press his suit.

''Are you certain you did not wish to accompany us to Lady Worthington's?'' Castalia inquired of Katherine as they filed out of the music room an hour later.

''Please do,'' Belton encouraged.

Katherine felt trapped. To decline now would label her as rude; she could hardly plead overwhelming weariness after venturing out this evening. With the Season at its height, there was a multitude of *ton* parties for Knowlton to choose from. The chances of his attending this particular party were slim when he had so many other sources of entertainment. She nodded in acquiescence, but vowed she would have a long talk with Castalia in the morning.

She was disappointed to find that the Worthington rout had turned into a severe crush even before their arrival. That was another element she found so disturbing about the city—the sheer numbers of people everywhere. She longed for the solitude of a quiet country lane.

''I think half the city is here tonight,'' Castalia whispered from behind her fan. ''That ball in Grosvenor Square must have been a sad affair.''

Katherine made a futile attempt to wave cool air over her face with her own fan. ''I suppose it is too much to hope that there will be anything left in the refreshment room.''

''One can always hope, Lady Robert,'' Belton said. He took her elbow and carefully pushed their way through the crowded room, leaving Castalia to trade gossip with a friend in the overheated saloon.

The supper room was astonishingly empty; Belton easily appropriated a corner table and chairs, returning swiftly with two overladen plates and glasses of champagne.

''This is much better,'' he said, saluting her with his glass. ''An unexpected oasis of quiet.''

Katherine took a sip of her champagne and wrinkled her nose at the tickling bubbles. She had not intended to find herself in such an intimate setting with Belton, and she struggled to find an innocuous topic of conversation. One that would not lead to topics she wished to avoid for the present time.

"How are your library acquisitions coming? Have you purchased any new finds?"

"There is a sale tomorrow I am attending, as a matter of fact."

"Another estate disposition?" She tilted her head in feigned interest.

Belton shook his head. "A private sale, I am afraid. For collectors, so the prices will be high. I may not find anything I even wish to buy, but I thought I would attend just in case."

"Robbie is very much enjoying the copy of *Robinson Crusoe* you sent him." She flashed him a grateful smile. "He is struggling now with the choice of whether to join the cavalry or become an adventurer when he grows older."

"Have you settled on a school for him yet?"

She shook her head. "It is such a difficult decision. Winslow, of course, wishes him to go to Eton, like his father. But I cannot forget how much Robert disliked the place." She paused, as if in embarrassment. "I hope you did not attend Eton."

Belton laughed. "Harrow. So you may malign Eton to your heart's content."

"I must own that Harrow sounds to be much like Eton. I am very intrigued with a school in Norfolk. It is small and features a more varied curriculum." She sighed. "Robbie must choose a career of some sort, and the better his education, the better he shall do. I detest the idea of his entering the army, but if that is his choice, unending years of Latin and Greek will do him little good. Mathematics and geography will certainly prove more useful."

"Was the school recommended to you?"

She nodded. "The Duke of Hartford sends his son there—precisely because he hated his years at Eton." The thought of Hartford caused her mind to drift back to those easy weeks at Warrenton. When she still had hopes and dreams.

* * *

Standing in a shadowed corner, sipping his champagne, Knowlton watched Kate and Belton with increasing distress. She looked entirely too *comfortable* with the viscount. He winced as she smiled brightly at some comment her partner made. Entirely too comfortable. They almost looked like a married couple. The thought caused a wrenching feeling somewhere in his middle. Knowlton quickly tossed off the glass of champagne and searched for another.

He had half a mind to saunter over to their table and pull up a chair. He would like to see the look on Katherine's face if he did. But he had resolved, after their last disastrous encounter, that he would keep his distance. He had enough honor left to know she did not wish for a casual liaison, however much her body might protest to the contrary. She simply was not that kind of woman.

Watching them through narrowed gray eyes, he tried to objectively evaluate Belton as a partner for her. There was little to criticize. Belton was as solid as they came. A bit boring at times, of a certainty, but he would never be caught making love to an unmarried lady in the library of a friend's house. That alone would do much to commend him to Kate.

Knowlton hoped his contrite note and floral peace offering had mollified her slightly. How could one woman goad him into such a mixture of anger and lust? He began to think there was something seriously amiss with his life. He had offended a woman he genuinely liked, and embarrassed himself in the eyes of one of his closest friends. In short, he had acted like a total fool. Which was entirely unlike him. He was rarely ever rash or foolish; his life had long been one of cold, calculated deliberation. Why was it suddenly becoming so difficult to act in such a manner?

He shrank back further into the shadows as Katherine and Belton left the room. Setting down his now-empty glass, Knowlton followed them back to the crowded main rooms. Knowing there was no point in his remaining, he continued to the door and called for his carriage. Despite the early hour, he gave the order for Upper Brook Street. He was in no mood for company tonight.

Settled at last in his comfortable leather chair, Knowlton stared morosely into the flickering flames of the fire before he tossed back the last of the brandy in his glass. With an unsteady hand he refilled it and took a large swallow.

He wished Katherine had not been there tonight, even though he had gone entirely on the possibility that she would be. But he had thought . . . Just what had he thought? That seeing her with the adoring Belton at her side would free him from the ghost of her presence that haunted him every waking moment and drove the sleep from his brain at night? He uttered a mirthless laugh. More fool he. He had only added months, if not years, onto his torture.

She had looked so exquisite in that clinging blue silk. Cut low over the swell of her breasts, the sleeves barely skimming her bared shoulders, it had made the blood run hot and thick through his veins. God, how he wanted her. He had tried to quench the fire with the body of every willing woman who crossed his path, but that excess had only heightened, not dimmed, his lust. Each unsatisfying sexual encounter only sharpened his sense of loss and enhanced his memory of that last evening at Warrenton. Her passion would be wasted on Belton.

So what was he to do? Live celibate for the remainder of his life? Lose himself in more displeasing liaisons? Cavort and carouse with every piece of muslin he could find until he had at last exorcised her image from his brain? And how long would it take? Weeks? Months? Years? The rest of his blighted life?

She *was* a witch. There could be no other explanation for the power she held over him. Never had a woman so filled his mind, pushing all else aside to become the dominant thought during all his waking hours. And unsatisfied with that achievement, she made his nights a torment.

There had to be a way to free himself from her grip.

Katherine took her seat at the breakfast table, eyeing the groaning sideboard with distaste. She had eaten far too much at the Worthington rout last evening, but it had been easier to eat than to talk with Belton. She reached for a piece of toast, nibbling on it while the waiting footman poured her tea. The marquess ignored her presence, his head buried in the newspaper.

"Well, my dear, when can we expect an interesting announcement?"

His abrupt question startled Katherine out of her reverie.

"An interesting what?" She directed him a puzzled look.

"Belton. Has he talked to you yet?"

"About what?" she asked casually, although she knew perfectly well what the marquess meant.

"Good God, girl, are you obtuse? No man pays a lady that much attention unless he is considering marriage."

"The subject has not come up," Katherine replied primly.

"And I wager that is more of your doing," said the marquess, laying down his paper with a disgusted snort. "You are no miss fresh out of the schoolroom; you know how these things are done. You have to maneuver him into the right position."

"I have no desire to maneuver Lord Belton into anything," she said obstinately.

"You could not do much better," the marquess mused. "He has a very good income, a prosperous estate. And he dotes on you."

Katherine had the grace to blush. "Lord Belton is an amiable companion. Nothing more."

"If I thought you were still wearing the willow for my son, it would make sense," the marquess said, his voice rising. "But you ain't, and that's a fact. You are acting like a skittish filly at her first mating. Good God, woman, you're a nearly thirty-year-old widow, with a son to boot. Husbands don't grow on trees for the likes of you."

"I am not looking for a husband," Katherine said, her anger rising. "As I have tried to tell you and Castalia more than once. But you both refuse to listen."

He brushed off her objections with a dismissive wave of his hand. "Of course you want a husband. You need someone who can give young Robbie some guidance."

"I can give Robbie all the guidance he needs." She pressed her lips together tightly to forestall a more heated response.

"The boy needs a man," the marquess roared. "You have been given every opportunity to find one. If you let Belton slip

through your fingers, you are a worse fool than I thought."
He picked up his newspaper again and retreated behind its printed pages.

Katherine left her half-eaten toast and took her teacup into the library. She was not going to let the marquess goad her into a display of anger.

The marquess, despite his lack of tact, was right. She was acting like a skittish filly. She knew that the sightest word of encouragement would bring a declaration from Belton. Why did she hold back?

It was foolish of her, really. Belton would make an excellent husband. He liked Robbie, and more important, Robbie liked him. He was steady and dependable. She never need worry that he would squander his money on gaming or lightskirts. As his wife, she would have the security she longed for, a house she could call her own. Why, then, was she so reluctant to bring him to the point?

Simply because the sight of him did not take her breath away. The touch of his hand did not send thrills coursing through her body. And she suspected that kissing him would be about as satisfying as kissing a brother.

It was unfair, but she simply could not help comparing her reaction to him with the one she had to Knowlton. And there was simply no comparison. With Knowlton, her pulse raced, breathing became an effort. He had treated her abominably that night at Elizabeth's, and still she found herself melting in his arms. It was a continuing revelation to discover how he could tempt her to throw all her good sense and judgment out the window at the crook of his beckoning finger.

Knowlton did not enjoy his solitary ride through the park that morning. The signs of spring grew more evident each day and hinted of the summer to come. Anyone else would have been cheered by the thought. To Knowlton the idea of summer brought only gloom. He could not think of summer without thinking of Warrenton, and Kate.

"Knowton! Lord Knowlton!"

He froze at the eager, familiar voice. One more reminder of his damnable folly. "Hello, Robbie."

"I say, Knowlton, it has been ever so long since I saw you last."

"That it has, Robbie." A genuine smile crossed his face. "Still riding Atlas, I see."

Robbie smiled and patted his mount's neck. "He is a good pony. Although Grandfather says I may have a full-size horse this summer."

"Planning on spending the summer with Winslow, are you?" Did that mean Katherine would be there also?

"Mama says we might go to the seashore, but I am not certain we will." He looked glumly at Knowlton. "Aunt Castalia says Mama might have other plans."

Knowlton hastily sucked in his breath. It did not take much effort to guess at Lady Durham's meaning. "I saw your mama just the other night at a party," he said with a forced casualness. "She was with Lord Belton." He watched Robbie carefully to gauge his feelings for his mother's suitor.

"She is with him often." Robbie gave Knowlton a wistful stare.

It was cowardly of him to discuss this with Robbie, but he had to know which way the wind blew. "Do you like Lord Belton?"

"He is nice," said Robbie with a self-conscious smile. "He brings me things a lot. Mostly books. Mama says he collects books. The last one was about a man who is stranded on a desert island all by himself except for a friend he called Friday."

"*Robinson Crusoe*." Knowlton smiled in remembered pleasure. "And now I wager you wish to go to sea when you are a bit older."

Robbie colored. "Maybe. I still think about the cavalry."

"We never did get you to Astley's last fall, did we?" Knowlton frowned in remembrance. "It was forgotten in all the business after the queen's death."

"Oh, I have been twice this spring. Lord Belton took me once, and Mama and Grandpapa came with me one time."

Knowlton tried to ignore the sharp pain that stabbed through him. How he would have liked to see Robbie's wide eyes at his first glimpse of the delights of Astley's. He would wager a monkey the lad had talked of nothing else for weeks. A deep regret assailed him.

"What else have you been up to these last months?" If Knowlton had been cut out of Robbie's life as effectively as from Katherine's, he could at least hear what he had missed.

"Studying a lot." Robbie grimaced. "I have a tutor now because Mama says I will be going away to school in the fall. Did you go away to school when you were eleven?"

Knowlton remembered those first terror-filled weeks at Eton, when the older students had mercilessly tortured the new ones. Perhaps things were better now. He hoped Robbie would have an easier time. "I was about your age when I went to Eton," he said carefully. "You will make lots of new friends at school."

Robbie shrugged gently. "I hope so. I wish my cousins were older so I could play with them. I miss Sam sometimes."

"Sam is doing well, I hear. I saw him when I was at Warrenton last month. I will tell him you asked after him when I see him next."

"Thank you," Robbie said, smiling.

"Do you think your mama will marry Lord Belton?" The moment the words left his mouth, Knowlton was appalled at his question. But he had to know.

Robbie gave him a curious glance. "I do not know. I think Grandpapa wants her to. She has not said anything to me. What do you think?"

"I am not privy to your mother's thoughts," Knowlton replied stiffly. He would be the last person on earth to have that news.

"Sometimes I wish we were back at the Rose Cottage," Robbie said quickly. "So I could walk over to Warrenton and visit you."

A sudden impulse seized Knowlton. "Do you still play chess?"

Robbie nodded.

"Then come home with me now. We can have a quick game."

Robbie's eyes lit. "Really?"

"Really." Robbie's enthusiasm bolstered Knowlton's spirits.

"You can send the groom back to your grandfather's with the message; I can escort you home later."

"Capital!" the boy exclaimed.

As they swung the horses toward the park exit, Knowlton felt a twinge of regret for all that he had missed and was going to miss. One morning of chess would not count for much over a lifetime.

21

Sweet seducer! blandly smiling;
Charming still, and still beguiling!
Oft I swore to love thee never
Yet I love thee more than ever!

—Thomas Moore, *Song*

Katherine looked up in surprise as the butler ushered Belton
into the morning room. For a moment she was confused. Had
she promised to accompany him somewhere today and forgotten? In the jumbled state her mind was often in these days,
it was a distinct possibility.

"I had hoped to find you at home this morning," Belton said.

She let out a relieved breath and flashed him a welcoming
smile. "How nice of you to call," she said, setting her sewing
aside.

Lord Belton took his seat across from her. Katherine thought
he looked oddly uncomfortable today, and the first hints of
apprehension teased at her brain.

"Katherine," he began, "you cannot be surprised when I tell
you how much I have grown to admire you."

Dread swept over her body. That which she had most feared
was happening, and she was beset with panic. What was she
going to do? What could she say to him?

"It is always pleasure to be in your company," she said
slowly. How, exactly, did one go about forestalling a proposal?
She abruptly stood up and crossed the room to the window,
certain that her nervousness was obvious. "The weather looks
to be clearing."

He came up behind her. "Katherine, there is no need to be
skittish."

She whirled and faced him. "Do you imagine that I am
nervous, my lord?"

"It has not escaped my notice that you have been taking great pains of late to avoid being alone in my company. I begin to think I have offended you in some manner."

She uttered a nervous laugh. "Certainly not, my lord. I am sorry if I have given you that impression, for I assure you it was not my intent."

Belton took her hand in his and led her back to the sofa. She sat gingerly on the edge, half-dreading what was to come and half-relieved that it would be out in the open at last.

"Katherine, I find I am no longer able to enjoy a day if I am not able to spend some small part of it in your company."

She forced her gaze to meet his, and the fond emotion that shone in his bright blue eyes pained her. "My lord—"

"Richard."

"Richard." The name sounded strange on her tongue. Could she speak it every day for the rest of her life?

"I think we have spent enough time in each other's company to have a fair estimation of one another's character. There is much to be admired in yours, Katherine. You have grace, and beauty, and serenity."

She stilled the urge to laugh. Serenity. That was one thing she completely lacked. Serenity had fled from her life the day she had met Knowlton.

"You make me sound too much of a paragon," she said lightly. "I fear I could not live up to such standards."

He smiled warmly. "I cannot imagine any such thing," he said, taking her hand again. "I had hoped to invite you to Belton House this spring so you could determine whether you could be happy there." His eyes searched her face. "But I find I am too impatient to wait for such an opportunity. You would do me great honor, Katherine, if you would consent to become my wife."

She dropped her eyes, looking dispassionately at their clasped hands. A proposal. A most honorable one. Castalia and the marquess would be thrilled. Katherine could not put a name to the emotion the offer stirred within her.

As if sensing her hesitation, he sought to further his case. "I cannot pretend to replace Captain Mayfield, either as a husband or as a father to his son. But I know I could be a good guide for your Robbie. And I hope I could be the kind of husband you would wish.''

She shut her eyes, feeling the tears welling in them. Why could he not have waited a bit longer, waited until she had her emotions more closely under control? Now she was going to have to say something, and she did not know what her answer would be.

''You honor me with your attention,'' she said at last, choosing her words with infinite care. ''And I cannot say that your offer causes me displeasure. But I do not feel that I can give you an answer immediately.''

She looked toward him and smiled pleadingly. ''I entertained no intention of seeking another husband when Robbie and I rejoined the family. I felt that the happiness I had enjoyed with Robert was all that one person could expect from a lifetime. To marry again . . . There have been so many changes in my life this past year, I do not know if I am ready for another yet.''

She saw the disappointment in his eyes as he sat back.

''I certainly understand your hesitation, Katherine,'' he said. ''I in no way want to make you feel that I am forcing a decision upon you. Perhaps my original plan was best. Later in the spring I could arrange a party at Belton—''

''I cannot expect you to wait so long for an answer,'' she said, deciding in that moment that she would have to make up her mind soon. ''I ask for only a short time to consider your very flattering offer.''

''I will await your decision, then,'' he said in a lighter tone. He brought her hand up and gently brushed his lips against it. ''You know that I will hold out every hope that you will find me worthy of your affections.''

She wanted to scream at him to stop, to cry out that she was not worthy of his affections at all. That she had given her heart to a callous rake and was almost willing to throw away a good and kind man like Belton because of it. But she remained silent.

Belton rose to his feet. ''I will take my leave now, Katherine.''

She stood and walked with him to the morning room door. ''I thank you again for the honor,'' she said quietly. ''And I promise to give the matter great thought.''

He nodded and took his leave.

Katherine collapsed weakly upon the sofa. Dear God, what was she going to do? She laughed bitterly. Last year she had been a near-penniless widow; now she was being offered a life of luxury and ease she could only have dreamed of then.

She tried to school her mind along objective lines. There was no denying that Belton would be a good father for Robbie. They got along well. Belton never talked down to her son, and paid him respectful attention at all times. They dealt well together. And she could not underestimate the importance of Robbie's happiness to her.

It was not any apprehension about Belton's dealings with Robbie that caused her reservations. And she did not hold any concerns about the way Belton would treat her. He was always a perfect gentleman, solicitous, concerned, and willing to do anything to please her. As his wife, she would be worshiped and adored. He would indulge her whims, surprise her perhaps with presents, and be as attentive as she could ever wish.

No, what caused her to pause was the fear that she would be a dismal failure as his wife. Could she truly be content in that role? Or would the ghost of a cynical earl with mocking smile and cool gray eyes always come between them? With Knowlton forever in her heart, would there be room for anything other than warm affection for Belton? He deserved far more.

She wrapped her arms around herself, feeling chilled even in the warm room. Was there any hope of escape from this coil?

Katherine forced her lips into a smile as Robbie entered the room.

"Finished with your studies already?"

He nodded, standing awkwardly, as if considering something in his mind. "Are you going to marry Lord Belton?" he blurted out.

Katherine was taken aback. In all her confusion, she had never once discussed the matter with Robbie. Of course she must speak to him before making her decision. He would be as affected by the matter as she.

"Does that idea displease you?" she asked, carefully watching for his reaction.

He shrugged. "Lord Belton is nice. I just wondered."

"Has someone been talking to you about this?" If the marquess had gone behind her back and hinted to Robbie, she would be furious.

"I saw Lord Knowlton in the park yesterday. He wanted to know."

Just the mention of his name was enough to send her pulses racing. Knowlton's interest puzzled her. But she was certain it meant nothing. It was obvious her relationship with Belton was on everyone's mind.

She reached for Robbie's hand and drew him to the sofa. "We have never talked about the possibility of my remarrying. What do you think about the idea?"

Robbie wrinkled his freckled nose. "It would be all right, I guess. As long as it was someone like Lord Belton or Lord Knowlton. They are fun."

"I do not think it very likely that I would marry Lord Knowlton," she said quickly, the words cutting into her like a knife. "Lord Belton was here this morning, and he does wish to marry me."

"Did you say yes?"

"I did not give him an answer," she explained, relieved that Robbie showed no signs of distress. "I told him I needed some time to consider. I knew that I needed to discuss it with you. I have thought that you two dealt well with each other."

Robbie nodded absently. "If you married him, would we go to live at his house?"

"We would."

"So I would not go to Grandpapa's for the summer?" The disappointment in his voice was clear.

"You could certainly go for a visit," she said. "Lord Belton has a country house of his own, you know, in Dorset. I imagine there are lots of things you could do there."

"And I would still go to school in the fall?"

"Yes."

Robbie stared down at his feet, as if he found them the most fascinating objects. "If you married him, would I have to call him 'Papa'?"

She sensed the anxiety in his question and hugged him close. "Not unless you wished to. Lord Belton knows you remember your papa. You can call him what you wish.'' Robbie's sigh of relief told her she had mollified his worry.

"Mama?"

"Hmm?"

"Would we ever see Lord Knowlton again if you marry Lord Belton?"

The pain of that thought tore through her. "We might see him in town on occasion," she said slowly.

"I will miss him," Robbie confided. "We played chess at his house yesterday and he said I was getting much better."

"You were at Knowlton's house?" She stared at Robbie in surprise.

"He invited me," Robbie said defensively. "I think he wanted to take me to Astley's, but when I told him I had gone already, he suggested we play chess. It took more than an hour for him to beat me."

"I am pleased your chess is improving," she said quietly. Astley's? How like Knowlton to confound her again. It was nearly impossible to conjure up the picture of him there. She was grateful he had not totally forgotten Robbie. She still felt twinges of guilt at having allowed their friendship to develop so last year.

"Atlas is probably ready now," Robbie hinted.

She pulled him close again. "And ponies must come before mothers, I know." Her voice turned serious. "You are certain you would not mind if I marry Lord Belton?"

"No, Mama," he replied, squirming to be free of her arms.

"Ride carefully," she instructed as he headed for the door.

For a brief moment she wondered at Knowlton's purpose in renewing his acquaintance with Robbie; then she firmly resolved to push all thoughts of him from her mind. She had another man to consider.

But try as she might, she simply could not rid her mind of Knowlton. He had the annoying habit of popping into her thoughts whenever she tried to look favorably upon the idea of marriage to Belton. And she feared that the situation would continue if she agreed to marry Belton.

Knowlton closeted himself in the study at Upper Brook Street for several days, unwilling to make the effort to go out. The simple act of opening the paper filled him with dread, for he daily anticipated seeing in black and white that which he feared most. Robbie's answers had only confirmed what he had long suspected. Any day now, Katherine would be affianced to Belton and lost to him forever. He had seen the closeness between them at the Worthington rout. It was only a matter of time. Knowlton desperately wanted to be able to wish them well, for he desired Katherine's happiness above all. If Belton could provide it . . .

It took no effort to imagine Katherine in several years, laughing and content with a doting Belton at her side and adoring children at her feet. Knowlton sucked in his breath at the sharp stab of pain that scene evoked.

He groaned in despair as the realization hit him. He loved her. It would be laughable if it were not so horribly true. For so long he had thought himself incapable of that emotion. Yet he knew no other word to describe the hold Katherine had over him, the unbearable yearning and need he had for her. His life had been hollow and empty since the day they had parted, and he knew that he would not be at peace again until she was at his side.

He had to have her. But, oh, the price she demanded. Fear clutched his heart. She wanted a boring, respectable marriage. Could he honestly agree to such a thing?

Marriage would require so much of him. More than he had ever given anyone. Companionship. Dependability. Fidelity. The very words made him cringe. He had demonstrated none of those qualities in his five-and-thirty years. Was there any reason to think he could adopt them now? Could he truly change himself to become the type of man Katherine wanted? Was this newly acknowledged feeling strong enough to carry him through?

He was not even certain he knew exactly what marriage would entail. Was it not laughingly said that every woman changed once the ring was safely on her finger? Or that the thrill quickly faded after the honeymoon period had ended? What would ultimately happen to him and Kate if they joined their lives together?

Somers would know. Somers, who had once been as opposed

to marriage as he, could tell him what happened after marriage. Did he now have any regrets over taking Elizabeth as his own? Knowlton abruptly jumped from his chair. He knew Somers had intended to spend only a short time in town. Was he still here? Racing into the hall, Knowlton grabbed his hat and gloves, hastening down the front steps for the short walk to the square. Somers was the one person he could trust to tell him the truth.

"Knowlton, how delightful." Elizabeth held out her hand in greeting.

"You are as lovely as ever, my dear." He smiled, bowing low over her hand, relieved to have found the Wentworths still in town. Elizabeth did look well. Was it true that pregnancy made a woman lovelier?

She laughed. "How well you lie. I know I am horridly huge, and with three more months to go. Somers has already taken to calling me 'the whale.' "

"Shall I call him out for the insult?" Knowlton asked, his eyes twinkling.

"A duel?" Somers asked, strolling into the room. "How exciting. Who is the poor fellow?"

"You," Knowlton replied with a grin. "Elizabeth tells me you have been casting grievous insults at her."

"Nonsense," Somers said, planting a fond kiss on his wife's cheek. "You must have misunderstood. Besides, we are leaving for home on the morrow, so I am not free to indulge your thirst for bloodshed."

"Do I have your leave to withdraw the challenge, my lady?"

"Only if you stay to dine with us tonight," she replied. "For I know it will be ages before we see you again. Babies have such an annoying habit of driving all our friends away."

"Then I shall stay," he promised. He looked to Somers. "I should like to have a word with you, if I may. If your lovely wife will excuse us?"

Elizabeth laughed. "I see even the mention of babies sends you fleeing. Go ahead, leave me here with my book. I shall be content."

Somers nodded toward the door. "We can repair to the

study.'' He gave Elizabeth another kiss and followed Knowlton into the hall.

"You sound filled with mystery," Somers said when they had ensconced themselves in the comfortable leather chairs that flanked the fireplace, glasses of brandy in their hands.

"Elizabeth does look marvelous," Knowlton said, unsure how to gain the information he needed without revealing his thoughts to Somers. "Do all women look so when they are . . . ?"

Somers laughed. "You should have seen her over Christmas, when even the sight of breakfast caused her to turn green. I would waken every morning to the sound of her retching in the washbasin."

His blunt description made even Knowlton feel a bit green. "You did not . . . I mean, it did not bother you?"

"How can I complain when I am the cause of it?" Somers smiled smugly.

"Do you ever regret giving up your freedom?" Knowlton asked bluntly.

Somers eyed him with a guarded expression. "I do not think there is a man alive who has not asked himself that question— particularly after a long night spent in the company of a screaming baby. But an honest answer? No. Never."

"Why?" Knowlton leaned forward, eager for the answer.

Somers smiled enigmatically. "It is Elizabeth, pure and simple. I cannot imagine a life without her." He set down his glass and quickly refilled it. "The night Caro was born filled me with sheer terror. I had thought I was well aware of my feelings for Elizabeth, but that night showed me just how deeply they ran. If anything had happened to her, I honestly do not think I could have gone on."

Knowlton did not realize he was nodding in agreement. Somers noted the action and smiled inwardly. The point of this odd conversation became clearer.

"Is it not frightening to feel so strongly?" Knowlton took a careful sip of his brandy.

"It is terrifying," Somers agreed. "But I would not change it for the world. You cannot know the indescribable joy I feel when I wake each morning and find Elizabeth at my side. I would do anything in my power to make her happy, even if I had to lay down my life for her.''

Knowlton pondered this in silence. Somers' words echoed his own thoughts about Katherine, confirming his worst fears. It was love, this strange, unfamiliar feeling that had him in its grip. He did not know whether to laugh or cry at the finality of his knowledge.

''It is funny,'' Somers said thoughtfully, ''for I did not realize for the longest time that I loved her. Oh, I knew I admired her and wanted her in a physical way. But it was not until I realized that her happiness was more important than my own—even if that meant she would be lost to me forever—that I finally understood what love really is.''

Knowlton stared morosely into his glass. Could he selflessly let Kate walk out of his life, knowing it was best for her? Was his desperate desire to find some way to possess her an indication that he was still more concerned with his own selfish needs?

Somers eyed his closest friend with curious interest. He well remembered the utter panic he had experienced when he had arranged matters to provide Elizabeth with an independent competence, giving her the option to refuse his offer of marriage. There had been that agony of indecision, knowing he was giving her the very excuse to reject his proposal. That she had accepted sometimes seemed nothing short of a miracle to him. And Knowlton's situation could only be worse. Somers had been no angel, but he had certainly been more discreet in his behavior than Knowlton. Katherine Mayfield could harbor no illusions about him.

He began to understand the reasons underlying Knowlton's erratic behavior this spring. Why he had been seen with a new companion at every turn. He was trying to exorcise a woman from his mind. Somers shook his head, a fleeting smile touching his face. Did Knowlton not know that course was doomed to failure?

He saw Knowlton pour himself another glass and drain it nearly as quickly. It looked to be a long afternoon. Somers refilled his own glass, remembering the night he had walked in on Knowlton and Katherine in the library. She had looked to be a willing participant in that heated embrace. Yet gossip said she was close to wedding another. He decided to test his theory.

"I understand everyone is looking to Belton for an interesting announcement." Somers watched Knowlton carefully and did not miss the whitening of his friend's knuckles on the glass he held.

"So it is said," Knowlton said curtly, taking another large swallow of brandy.

"It seems a rather odd match," Somers said with feigned casualness. "Katherine struck me as a bit too spirited for a prosy fellow like Belton."

"One can never account for taste."

"I had once thought her taste was excellent. A little adventuresome, perhaps, but pointed in the right direction."

Knowlton pierced him with a withering stare.

Somers grinned. "Of course, I might be mistaken. Perhaps she is in the habit of kissing any number of men behind closed library doors."

Somers was tempted to throw up his hands in a defensive posture against the glare Knowlton directed at him.

"What I think," Somers said, weighing his words carefully, "is that we have a man who thinks he has newly discovered he has a heart, yet is terrified to find out for certain. It is odd, since he has never struck me as a cautious sort before. Perhaps age is beginning to tell."

"If I thought that there was any hope," Knowlton said finally, "I might be tempted to speak. But I see no point in pursuing an impossible quest."

"Are you so sure it is impossible?"

Knowlton laughed sardonically. "What woman in her right mind would have anything to do with me?"

"You do have a point," Somers said, torn between amusement and sympathy. "But do you want to go through the rest of your life never knowing the answer? I suspect you will always be plagued by doubt if you do not speak now. Who knows? Perhaps the sun has touched her brain and and she will say yes."

"It is not even her refusal that I fear the most," Knowlton said in a low voice. "It is her acceptance. I know I shall disappoint her. I can never be the man she deserves."

"Should not the choice be hers?"

Knowlton shook his head in despair. "I want to believe it is possible. But if I bring her pain, I will never be able to forgive myself."

"One could argue very effectively that she has certainly seen you at your worst," Somers said. "You have put on a striking demonstration this spring of the very definition of the word 'licentious.' "

"Would to God that I could go back and have it to do all over again," Knowlton moaned, the liquor slightly slurring his speech. "Everything, from the very start."

"You cannot, however, so you may as well stop wallowing in self-pity and decide what you can do now to rectify matters," Somers said bluntly.

"I knew I would get consolation if I came to you," Knowlton retorted.

Somers tossed back his head and laughed. "Is that not what friends are for?" He poured more brandy into their glasses. "Elizabeth will probably not speak to me for a week," he said, beginning to feel the effect himself, "but I think the occasion calls for some serious drinking."

Elizabeth was more than a bit disgusted when Somers and Knowlton finally staggered out of the study at the dinner bell. But she bit down on her lip and did her best to ignore their boisterous display at the dinner table. Besides, if she treated Somers too harshly he would never tell her what had transpired to bring them to such a state. And she had an overwhelming desire to know.

22

How shall ever one like me
    Win thee back again?

                      —Shelley, *Song*

Knowlton groaned aloud at the bright morning light streaming into his room. He was not certain whether to blame himself or Somers for his sad state.

Despite yesterday's talk with Somers, he was still apprehensive about speaking to Kate of his feelings. Somers had almost convinced him he should make the attempt, but in the harsh light of morning Knowlton was no longer as certain.

He had spoken the truth when he said he feared her acceptance more than her rejection. Because that would put the burden of success squarely on his shoulders. And he could not fail. He himself could live with his failure, for his expectations of himself as a doting husband were low. But other people would be relying upon him, and if he failed them, he was not certain he could ever live with himself again. The hero worship he had often glimpsed in Robbie's eyes frightened him silly. Could he take on the mantle of fatherhood and be a success? He was fond of Robbie, but that was not enough to make him a good father. Lord knew, he did not exactly have a shining example from his own childhood to guide him. The thought of the adoration dimming in the boy's eyes made him wince. He could not bear to see that happen.

And Kate. If he failed her . . . how could he ever live with himself? It was enough to send braver men fleeing in terror. He had disappointed her so many times already. Breaking his promise not to pursue her while she sheltered under his roof. His abominable tormenting of her at that wretched dinner at Somers. His blatant flaunting of every Cyprian in the town. If she had only heard half the tales of his recent licentiousness, she was certain to have been filled with disgust. How could he possibly think she would ever seriously entertain the thought of a union with him? The idea was ridiculous.

Yet he knew, somehow, that he had to make the attempt. For his sake, more than hers. He felt that Kate was truly his last hope. If he could not acknowledge and live with his love for her, he would never be granted that chance again. She held out to him a great prize—love, tenderness, compassion, and trust. All the emotions that he had scorned through his five-and-thirty years. All emotions he had not thought a necessary component of a man. Yet he now realized that without them, he was less than a man.

What, in all honesty, could he offer her? He knew she had no care for his title. She had lived too long in the shadow of the power of the Winslow name to hold any affection for that. He knew she would have no qualms about his relationship with Robbie. He could not have been fonder of the boy if he was his own son. But with Robbie's future secured by his grandfather and the rekindled contact with that family, Katherine would not be so needing of a male influence in her son's life.

Of course, he offered financial security. Quite a bit more than that, in fact. Katherine would never want for anything material. He would buy her the moon if he could. But with Winslow's patronage, she would not be perched precariously on the edge of poverty anymore. And Knowlton knew her wants were simple. She was no more averse to pretty things than any woman, but she was neither avaricious nor accumulative. Money would not be a critical point with her.

When all his other advantages had been stripped away, there was really only one thing he could offer her that no one else could—himself. And he feared that was the poorest part of the bargain. One rather cynical earl, with a history that would recommend him only to the boldest lady or the most grasping Cyprian. Certainly not a past that would make Katherine confident of the outcome of any connection.

He would do his best to persuade her that his previous actions *were* all in the past. That he yearned to settle for constancy, for it was the only way he could have her—and be able to live with himself. Would words be enough to convince her of his sincerity when he half-feared his ability to fulfill his pledge? If he had time, he could show her that he intended to follow the new course he had laid out for himself. But with Belton hovering in the wings, Knowlton had no time.

His gut wrenched at the thought that perhaps he was already too late. The bets had not been settled yet at White's, but oftentimes a betrothal remained secret at first. What if Belton had already made the offer—and Katherine had accepted? She would be a fool not to. He could go down on his knees before her, baring his soul, humbling himself, only to find that she was no longer free to accept his suit. That would be the worst torture of all. He would have to speak to her. Today.

Katherine did not look forward to today's outing. She had done everything in her power to forestall Belton from pressing her for a decision. If only she could hold him off a little longer . . . But she suspected that the chances for a secluded *tête-à-tête* would be great today, and once he got her alone, there would be no way to deflect his offer. And it would be difficult to put her answer into words.

It would be cruel of her to refuse him, after she had given him every indication all these long weeks that his suit would be welcome. Yet it was better to cause him pain now than to bind him to a lifetime of torture. He was a wonderful man, kind, generous, caring. But she did not love him. Or at least she did not love him in the way she loved Knowlton. She could not sentence herself and Belton to a lifetime of marriage when her heart and soul were given to another.

She would not mind, terribly, having to say him no. She had never intended to find herself a husband when she had brought Robbie to London. That had been the plan of the marquess and Castalia. Katherine had allowed herself to be swept up in their enthusiasm. It might have been foolish on her part, but she had not anticipated the harm that would come from it. Now there would be hurt enough for everyone.

She at least would have the satisfaction of knowing that she had done the right thing for Robbie by coming to London. She could be filled with pride as she watched him grow to manhood. There were nieces and nephews for her to dote on. Life as Aunt Katherine would not be unpleasant. Moving from country house to country house, she could stay with each member of the family until her welcome had worn off; then she could move on. For herself, she could keep a small cottage as a retreat when the demands of family grew too strong.

And if she was sentencing herself to a life of unbearable loneliness, well, she was the one who would have to live with it. If there were nights when she cried herself to sleep for what might have been, she would have the satisfaction of knowing that she had not dragged another human into her circle of unhappiness.

She dressed carefully for the trip to Richmond, in a round dress of figured gray silk, with a gray velvet pelisse. As she fingered the ribbons of her leghorn bonnet, Katherine allowed her thoughts to drift again. How content she had been a year ago! If it were not for the advantages to Robbie, she would wish the last year had never transpired. Her mind would be the less unsettled for it.

Lord and Lady Durham soon arrived in the barouche. Frederick waited outside while Castalia came to retrieve Katherine. She was grateful they were meeting Belton at the breakfast, knowing she needed to conserve all her strength for the interview she knew would come.

Despite the title of "breakfast," Lady Gresham's party was closer to a luncheon, not starting until half-past eleven. The sun had rallied its feeble spring rays to make the event a success, and tables dotted the south lawn, groaning with the weight of the food upon them. When Katherine and Castalia arrived, guests were already helping themselves to the massive repast.

"One would think some had not eaten for a week," Castalia noted as her husband trailed behind them with the carriage rugs. She jabbed the point of the parasol into a spot of ground she declared to be dry, and her obliging husband spread the rugs around.

Katherine casually glanced about the lawn, wondering if Belton had yet arrived. Now that she had made her decision, she was eager to have it over. She determined to make her refusal as gentle as possible.

Frederick had gone to fill their plates when Belton strolled over to Katherine and Castalia.

"A lovely day for a spring outing," he said, doffing his hat. "And here I see we have two of the most enchanting flowers of the season."

"Sheer flummery," Castalia laughed. "But I will accept it gladly. Do join us. Frederick will be back shortly."

"I thought to ask Lady Robert for a few moments of her company," Belton replied. "The grounds are very lovely this time of year."

Katherine sighed inwardly, knowing the time had arrived. "That would be nice. I should like to stretch my legs after the long drive."

Belton obligingly took her arm and they strolled about the gardens, admiring the view of the Thames and appreciating the riot of color afforded by the spring blooms.

Katherine swallowed hard, trying to decide on a proper method of introducing the subject. But she realized there was no simple away around the matter.

"Lord Belton, I—"

"I asked you to call me Richard."

"I . . . I do not think that would be appropriate." Katherine kept her gaze firmly fixed on the distant vista of the river. "For as honored as I am by your declaration, I feel I must decline your offer of marriage."

"I see."

Katherine dared to glance at him, and she winced at the disappointment she saw in his bright blue eyes. Yet, better a slight disappointment now than the crushing one he would later experience if she had accepted his suit. This way, he would be free to find a woman who could return his affection.

"I am sorry," she said, wanting to make certain he knew that he was not the cause of her refusal. "I wish that I could accept. But I fear that I would make you a very poor wife."

"Am I not a better judge of that?" he asked.

She shook her head. "I am not free to love you as a wife ought," she said quietly.

She saw Belton's startled look.

"I had no inkling there was a rival," he said quietly.

Katherine berated herself for having revealed so much. "It is not that, precisely. It is as I said, I do not feel I would be the right wife for you."

"Should not that decision be mine?"

"No," she replied. "For I know myself better than you do. I am very honored that you think me suitable, my lord, but I fear I am not."

She watched his silent sigh with sadness. In other circumstances, such a proposal would have been most welcome. But it was precisely because she thought so well of him that she could not accept his suit.

"I will regretfully accept your decision, then, Lady Robert," he said, offering her his arm.

In silence they walked back toward the spot where Frederick and Castalia sat, and Belton quickly took his leave. Katherine deliberately ignored Castalia's quizzical expression. She wished she had never consented to come to this breakfast.

Knowlton seethed with frustration as he paced back and forth outside the blacksmith's shop. Why, on this of all days, had his horse decided to throw a shoe? He was half-inclined to unhitch his other mount from the curricle and continue to Richmond on horseback, but the foolishness of that plan struck him at once. It would only be scant minutes before his horse was shod and ready to go on. What did it matter that he had been delayed an hour?

His temper was short from impatience and frustration when he finally arrived at Lady Gresham's. He now had the onerous task of locating Katherine, extricating her from her companions, and attempting to convince her in a very short time that her future should be entwined with his. Only a very small task.

He looked first for Belton. It would be a miracle if he had not escorted her here. Knowlton smiled for the first time that morning. He could only imagine how he was to walk up to Belton and ask leave to speak with Katherine alone. Belton would as lief plant him a facer as allow him a moment with

Katherine. Knowlton knew he had not imagined the hostility that came over Belton every time he drew near. But Belton or no, he meant to speak with Katherine. Today.

He spotted them at last, Katherine and the Durhams. He was surprised not to find Belton with them. Kate's new family would have no objections to that man as her husband. Would she be willing to fly in the face of their probable opposition and marry him instead? He was much the poorer bargain.

Knowlton shrugged off these new doubts. He strolled over to the gathering, donning a mask of feigned boredom.

"Ladies. Durham." He sensed Durham's cautious appraisal.

"We have seen so little of you of late, Knowlton," Castalia said with a welcoming smile. "Too busy for old friends?"

"You understand the press of the London Season," he said smoothly. "So many obligations . . . so little time." He turned to Katherine. "I had thought, Lady Robert, in recalling your fondness for gardens, that you might like to examine them with me. Lady Gresham prides herself on her narcissi."

Katherine started to decline, but the pleading look in his eyes changed her mind. She extended her hand and he assisted her to her feet.

"I will bring her back in good time," he assured Castalia.

"You are being so mysterious," Katherine said once they were out of earshot of the others. "What dramatic news do you have to impart?"

"You ascribe more significance to my attitude than is necessary," he said lightly. "I did wish you to see the gardens. They are lovely in the spring." He took her gloved hand and placed it on his arm as they strolled past the end of the house.

They walked along the gravel path for some time in silence. Katherine appreciated the display of spring blooms, but hardly thought it worthy of such a conscious effort on Knowlton's part. What was his true purpose?

Not until they were a far distance from the house did Knowlton speak.

"Is Robbie getting along well with his tutor?" It was an inane remark, but he could think of no other topic to start the conversation.

Katherine looked at him with a puzzled expression. He wished to speak to her of Robbie? "He is. Not so much for the work, but he is excited about the prospect of school in the fall."

"And where shall he go? Eton? Harrow?"

"Neither. I have decided he would do best at the school the Duke of Hartford's son is attending in Norfolk. It is small, without the traditions of Eton or Harrow, but he will receive a much better education there."

Knowlton, remembering his life at Eton, agreed. Her wisdom pleased him.

They soon reached the end of the formal garden. Katherine turned, anticipating the return walk, but Knowlton stopped her with a staying hand.

"I should like to talk for a moment," he said. With each passing minute, his cravat felt as if it were tightening about his neck. Much like a hangman's noose.

Katherine looked at him expectantly. He was behaving very oddly today. Was he still uncomfortable about their last encounter? He had apologized most graciously in his note, but perhaps he wished to do so again in person.

"I understand that congratulations may soon be in order." He would not make a fool of himself if it was too late. He could spare himself that embarrassment at least.

She wrinkled her brow in confusion. "Whatever for?"

"The wagering in the clubs says it is only a matter of days before your betrothal to Belton is announced." He watched her carefully, with mingled fear and hope.

"And where does your money lie?" A flash of anger filled Katherine."

"As a lady I know once said, it is folly to wager on the happiness of other people." He clenched and unclenched his hands nervously.

"I am glad you have developed some sense." Katherine grew impatient to return to her friends, if this was all he had to say. Her emotions were already rubbed raw from that uncomfortable conversation with Belton. It was too difficult to keep herself in check, standing here next to Knowlton.

"You have not answered my question."

"What was the question?" She looked him directly in the eye.

He met her gaze without wavering. "Are you going to marry Belton?"

"No," she replied.

Knowlton felt as if he had been holding his breath for the last five minutes. He expelled the air in his chest in a long outrush. It was not too late. Now, if only he could find the right words . . .

"Katherine," he began slowly, "I hope you can appreciate how difficult this is for me. I have done a great deal of thinking these last weeks. Many nights I lay abed, staring at the ceiling, because I was afraid to go to sleep."

"Afraid?"

"Afraid. Because each night I dream of a beautiful red-haired witch who has cast a spell about me. I struggle and fight against it, but to no avail. She has bound me to her with magic as tightly as any rope."

Suddenly intent on his words, Katherine almost forgot to breathe. "I had not thought there were witches in our modern age."

"Neither did I, or I would have taken greater pains to protect myself." He smiled ruefully. "I am well and truly caught now, and there is no hope for me."

Hardly daring to believe what she was hearing, Katherine took a deep breath. "Perhaps if you spoke with your witch, she would free you from her spell."

"I am not certain I wish her to."

The deep longing she saw in his eyes, the nervous smile that flitted across his lips, sent a strange trembling through her.

Knowlton paused, taking her hands in his and bringing them to his chest, drawing her closer, as if he could transmit his intent to her.

"This is probably the most difficult thing I have ever done in my life." He looked down at their joined hands, then lifted his gaze to hers. "I love you, Kate. I am being driven mad with wanting you. I will not know any peace in this life until I can have you with me again." He paused, his gray eyes reflecting mingled hope and fear. "I know I have little to recommend me as a husband, but I am begging you to marry me."

Katherine could not suppress her stunned surprise. "Marry you?"

"If it is what I must do to have you, well then, I shall do it."

The hope that rose within her fell again. "Hardly an enthusiastic declaration."

"Dammit, Kate." His voice was harsh. "What do you want of me? I have wrestled with this for weeks, arguing with myself, telling myself it would only lead to disaster for both of us. But I have not known a day of peace since you left Warrenton, and I know I will never have another until you agree to be my wife."

Katherine gently freed her hands and stepped back a pace. "I do not wish to cast doubts on the sincerity of your motives, Edward," she said slowly, carefully. "But you were certainly able to put on a very convincing demonstration last fall of a man who scorned the idea of marriage."

"I did. Then." There was an edge of panic in his voice. He had known it would be difficult to persuade Kate of his change, but nothing was going as he had planned. She did not sound the least convinced, and he did not know what new words would convince her.

"I want you," he said. "I . . . I simply cannot imagine life without you, Kate."

She turned away so as not to see the pleading look in his eyes. Damn the man! What was she to do? One part of her wished to fling herself into his arms, accepting his offer joyfully. But she was no longer the impetuous child she had once been. What Knowlton proposed was in direct opposition to all he had said and done since she had first met him. Could one man change so, in such a short space of time?

"Kate?"

The note of raw terror in his voice made her turn. He stood there, hands limply at his sides.

"I am frightened, Kate. I am terrified of what you are doing to me, what I want to do with myself." He closed his eyes as if seeking strength. "Help me. Help me through the fear."

Katherine took a step toward him, reaching out her hand to touch his sleeve.

"I am frightened also," she said softly. "Of what loving you could bring. If I let myself believe, only to discover I was in error, I do not know how I could endure."

He clasped her to him in a crushing hug. "Oh, Kate, I swear I will do everything in my power to make you happy." As quickly as he had grabbed her, he held her away at arm's length. "You have my solemn promise that I will never, ever do anything to hurt you."

Katherine's eyes filled with tears. She wanted so much to believe him. But could she ever be truly certain of his faithfulness? The man whose legendary collection of mistresses was the talk of London? Only a fool would take such a man for a husband.

"I know I have not set much of an example of correct behavior these last few months," he said slowly, evenly, his gray eyes wide with the effort. "It was only a vain search to rid my mind of you." He pulled her to his side again. "You have thoroughly ruined me for any other woman, Kate Mayfield. No matter whom I was with, your face and form always intruded upon my mind until all else became a torture."

He looked down at her, his expression filled with tenderness. "Had I thought there time, I would have reformed myself, to show you how I could behave. And if you should like to put me on trial, I would be more than willing to demonstrate my ability to change. But with Belton so assiduous in his attentions, I feared there was not time, and I—"

"Hush," Katherine said, placing a finger against his lips. It was that, then, which decided her. His jealousy of Belton. It explained so much of his abominable behavior—it had all been sheer, jealous anger. She laughed at the joy of it. Knowlton. Jealous. For her.

Her laughter sliced painfully through him and he quickly released her, a hurt expression filling his eyes.

"You were jealous!" she exclaimed, beaming in her joy. "It was pure, simple jealousy."

"Of course I was jealous," he said, puzzled by her reaction. "Watching Belton cozying up to you at every opportunity? It nearly drove me mad."

"And are you certain that it is not madness driving you now?" She searched his face, looking desperately for a final sign of his sincerity.

He leaned down and softly brushed her lips with his. "If it is madness, I welcome it gladly."

She stepped back once again, and he saw the apprehension in her eyes. "Lord knows, you have cause to doubt me, Kate. I do not know what else I can do to convince you. I can only ask for your trust."

"If you so much as touch another woman, I will cut your heart out." Her smile belied her words.

"And I will willingly hold the knife for you," he said, pulling her into his arms once again. "My dearest, darling Kate, say you will."

She smiled up at him, her face lit with a radiant joy. "I think, my Lord Knowlton, that you have yourself a wife."

He stopped any further words with a kiss.

Some minutes later, when he at last released her from his arms, Knowlton slipped his arm around her waist and guided her slowly back to the house.

"It there not something you are forgetting, Lady Knowlton-to-be?"

"What is that, Edward?" How wonderful to speak his name again.

"You have yet to say you love me." His voice was low and husky.

"And are you so certain that I do?" Katherine could not resist the impulse to tease him. She loved him all the more for his newly revealed vulnerability.

He stopped and looked at her in mock despair. "Do not say you are marry me only for my title!"

"Or your money?" Her mouth curved in a teasing smile.

"Or my body?" He raised an impish brow.

Katherine laughed and wrapped her arms about his neck. "I love you, Edward Beauchamp, foolish as I have often thought that to be. I have loved you for a dreadfully long time, and if you love me half as much as I do you, we will deal together famously."

"Impossible," he said, leaning down for another kiss. "No

one could possibly be more filled with love than I." He lifted her in his arms and twirled her in dizzying circles. "Kate, Kate, my lovely Kate," he murmured over and over until they were both breathless and laughing with love and hope.